TREACHEROUS

BEAUTIES

Other Fiction
by Cheryl B. Dale

Romantic Suspense

Intimate Portraits
The Man in the Boat
Set Up

Paranormal Romance

The Warwicks of Slumber Mountain

Light Mystery

Taxed to the Max
Overtaxed and Underappreciated

Vintage Mystery

Losing David

This book was previously published in 1993 by Silhouette Books. Updated and revised in 2012 by Cheryl B. Dale

Copyright Information
Copyright 1993-2014 by Cheryl Dale
Published by J&H Press
Cover Art by Calista Taylor
Proofed by L.F. Martin

ISBN: 978-0-9908695-0-4

www.cherylbdale.com
cherylbdale.blogspot.com
cherylbdale@hotmail.com

TREACHEROUS

BEAUTIES

by

Cheryl B. Dale

J&H Press

CHAPTER ONE

HAD I BEEN IN my right mind, I would never have attempted such a masquerade.

Sometimes, on looking back, I marvel that I had the nerve. By nature I'm a cautious person. I don't take any unnecessary risks nor give in to foolish impulses.

"Prudent," my fond mother had always said of me. "I'll never have to worry about Annabelle getting into scrapes. She doesn't believe in taking chances."

She was right, too. I never gambled on anything, never in my life. Except during that time in Rahunta.

And even there, after daring so much, I turned away from the one big gamble I should have taken because I couldn't bring myself to take a chance on my heart being right and my mind being wrong.

That was when my stupidity nearly cost my life.

Normally I'm not stupid. I'm calm and rational and some think me intelligent. Only when my brother, husband and mother died within one six-month period did depression take over.

That was when the nightmares began.

I blame them for that first desperate step, those nightmares where Alan came with his hand held out in supplication.

My psychiatrist suggested that they reflected guilt.

I hadn't been able to go with my mother to get Alan's body and bring it home, nor had I been able to attend the funeral. When we learned of Alan's death sixteen months before, I was in Illinois where my husband was undergoing surgery to remove one lung and part of the other.

Mother had called during the afternoon. "Your brother's dead, Annabelle." Her voice was tightly controlled. "Shot during a robbery. He fell into that dreadful gorge and died. He never should have gone up there."

Stunned, I'd stared at the beige walls of the lobby where I awaited word on my husband's condition. My mother knew as I did that I had to stay with Bob. Indeed, she'd urged me not to come home.

Yet perhaps there *was* guilt. And perhaps that guilt had begun to surface once my mind was free to dwell on Alan's death.

It was true that now, a year and a half later, he consumed my thoughts for the better part of each day, and at night he appeared in macabre dreams with a regularity that failed to make them any less painful. They would never cease, I sometimes felt.

"Do you think, Anna, that Alan's spirit is trying to contact you?" Dr. Brunweld had prompted toward the beginning of our sessions.

His reassuring presence was inevitably spoiled by a cluster of flowers on his desk, reminding me of hospital rooms and funeral chapels. The bright chrysanthemums that day were colored replicas of the white monsters adorning graves, and their presence sickened me. "No. Of course not."

Dr. Brunweld gave his noncommittal little "Hmmm," before probing: "Was Alan your mother's favorite, Annabelle? Do you feel guilty because it was he who died and not you? Is there a latent hostility toward your brother?"

My laugh startled him.

"No," I'd assured him. "Oh, no."

Six years my junior, Alan had been my doll, my pet, and finally my friend. There was no resentment in Alan's memory, only love twisted by grief.

Why I dreamed about him and not Mother or my poor Bob, I couldn't say. But the dreams always centered around Alan and were always the same. He would look directly at me, his usual sunny expression changed to an alien intensity as he struggled to tell me something.

Something important.

I, painfully slow to comprehend as such dreams inevitably make us, could never quite grasp what he wanted.

"Belle, you of all people should understand," were the urgent words he repeated each night as I tossed and turned. His hand would stretch out in a pleading gesture he would never have used in life. "Belle, you must help me. No one else can."

The night before my life changed, the dream came again. At the point where Alan put out his hand, his appeals gave way to despair. "You've never let me down before, Belle. If you won't help me, what am I to do?"

I sat upright in bed, tears streaming. Despite all my efforts, there was no understanding what he sought, and my impotency drew out frantic remorse. "Alan, I'd help you if I could. I would. You know I would."

Wiping my eyes, I got up.

Predawn shadows transformed the snug house Bob had loved. The stairwell, cheerful wallpaper shrouded in gray light, loomed chilly and forbidding.

Like a wraith, I crept down familiar steps turned hostile and glided past lonely rooms to the kitchen. Light from a passing car startled me before the sound of its motor broke the silence of the sleeping neighborhood.

I froze, rooted to the spot until my pounding heart returned to normal. *What's wrong with me? It's only a car.*

My north Atlanta subdivision was peaceful and without through streets, the large yards screened from other houses by heavy shrubbery. Its old trees suggested tranquility. There was absolutely no reason for my shaking hands.

In pajamas and bare feet, I made myself coffee before going into the den and drawing back curtains from French windows. A rich September sun came up behind the dogwood trees and tinted the horizon pink.

Surely by now the nightmares should have gone away, or at least lost some of their vividness.

"What do you want, Alan?" I remember whispering into the rosy dawn of the day that changed my life. I remember, too, the aroma of the steaming coffee, the heat of the cup in my hand, the bloodred reflection of the rising sun in the pool, the wetness of the tears on my cheek, the taste of their salt on my lips.

But most of all, I remember my sense of helplessness.

Alan was dying all over again, and this time my imagination lifted me there to him in the lovely, treacherous hills, unable to reach him in his final moments, watching from atop a wind-strafed ravine as he lay defenseless at its bottom. "Why can't you tell me what it is you want me to do?" I cried.

Streaming eyes lit upon some of his books that Mother had given me before she died.

"They were in his bedroom up *there*." Her thin face revealed the strain of the past months. Alan was her baby, her only son. Because the north Georgia hills had taken him away, she would never again speak of them without loathing. "You enjoy reading so I thought . . ."

But not anymore. Alan's books had remained in their box until yesterday, when one of my frenzied attacks of cleaning unearthed them from a back closet and thrust them haphazardly into shelves.

Now I drew out *Hiking Trails of North Georgia*, seeking comfort, some sign that Alan's ghost was at rest and that the haunting dreams came from my own mind.

Riffling its pages produced a ticket stub, a grocery receipt, a postcard of the gorge, and a wallet-sized photo.

In it a girl, chin resting on hands laid on the back of a rattan chair, looked out from a three-quarter angle. A mass of red-gold hair flattered the oval face and framed green eyes that smiled into the camera.

I recognized her from the newspapers and from my mother's

description. On the back, a clear, feminine hand had written the expected name.

Like other women before her, Tiffany Underwood, despite her engagement to Jason Forrester, had fallen head over heels in love with my brother. Alan had enjoyed beautiful women, and they'd been drawn to him, too, with his blond hair, blue eyes and strong body. We'd teased him that he'd never be able to settle for one girl, but it seemed we were wrong. This time, according to Mother, Alan had been ready to commit.

Poor girl.

Poor Alan.

With an aching heart, I closed the book on the smiling face.

A folded piece of yellow paper fluttered to the carpet. A page from a legal pad.

Alan had used such pads to jot down things to do, articles to buy, places to go, people to meet. He'd kept pad and pen beside his bed, and everything he intended to do each day was religiously recorded when he first woke up.

It was a wrench to see the familiar chicken scratch, but the mere existence of this page brought an involuntary smile. How many times had he pulled a rumpled yellow sheet from his pocket to methodically cross off each completed item? How many times had I teased him about his addiction to making lists and schedules?

"You're as bad as an old maid," I would scoff.

"You're jealous because I'm organized and you're not," he would retort, certain that his method of keeping up with the world was the best.

Ah, Alan, if I could only tease you one more time.

I blinked away tears and looked over the paper.

> *PE test - 10 am*
> *Lunch with the council @ noon: WEAR TIE*
> *Lecture on local history @ 3 pm: bring book*
> *Make dinner for T @ 6 – pick up steaks*
> *Meet @ fork - 10:30*

Under this last heading, there were several subtopics:

Make sure of truth and accept responsibility

> *EMPHASIZE HONESTY and fairness of F*
> *Insist on facing situation together*

It was a strange list, the last part puzzling.

T was probably Tiffany. If he was seeing her at six o'clock, who was he meeting later?

I glanced at the date scribbled at the top of the page, and the hairs on the back of my neck stood up.

Alan had made this list on the same day he'd fallen from the top of the gorge.

The paper became a yellow blur.

When the phone rang, I jumped five inches.

Charles Raite, the company's attorney, said, "Hullo, Annabelle. Sorry to call so early, but I wanted to be sure I caught you. One more set of papers for you to sign and then Bob's boys will have your proxy and you'll be able to do whatever you want in good conscience."

"Oh. That's great, Charles." I hoped my concession would salve the feelings of Bob's sons, all older than I. They had been astonished and annoyed when he'd bequeathed me fifty-one percent of the business during my lifetime. Since Atlanta Ice Cream Company held no interest for me now that Bob was gone, I thought it politic to let my stepsons run it.

"Can you drop by this morning?" Charles asked.

"It'll be eleven-thirty or so before I can get there. Is that okay?"

"Fine. Why don't you plan to have lunch with me?"

"Lunch?" I echoed. "I don't know." Lunch meant dressing up and putting on makeup.

The hallway mirror reflected an apathetic human being: brown hair pulled back carelessly, heart-shaped face haggard, shadows below dull eyes. Even the expensive silk pajamas looked like a yard sale find, so baggy were they on my thin frame.

"Am I losing my mind?" I'd asked Dr. Brunweld on my final visit.

His answer was quick and cheering. "Don't be silly. Aside from the dreams, you've come through a bad time quite well. When you come to terms with the past, they'll go away. In the meantime, get on with your life. Take a trip, get a job, go back to school. Do something for yourself for a change."

Looking at the sorry specimen of womanhood in the mirror, and remembering my psychiatrist's parting advice, I squared my shoulders. "I'd love to have lunch, Charles."

"Good. I'll see you about eleven-thirty."

Hanging up, I stared at the yellow paper in my hand. I wished it hadn't fallen out of the book, after last night's variation of my nightmare. It seemed more than coincidental.

Meet @ fork . . . Fairness of F. What could it mean? Could the note have anything to do with the Forresters? With Jason Forrester?

Surely Alan hadn't agreed to meet with Tiffany's fiancé that night. There were hundreds of names beginning with *F.* Frank, Fred, Fleming, Fullerman.

Forrester.

Unbidden, a grainy newspaper picture of Jason Forrester with his mother sprang to mind: a strong nose beneath wraparound sunglasses, a dark mustache sheltering an unsmiling mouth, his whole attitude one of hostility toward the reporters around him. The elderly woman encircled protectively by one of his arms was tiny next to his large form. She seemed oblivious to the anger emanating from her son, but it had jumped out of the photo to everyone else.

Jason Forrester. A volcano waiting to erupt. He was the one who'd discovered my brother. According to Mother, he was also the one Tiffany Underwood blamed for Alan's death.

The official version stated that Alan had died from the impact after falling hundreds of feet onto the rocks at the bottom of Rahunta Gorge, a spectacular ravine that split the north Georgia countryside and drew hordes of tourists each year.

There was no explanation as to why a .45-caliber bullet was lodged in his right shoulder. Light powder marks on his hands and clothes suggested suicide, but no gun had been found. His missing wallet and jewelry supported the belief that he'd been shot in a struggle during a robbery. The valuables had never been recovered, and the case remained unsolved.

Death at the hands of a person or persons unknown.

Except that Tiffany Underwood had told Mother Jason Forrester had murdered him.

And Alan's ghost haunted me night and day.

When it came time to leave for my appointment, I was no closer to a solution of his cryptic list but my curiosity was aroused. I'd had a year and a half to let the doubts about Alan's death simmer. The nightmares had heated them to a boil.

* * *

FINDING ALAN'S LIST WAS the beginning, but not until after my lunch with Charles Raite, when I was getting into my car to go home, did it hit me.

I was a free woman. Free to take Dr. Brunweld's advice. There was nothing to keep me rattling around my big empty house. I could take a vacation. I could go away for a week, a month, a year.

To the seashore or Mexico or Canada.

To Rahunta.

I'd considered it before, but my responsibilities in settling Bob's and then Mother's affairs had always intervened.

That was no longer true.

So I sat in my small car with my hands gripping the wheel and faced my subconscious promptings squarely. The autumn sun streamed in, its rays enveloping and warming me almost as much as my decision.

I would go to the hills where Alan had died.

Maybe then his ghost would be satisfied.

* * *

I PRETENDED CURIOSITY BROUGHT me to Rahunta and led me to saunter its streets like any other tourist come to see the hills.

I told myself I would look over the town and view the gorge and go back home, Alan's ghost finally put to rest.

Maybe I even believed it.

So as I strolled down the sidewalks of the main town, sanguine in my hopes of banishing the dreams, there was no intimation of what was to come. How could I know, as too often happens, providence was about to take a hand?

I couldn't and didn't, even as my feet wandered past the square and toward the office of Forrest Land Company.

The small building sat facing the street, with parking on the side and directly in front. A pickup truck by the door blocked the sidewalk so that I had to move onto the asphalt to skirt it. Circling back brought me in front of the window.

A sign stood out.

It was one of those cardboard signs, black lettering on white, and it read: RECEPTIONIST NEEDED. APPLY WITHIN.

There was no explaining my actions.

To this day, I don't know why I looked at the sign, stopped and then went inside.It was as if I had no mind of my own, no will of my own. The sign beckoned and I responded.

Destiny, fate, karma. Whatever one cared to call it, mine looked me in the face that day and challenged me.

I could no more have resisted it than I could stop the nightmares from coming every night.

"I'm Anna Levee," I told the elderly lady who stood behind the desk in front. "I'd like to talk to someone about the receptionist job."

Candid blue eyes under bushy gray hair inspected me. Short and stocky, she seemed friendly and easygoing, the type woman people would be comfortable with.

Right now doubt tinged her vaguely familiar face. "We had in mind a more mature type. Someone settled and experienced. With enough common sense to handle whatever comes up."

"I have plenty of common sense. And I'm older than I look. I was thirty last June." I wanted this job. "Who should I talk to, please?"

"I'm Mrs. Forrester. You talk to me. And I'm afraid you won't do." She didn't say it rudely.

I finally recognized her. Jason Forrester's mother.

"But Mrs. Forrester, you aren't giving me a chance!" Some desperate need overwhelmed my normal reticence. "I'm sure you'll find I'm very well qualified."

She was skeptical. "Are you really, Miss, er . . . ?"

"Mrs. Levee, and I'm very experienced." I rattled off my qualifications. "Twelve years ago I started as receptionist for Atlanta Ice Cream Company and moved up to public relations and then assistant to the president. I know everything there is to know about handling people. You'd be getting a bargain if you hired me." Afraid I was laying it on a little thick, I paused to gauge her reaction.

My aggressiveness didn't offend her. In fact, the slightest hint of a twinkle appeared. "I see. Do you have a résumé?"

That small matter didn't deter me. "Back in my room." Circumspect Annabelle, she who'd never distorted the truth in her entire life, was lying as if she did it every day. I tried not to cringe at what Mother would have said.

"Your room?"

"I'm staying over in Steve's Bend. At the Arms Inn."

"Ah. While you look for a job, no doubt."

I didn't miss the irony. Arms Inn was an expensive place for a job hunter to stay.

"Not at all. I wasn't really looking. I saw your sign outside and . . ." Time to beg. "Mrs. Forrester, I love north Georgia. My husband died a year ago and I've recently got his affairs straightened out. I came up here to, to recover. I was just thinking what a wonderful place this is and how I'd like to live here when I saw your sign. It seemed like an omen. Won't you give me a chance? Let me work a month, and I promise you'll let me stay."

She hesitated.

I put on my most appealing expression.

"All right." The smile lurking in her eyes broke loose and lit up her entire face. "We'll take a chance on you. But just for two weeks," she added sternly. "After that . . . Well, we'll see. Okay?"

"That's fine." By now I would have agreed to anything.

"Our hours are eight-thirty to five, five days a week," she went on. "Do you have any idea of what we do?"

"What you do?" I had an excellent idea of what Forrest Land Company did. I even knew Letitia Forrester ran the office while her sons Brent and Jason designed, sold and developed commercial projects throughout the country.

My stroll past Forrest Land Company on this fine September day was to catch a glimpse of Jason Forrester. I had some vague idea of seeing the man and taking his measure.

Mrs. Forester was waiting for an answer.

"Why no." My coo sounded so much like my mother's socialite sister that I nauseated myself. "Why don't you tell me?"

CHAPTER TWO

"MATT, THIS IS ANNA Levee. She wants to see our vacant cottage."
With that introduction, the president of Rahunta Preparatory Academy
and Day School left me with the purchasing manager.

Letitia had suggested I go there when I'd asked about apartments
near town. "There aren't any. Rahunta Prep owns several houses close
by and occasionally rents them out. That's your best bet."

My heart had stopped at the name.

Was it coincidence that she directed me to the school where Alan
had taught?

"Rahunta Gorge Preparatory Academy and Day School!" he'd
exclaimed when landing his interview. "Ain't that a mouthful?"

"Oh, Alan," Mother had reproved halfheartedly. "And you an
education major."

He'd laughed at her. "Time enough to watch my language when I
get a roomful of brats to teach."

Seizing my hands without warning, he'd pulled me to my feet and
twirled me around. "Ain't gonna say *ain't* no more! Ain't gonna say
ain't no more! Ain't gonna say *ain't* no mo-o-ore!" he sang to the tune
of "Jimmy Crack Corn" while we danced round and round. "'Cause
the brats will say it too!"

And we'd collapsed in giggles while Mother struggled to keep her
frown before giving up and laughing with us.

He should never have come to this place.

The man before me wearing a doubtful expression brought me
back to the present. I extended my hand for him to shake.

"We do have a cottage that's vacant right now," Matthew Graven
admitted, "but you may not be interested."

When he wasn't more forthcoming, I prodded. "I'd love to see it."

"Oh." He blinked, looking out from his thick lenses like a wise old
owl. "Uh, all right. Now where . . .?"

Rummaging through his desk, he came up with a key.

At a sedate pace, he drove us about a mile before leaving the main
road. A twisting, tree-lined route led to the cottage, which sat about
fifty feet back from the gorge.

Getting out, I walked over to a low stone wall at the chasm's edge
and caught my breath.

I forgot the last terrible sixteen months. I forgot the exhilaration of getting the job at Forrest Land Company. I even forgot the dreams that dogged me each night.

The spectacular cleft was laid out like an offering. Shrubs and ferns and trees and windflowers softened its rocky sides while along the bottom, the Rahunta River snaked among the boulders, the silver rivulets reflecting sunshine. Such splendor trivialized human problems.

"Beautiful, isn't it?" Matt Graven's genuine smile made me overlook his copious sprinkling of freckles.

"That's an understatement. What's that down there?" I almost didn't notice it, so skillfully was the structure built to blend into the rocks and trees. Halfway down the gorge, a wooden deck skirted an ultramodern house that literally hung over the edge. One wing was long and low with slits for windows. The other side was a smoky gray bubble that seemed to melt into the background.

Matt's smile diminished. "That house belongs to Brent Forrester. He's an architect and developer. Fairly well known."

I knew who Brent was. Lettie's son and Jason's younger brother. "It looks precarious. I'd be scared to live perched over the gorge like that."

"It's perfectly safe." As if anxious to draw my attention elsewhere, Matt pointed in the opposite direction. "The white house up on top belongs to his mother."

I followed his finger to see a two-story frame building with a double wraparound porch. Big and rambling, it looked like a successful rancher's house in a western movie. "The Forresters must do pretty well for themselves."

"You could say that. They're the local bigwigs. Own half the county and most of the gorge."

"The gorge?" I opened my eyes wide. "You mean the gorge isn't public property."

He chuckled at my ignorance. "Nope. Not all of it. The Forresters own all that over there and then back around nearly to here. They lease some of it to the school. The county owns a tiny little slice on the far end."

"I didn't realize it wasn't public."

"Most people don't. Ready to go check out the house?"

I liked the cottage.

Its boxy lines blended with the hillside. Inside, curtains of yellow gingham, their pattern repeated in occasional cushions, cheered up pine flooring and red maple furniture.

The floors had been swept, the walls newly painted, every drawer and cabinet lined with fresh paper. There was no dishwasher or garbage disposal, but a washer and dryer were tucked away behind folding doors and the bathroom boasted a shower. The white porcelain and yellow tiles fairly sparkled, so clean had they been scrubbed.

"I'll take it."

"We-ell. Why don't you think it over?"

Was that reluctance? "Oh, no. I love it. I'm ready to sign a lease right now."

"Well. Okay then. If you're sure you don't want to think about it."

Matt didn't want me to rent the cottage.

We went back outside onto the wide front porch, half screened and half enclosed in glass. Facing west, the perch was perfectly situated for watching sunsets and offered a great view of the gorge as well, overlooking the wooded side that rose up to meet the sky in mesmerizing splendor. Again awe filled me.

How puny we animals who call ourselves humans really are.

Matt interrupted my reverie, still uncertain he wanted me for a tenant. "The thing is . . . Oh, well, you're bound to hear anyway. It's like the cottage is, um, not exactly haunted . . ."

I waited, knowing what was coming before he blurted the words, certain that my being here was part of the same pattern that had landed me the job with Forrest Land Company and led me to the school where Alan had worked.

Matt rushed his words, anxious to tell me the worst. "See, one of our teachers lived here, and he was killed. Since he died, we've kind of avoided putting anyone here."

Perhaps in the back of my mind I'd known all along. "Oh, yes. I remember." I marveled at my steady voice. Had I really had trouble lying in the past? "The teacher found in the gorge. Did you know him?"

"No. It's been, let me see, May a year ago, and I didn't start my job here till last September. Of course, they don't know for sure what happened."

"He was shot, wasn't he?"

"Uh huh. That's why I suggested you might want to reconsider. Some people are nervous about living in a cottage where someone's died violently."

I turned back to the view and took a big breath of air. North Georgia was cooler and clearer than Atlanta. Here the leaves were already hinting at the gaudy colors of the season to come while in the city I'd left two days ago, they remained a lush green.

"I'm not afraid of ghosts," I told Matt Graven.

Not this ghost, in any event. God knows I'd had enough experience with him.

As we walked back to the edge for a last glimpse of the impressive ravine, an unexpected chill shot up my spine like a mischievous spirit had zoned in on us. Goose pimples rose on my skin. My breathing became shallow. I crossed my arms and pulled my blazer close.

Alan, I thought, *if this is your idea of teasing me, I don't like it.*

There was no reason for unease. The whole area remained empty, the air quiet except for the occasional chirp of a bird.

My imagination had shifted into overdrive.

"Do people ever hike in the gorge, Matt?" As soon as I could, I'd explore the place where my brother had fallen.

"Sure do. There's a logging road up the way, but the Forresters don't encourage trespassers. You'll need permission."

My overactive imagination produced an angry face with dark sunglasses and a thin-lipped mouth that forbade me access to his property. "Perhaps I'll try it from this side."

"No way. You stick to the main path." He showed me what I'd not noticed, a beaten trail round the rim of the gorge. "This leads up by Lettie Forrester's house and it's pretty safe. But there're other paths that join it, and they get hairy. Don't go on them without someone who knows the ropes."

"I've done some hiking."

"Not like this. It's dangerous."

"Dangerous? You mean like snakes or bears?"

He shook his head. "No. I mean like getting down into the gorge without falling."

"It doesn't look too bad."

"Looks are deceiving. There isn't a year that goes by without this place claiming another life." He pointed past my shoulder. "There were two people rescued last month after slipping and falling down there."

I followed his gaze to see an innocent ribbon of water falling to a rock shelf before pooling among the boulders at the bottom of the gorge.

"They were lucky. A broken leg, two broken arms and some scrapes and bruises. I'm a veteran hiker and rock climber, but some parts scare even me. No, climbing in the gorge isn't for amateurs. Don't go down without a guide." This last was said sternly.

"Maybe you can go with me one of these days."

"Sure."

Behind his back, a distant patch of brilliant magenta moved.

I started, heart in throat. Not my imagination. Someone *was* watching us. Someone outside by the bubble house.

Matt turned to see what had scared me. "There's Simone." His plain face lit up as he waved enthusiastically. As noted earlier, Matt

Graven was attractive when he smiled. "Simone Forrester. She lives over there."

"Is she Brent's wife?"

"Yes." The answer was curt, the smile disappeared.

When the woman returned Matt's wave, the wind lifted her shining pale hair. He watched her, amiable again.

"Are they my closest neighbors?" I asked.

"No, I'm right behind you, off over the hill there toward the school." He pointed vaguely to the side. "And of course Lettie Forrester and her son Jason live up at the top."

"Not exactly a family compound, is it?" I turned around to look at the white two-story and then back at the modern gray bubble. "A lot of distance between them."

"I doubt they'd be happy any closer. At least Sim—some of them wouldn't."

"You sound as if you don't like them."

His lips compressed. "You'll hear anyway. That teacher we talked about, who lived in this cabin. His name was Alan McKenzie, and some people believe Jason Forrester killed him."

"Do you?" It might have been another person asking, so impersonal did my voice sound.

"I think Jason Forrester is capable of killing," he said slowly. "But I don't really know any of them. Except for Simone. She's a wonderful person, beautiful and susceptible to . . . It's a pity that . . ."

I waited. "A pity what?"

He shrugged. "A pity she's so unhappy. The Forresters give her a hard time."

"Yet she's married to one."

"Yes, but the family never approved. And he doesn't appreciate her. Someone as fragile as Simone needs lots of love and attention."

Better tell him and get it over with.

"Hmm, you're making me curious. Forrest Land Company is where I start work Monday."

Aghast, he stepped back.

"You haven't said anything you shouldn't," I reassured him. "Actually, I'd be glad for any advice you can give me on how to deal with the Forresters."

He shook his head. "I can't advise you, but I'll tell you this. Everything in the county is cleared with Jason or Lettie Forrester. They own most of the land and a lot of the businesses. And they don't mind using muscle to get their way."

"Like covering things up?"

"Like covering things up." He eyed me speculatively.

"Small towns often have families who run things." I backtracked, afraid I'd revealed too much. "It isn't uncommon."

"No, it isn't. And the Forresters are that family around here. I've learned that much in the year I've been here." His gaze moved back to the low house hugging the ravine, but the figure in magenta was gone. "It isn't a good idea to cross Jason or Letitia."

Before I could dig further, he changed the subject and we headed back to the school.

Once the lease was signed and keys provided, I returned for another look at the cottage before collecting my things from the hotel.

As before, the gorge's serene grandeur was awesome. But as Matt had reminded me, that serenity was deceptive. People died in this gorge. Alan had been another such fatality. The wound in his shoulder made his death more horrible, but he was only one of many who'd lost their lives here.

On the ravine bottom, boulders caught the falling waters of Rahunta River and split it between swirling rapids and tranquil pools. Somewhere down there my brother had died after his crumpled and battered body had landed.

I had seen a copy of the autopsy report.

I knew about the internal injuries, the external wounds.

Had he suffered? How long had he lain there before Jason Forrester reported finding him? Was he conscious? If so, what had he felt as his life slipped away? Would he have been angry or fearful or sorry?

Answers to those agonizing questions could come only from that exasperating person I'd loved so dearly. No. From his ghost. But I might be able to retrace his time in Rahunta, to find somebody who would talk about him. Tiffany, perhaps, when she came home from college. Or someone else.

Jason Forrester's image flashed before me.

Perhaps now that I was here Alan's spirit would leave me alone. Perhaps now I could find peace.

I was glad I had come to these hills. Passionately, unreasonably glad.

CHAPTER THREE

BY THE TIME I finished unpacking, the sun was a red ball sinking over the mountains. From my porch I could enjoy the scarlet sky give way to pink.

The sensation of someone watching made me shiver and retreat into the glassed-in section.

I looked down the gorge toward the bubble house, but Simone Forrester was not on the deck. On the other side, Lettie Forrester's house, too, was deserted and lifeless.

No one around.

Perhaps it was Alan's ghost, welcoming me into his old house.

He was always one for a little joke.

That night I slept better than I had in months. The dream returned, but not as a nightmare. Alan no longer despaired. "I'm glad you're here, Belle. I knew you'd never let me down."

"Darn you, Alan," I flung at him in this nocturnal illusion. "You know you can always count on big sister. One of these days I won't be there, mister. What'll you do then?"

"Tell Mother on you." His impish smile revealed the dimple in his chin. His blond hair was tousled. His blue eyes laughed at me. In my dream I laughed with my good-looking brother.

When I woke up, I was smiling.

The emptiness of the past months had faded to a manageable nostalgia, and I was ready for the Forresters.

* * *

READING GLASSES MASKED MY gray eyes and helped disguise the nose that turned up too impudently to be dignified. Light brown hair brushed severely back was professional rather than stylish. I had outlined my full lips to look thinner, and as long as I remembered to keep them pressed together, they did.

Getting out of my car, I smoothed the collar of my charcoal suit coat and made sure the maroon paisley scarf was precisely tied. The reflection in the long, shaded windows of Forrest Land Company showed a woman who looked exactly the way a receptionist should look.

Conservative but impeccable.

Worries about a background check had vanished after I told Lettie Atlanta Ice Cream Company had done one before I left, and if she liked, I would permit them to send a copy to her. "Save you some money."

Especially when I could control its contents.

But she flapped a hand, saying we'd wait till my probation was up to worry about all that. "No sense in dealing with more paperwork than we have to till we see what happens."

She still wasn't sure I could do the job but I'd show her. If she did her own check after that, she might note my maiden name, but I'd worry about that when it happened.

So, since I'd primed the personnel director at Atlanta Ice Cream on what to tell her when she called for former employment verification, I had no qualms about starting work.

Calm, confident and cautious. That was my motto.

Right. Taking a deep breath, I opened the door and entered the small lobby.

"Hello." A very blond, very attractive man about my age looked up from where he stood rifling through the drawer of the reception desk. "You must be Anna Levee."

Totally unprepared to meet Brent Forrester first thing, I gulped. "Um, yes."

I was also unprepared for his physical appearance.

Newspapers had not done him justice. Dull black and white photos made the yellow of his hair and the blue of his eyes indiscriminate grays while the photographers invariably caught him with an anxious frown that aged him.

The man who came toward me with his hand held out was tall, with the lean body of a runner. His mouth was kind and generous, like Lettie's. "I'm Brent Forrester. My mother's on the telephone in her office, but she'll be out in a moment."

"How do you do." I shook his hand.

Only in the very back of his eyes was there a shadow that made him akin to that worried man of the newspapers.

He gestured toward a chair in the small lobby. "Sit down. Mom'll want to go over everything with you. Do you want some coffee?"

"No, thanks." I took the chair.

"Fresh brewed." He had an easy manner and a sweet smile. "And we have country ham and biscuits to go with it. Made by one of the best cooks in Rahunta."

"Your mother or your wife?" I tried to match his light tone.

"Good Lord, neither of them. We'd have food poisoning." He chuckled. "I mean Maggie Mahone, Mom's housekeeper. And I'll have you know that grown men have been known to break down and cry when they get here too late for her ham and biscuits."

"All right." I gave in, not immune to his charm. "You've talked me into it. I'll take one black coffee and one ham and biscuit, if you please."

Against my will, I found myself liking Brent Forrester.

Of course, nobody's called him a murderer.

A young woman with mousy brown hair and too much mascara came in, breathless and eyeing the clock on the wall. Lois Bradford and I would be working together. "I'm glad you're here." She stowed her purse in her desk. "Things have been so busy it's impossible for one person to keep up. And Lettie's been away so much lately."

"And hopes to be away even more." Letitia Forrester herself came out from a back office. She was in stocking feet, her hair as disheveled as when I'd met her. "If Anna works out, that is."

"I'll do my best." I'd be successful in my deception if it killed me.

"Anna's going to get along fine with everybody," Brent soothed.

"We'll see." Frowning slightly, Lettie assessed me. Not only her mouth, but her candid blue eyes were repeated in her son. "After all, some of the people we see on a day-to-day basis are probably not the sort Anna's used to."

"Now, Mom." Brent shook his head at her then turned to me. "Most of the people we see are country folk. Rednecks or hillbillies, you might say. True, sometimes they're a little rough, but they're also decent, honest, hardworking people. They're easy to get along with if you give them a chance."

Lettie snorted. "Don't dress it up, Brent. I don't want her running away crying the first time some big clod yells boo."

Stiffening, I started to speak in my own defense, but a specimen of Brent's description came in. With unkempt beard and flowing hair, he sported overalls and a worn flannel shirt. "Where we s'posed to pick up them braces, Miz Forrester?"

"Use the doormat," she snapped. "You know this is new carpet, Bill Tompkins."

He growled but meekly did her bidding before going back to the kitchen and coming out with a biscuit.

And that was how she spoke to all the workers coming in and out of the office. None took offense, and all of them wiped their feet as instructed.

I resolved to be equally firm when I had to deal with them.

But that day was spent in going over my duties: answering the phone, getting used to the computer and learning the eccentricities of the copier. The usual office routine.

Brent shut himself up, coming out about noon to tell his mother, "Going home for lunch. Simone wanted to get her hair cut. I'll bring her by afterward to meet Anna."

Letitia made no comment, but Lois gave a cheery, "Okay."

I recalled the small magenta figure standing beside the bubble house.

At lunch, Lois took me around town. She pointed out the one boutique, the gas station, the drugstore, the local discount store and Janie's Beauty Shop. "Kay and Tina are pretty good, but Janie listens to what you tell her. She goes to seminars in Atlanta and Chattanooga so she's up on all the latest styles."

I ran my fingers through my straight bob. "Thanks, I'll remember that, Lois. I could use a trim."

Lunch was a toss-up between the two fast-food places in town—hamburgers and pizza—or the local diner. The local diner won out, and we took back a plate for Letitia.

We hadn't been back at our desks long when the door flew open and a young woman danced in. "Oooh, Lettie, Lois, see what I have!"

A purple beret perched askew on shoulder-length hair pale as moonlight. Blue eyes sparkled above cheeks delicately pinked from the autumn air. She had a perfect little nose and straight white teeth, revealed when her bow-shaped mouth parted with laughter. The short jacket and black plaid slacks hinted at a voluptuous figure.

Simone Forrester was enchanting.

Her entry startled Lois. "What in the world, Simone?"

Simone held out her hand to display an amethyst ring surrounded with diamonds. "I saw it in Chattanooga last week and me, you know how I love purple."

Lettie sent the tiniest questioning look toward her son, and Brent gave the tiniest answering shrug.

What was that all about?

Unaware of the exchange, Simone spoke, her voice as delightful as the rest of her, its hint of lilting accent recalling steamy foreign films. "I haven't had anything new in so long. I've been saving my money, but I just had to have this. See, Lois?"

She flitted over to Lois, holding out her ring to be admired before, unable to remain still, she removed the beret and shook out long pale hair. Then she spotted me.

"Are you the new woman?" She came over to look at me in the delighted way a child examines a stranger. "Why, Lettie, I thought you wanted someone old and honest."

"Earnest," her husband said, looking a little harried. "Mom said she wanted an earnest woman, Simone."

"Honest. Earnest. What do I know?" She laughed at me, taking one of my hands into both her dainty ones and drawing me into her enthusiasm. "You're not old after all. I am so glad. I thought you would be sour and feeble." She wrinkled her exquisite nose in disgust. "But you, you're neither of those. I know we can be friends."

I couldn't help but smile at her.

"For heaven's sake, Simone, if you keep acting crazy, Anna'll decide she won't want anything to do with any of us." Lettie's words sounded crosser than her tone.

"Anna, I'm sure you realize this is my wife, Simone." Brent grinned at me ruefully. "Simone, this is Anna Levee."

The worried look at the back of his eyes was so pronounced, I wondered if it ever went away.

"Anna." Simone rolled my name on her tongue, pronouncing it *Ahna* rather than Anna. "How perfect. We don't know an Anna, do we, Lettie?"

"Not unless you count old Mrs. Wilkes," Lettie said dryly, "and I suspect you don't."

"I've got the Trenton preliminary laid out," Brent told his mother. "I think I'll take the rest of the day off."

Lettie's mouth may have tightened a fraction, or I might have imagined it. "All right." As the couple started to leave, she called, "I forgot to tell you, Brent. Jace called." For a moment, her troubled expression mirrored her son's. "He got to Nevada all right, but he wants us to be sure and check on when they'll pour the Cavalry Stable footings. You will, won't you?"

"Yeah. I'll do it." Brent tapped his wife's cheek lovingly. "Let's go, sweetheart."

There was nothing in the interlude to suggest anything besides a normal relationship between husband, mother-in-law and wife. Not really, I argued with myself while remembering the looks exchanged by Lettie and Brent. Certainly those weren't enough to indicate something was wrong between the Forresters.

Why did Matt Craven think Brent didn't appreciate his wife? And that the Forresters didn't care for Simone?

Perhaps he was talking about Jason Forrester. Perhaps Jason Forrester didn't like Simone.

I shivered inwardly, knowing I would soon have to face the man suspected of murdering Alan and dreading it.

CHAPTER FOUR

THE FORRESTERS' OFFICE BUILDING was pretty and functional, but not impressive inside or out. A stranger would never take it for the home of the most noted development group in the southeastern United States.

My desk sat squarely at the front door to greet anyone coming in while in my rear, Lois had a work space beside Lettie's office. Directly behind them were the kitchen and restrooms.

The brothers' offices took up about two-thirds of the building. Brent's was on the right, Jason's on the left. Spacious with large windows, they housed desks, drawing tables, computers, manuals, blueprint files and other paraphernalia. Brent spent long hours in his, designing projects on his terminal. Totally self-sufficient and absorbed in his work, he seldom made demands on either Lois or me.

Letitia hardly ever saw her office. She was always in and out, supervising work crews or running other errands instead of looking over our shoulders.

Which was fine with me. I hoped I was gaining her approval as I applied myself and listened in vain for some reference to Alan.

The one Forrester I particularly wanted to meet had yet to show up. Supposedly, Jason Forrester was still in Nevada buying cows, though Lois told me that he'd called the office one day and the background noise hadn't sounded like a cattle auction. "Not unless the cows have learned how to sing 'Light My Fire,'" she said, giggling. I'd quickly discovered she had a crush on the older brother. "He's something else, that Jace is."

As I waited for his return, I plodded away, learning how to work the computer and do the accounting, to deal with the sometimes surly customers and workers.

On this particular day I was alone out front. Lois had called in sick, and Lettie had an appointment in Chattanooga with a roofing manufacturer. "I'll be gone all day," she'd said before leaving that morning. "Will you be all right?"

"Of course," I said confidently. "Brent's here."

She looked dubious but had gone anyway.

All kinds of people—builders, contractors, salesmen—tramped in and out. The phone rang continuously. By the end of the day I was tired and cranky as I balanced out the general ledger.

The figures matched exactly so I clicked that program closed and opened up the purchasing program.

Thunk!

"Oh no."

The paperboy had missed our doorway and hit the side of the building again. After ten days I was accustomed to his habits, but his bad aim was still annoying. Hopping up, I went outside to retrieve the newspaper from the tall grass where he always managed to pitch it. Back inside, I sat down at the computer to enter last month's purchases before going home and putting my feet up.

A sudden movement in my blouse startled me.

Something was inside my sleeve.

Black widow spiders? Dirty cockroaches? It might even be a small mouse!

I yanked at the buttons, but they were small, round, mother-of-pearl ones, nearly impossible to undo.

I almost tore them off. "Damn!"

The biggest, blackest cricket I'd ever seen in my life stared out at me. Its long spindly legs made my skin crawl. It must have slipped into one of the cutout holes adorning my sleeve when I picked up the paper from the grass.

Cursing the paperboy, I slapped at the cricket. "Get away, you monster!" It disappeared when I took off my shoe to squash it. After several minutes with no sign of the cricket, I abandoned the fruitless search.

"Calm down," I told myself. "It's only a bug."

It would soon start chirping again, and I would find it and kill it. Or—I shuddered—catch him and throw him out. Meanwhile, I had work to do if I wanted to get out at a decent hour.

After putting my shoe back on, I sat down, careful to keep an eye and an ear open for the cricket.

It prudently remained silent until, absorbed in data entry, I forgot it.

The front bell made me jump.

My heart sank when one of the unkempt, bearded men with whom I'd become acquainted swept in.

Not this close to five o'clock! They always took forever to get their business done.

This one had driven his battered pickup right up to the front door, another strike against him. Thoughtful drivers parked so people had room to get into the office without having to turn sideways or walk in the street.

He had on jeans and high-laced work boots. Dark hair stuck out from a floppy felt hat that must be at least thirty years old. Topping off his attire was the most garish yellow parka I'd ever seen.

From the way he slammed the front door, I could tell he was going to be the aggressive type I so disliked and braced myself.

He froze, gawking at me as though he'd never seen a woman before. "Where's Lettie?" His voice was brusque, matching the rest of him. His eyes were dark and flat.

"Gone to Chattanooga." I dragged my gaze away from the fluorescent jacket and down to his boots covered with Georgia red clay. "Wipe your feet before you come any farther, please."

He gaped at me some more before condescending to notice his muddy boots, then halfheartedly stamped them on the doormat before starting forward. "I came by to pick up some plans."

"Go back and wipe those feet." These construction people were like little boys. One had to tell them and tell them and tell them again. Once they knew you meant what you said, they grudgingly obeyed. You simply had to let them know who was boss. I'd learned that from Lettie. "Surely you can see there's light carpet in here."

He bridled. I had never seen anyone bridle before, but he definitely bridled. What little I could see of his face beneath the hat and the beard and the thick eyebrows looked like a thundercloud. "I did wipe them. Ma'am."

"You did not. Otherwise you wouldn't have left that clump of red mud there behind you on the carpet that someone will now have to clean up."

He couldn't argue with that—the red mud was too obvious—and sullenly went back to make a show of wiping each foot.

"Now can I get my plans?" He looked me over pretty good.

I didn't like his attitude. "Stop staring at me. What kind of plans do you want? Does Brent Forrester know you need them?"

Realizing he wouldn't be allowed to run roughshod over me, he took off his hat and drew large blunt fingers through dark waves falling well past his collar. He needed a haircut as well as a shave. "No, ma'am. I reckon he doesn't."

He wasn't staring anymore, but his glance kept coming back to me.

I could almost read his mind. He was hoping that I would be put in my place and that he would be around to see it happen. His eyes weren't as dark as I had thought. They were a funny shade of brown, almost a deep gold.

His tone changed, becoming softer, more persuasive. "I can promise you Brent won't care if I get those plans. Ma'am."

Men like him didn't intimidate me and couldn't push me around, not with rudeness and not with fabricated courtesy. "What name?"

"The Cavalry Stables job, the one going up just over the state line in Tennessee. They're in that office right there." He pointed toward Jason Forrester's office.

"I meant what was *your* name"—he opened his mouth to answer but I held my palm up to silence him—"but it really doesn't matter. Jason Forrester is out of town and I don't know where to look for your plans." I was crisp. "I suggest you come back tomorrow when he's expected in."

He blinked twice, slowly, ominously. "No, I need them now."

I didn't like the way he glared at me. I liked even less his meaningful step toward Jason's door.

"You can't go in there." Jumping up, I scooted across to plant myself, all five feet six inches of solid female, squarely in front of him.

Goodness, I hadn't realized how large he was.

I had to tilt my head back to see his face. It was unnerving to be blocking the way of a battering ram. "If you insist, I'll see if Brent will talk to you. But you're *not* going in there."

He showed every sign of wanting to dodge me, but when I sidestepped in front of him a couple of times to head him off, he stopped. "Listen, lady, I don't want to dance. I want those plans."

"I told you," I said coldly, "to come back tomorrow. I'll call Brent Forrester out if you—"

"Well, fine!" He didn't bother to hide his exasperation. "Dandy. Just absolutely peachy. Let's call him out here and get the hell on with finding those goddamned plans then, shall we?"

"There's no need to use that sort of language. Mr. Forrester will be happy to come out here to deal with you." Despite being slightly breathless, I was forceful. "If you will kindly step back to the front, I'll get him. And for the last time, stop staring at me."

His mouth opened once and then closed. His strange eyes narrowed and he looked as if he might say something abusive. Instead, his mouth and mustache suddenly twitched. Taking off his ridiculous parka, he put it under his arm, turned on his heel and tramped back to the front with great dignity.

His hips were narrow beneath that huge set of shoulders and despite the work boots, he walked with the fluid grace of a wild animal. A shame that a lot of fine physiques owed little to education and nothing to intelligence.

Magnanimous in victory, I invited him to thumb through a magazine and, with a gracious smile, started toward Brent's office.

"Oh, miss," came a suspiciously honeyed voice behind me.

I turned my head frostily, to find him settling down with a magazine. "Yes?"

He crossed powerful thighs and swung one heavy boot. He did not look at me but kept his eyes on the magazine pages he idly turned. His mouth twitched again. "Your shirt is unbuttoned." The dulcet tones did not disguise the smugness.

I looked down at the lace of my exposed bra. Feeling my face flush, I turned away and hastily buttoned my blouse back up. "Thank you very much," I said frigidly. "There was a cricket earlier that got inside my blouse . . ." My words trailed away as he cocked a knowing eye at me.

"Yeah, you have to watch those crickets. They're real inclined to ravish the females," came that same saccharine voice. He didn't try to hide his leer. "And you're mighty welcome, ma'am. Glad to oblige. Any time."

Mortified, I fled to Brent's office.

Brent was studying some plans on his drafting table, but he offered me an absent smile. He was one of those people who are decent inside and out. It was hard not to like him too much, to remember that his brother was rumored to have murdered mine.

"Brent, there's one of your builders out front wanting to pick up some plans. For some stables? He says they're in Jason's office. Would you come talk to him, please? To tell you the truth, I'm a little afraid of him."

"Stables?" Engrossed in his work, Brent took a moment to understand what I was saying. "Cavalry Stables? I don't know of anyone who'd be picking up those plans." He got up. "Let me see who it is. As far as I know, the only set here is Jace's."

He walked out, saw the giant sitting sedately on the edge of the padded visitor's chair and stopped short. "Well," he said, putting his hands on his hips. "You back? What do you mean, scaring our new receptionist to death?"

"Whoa, you got that backwards, didn't you, bro?" The redneck uncurled his long frame and stood up. His eyes crinkled with amusement, though under the cover of the beard, I couldn't tell whether he was smiling. "Man, I've been afraid to move, she's got me so rattled."

They were obviously acquainted. I suspected the worst.

Brent went over to clap the other man on the shoulder. "You look like you've been on a two-week drunk. How was Nevada?"

"Like always. Fast. Fast food, fast money, fast women. And it was only a two-day drunk, not two weeks."

"Sure. And pigs have wings." Brent turned to me, grinning like he meant it, the anxious expression that seemed forever lurking, absent for the first time since I'd met him. "This is the black sheep of the family, Anna. Jason, this is Anna Levee, our new receptionist. Anna, this is the prodigal brother, Jace."

"How do you do," I said faintly, my poise deserting me as I recalled his stares. Finding my hand hovering protectively over my breasts, I immediately held it out without displaying any unwillingness.

Our handshake was not a success, as Jason Forrester took the opportunity to examine my wedding rings, and, in the process, held my fingers in his huge paw longer than necessary.

I yanked my hand away and took the offensive. "You should have told me who you were, Mr. Forrester. There was no need for all this to-do."

"You didn't give me a chance. I thought I'd run in and pick up those plans, but man, you sure stymied me. First the cricket and"—one brow wagged suggestively—"then jumping all over me for not wiping my feet. Where'd Lettie find you? The army?"

Before I could open my mouth, Brent came to my defense.

"Come on, Jace. Don't run Anna off now that we're just getting used to her. Tell me, what do you need Cavalry's plans for? They didn't get started on the footings till yesterday."

"The damned idiots have poured 'em backwards." Jason's smile changed to a scowl. "I stopped off there on my way from the airport. Which reminds me, I picked up Lochinvar for a cool hundred and bought two cows for fifty."

Brent raised pleased brows as if he understood. "Great."

"Anyway, went by the stable site for a quick look and damned if they haven't flopped the plans over and started backwards."

Brent blinked. "I don't believe it. They wouldn't do that. You were looking at it the wrong way, Jace."

"No, I wasn't. That's why I wanted to come get the plans, just to make sure."

The brothers went back toward Jason's office, still discussing whether or not there had been a mistake.

I sat down at the computer, hands shaking. Not from fright, as when I had discovered the cricket in my sleeve, but from humiliation.

So that was Jason Forrester.

He was not in the least as envisioned. He was supposed to be someone smoother, more sinister. Someone with an air of danger about him. Not that he didn't look like a criminal, with that heavy beard and long hair.

After the way he'd stared at my open blouse, I found myself *wanting* to believe the worst. The memory of his eyes on my exposed bra made me ill.

But any man would have stared at a woman whose blouse was undone.

Well, not *any* man, I amended, thinking of my gentle Bob. But certainly a lot of men would.

By the same token, lots of men up here looked like ruffians, with their stained work clothes and messy hair. By those standards, Rahunta was full of criminals.

Construction workers weren't known for their fashionable attire. Probably when one had to get out in the dirt and weather, one grew careless about such things as style, preferring to sacrifice it to comfort. Jason Forrester had certainly done so.

Strangely, I'd had an entirely different picture of him in my mind. Alan, the last time I'd spoken with him, had called Jason Forrester an egotistical lamebrain. But by that time Alan had been hopelessly in love with Tiffany Underwood. His opinion of Tiffany's fiancé was undoubtedly prejudiced.

As for my own image of Jason Forrester, it had been formed by the newspapers. They had shown him dressed in a suit and tie, his hair neatly cut, his cheeks and chin shaved smooth. Large sunglasses invariably hid much of his face, except for the forceful nose and the uncompromising mouth.

He had seemed distant in those pictures, disdainful. He'd *looked* like a dangerous man.

Just as I had been unprepared for the movie-star appeal of Brent, I was unprepared for the ordinary reality of Jason Forrester.

After a while the brothers came out, convinced that the footings had been poured wrong.

As Brent rolled up the plans, Jason strolled over to my desk. His glance brushed my breasts. "Welcome to the company. Decided whether or not you're going to like us?" He raised his challenging stare to mine.

His eyes were brown. They appeared golden at times because they had tiny yellow flecks in them. His mouth under the beard was like Lettie's and Brent's, wide with a full and sensual bottom lip that curved easily into a grin. Strange how the papers had made it look so thin and stern.

"I'm sure I don't know." I dredged up my usual aplomb. "I imagine I shall. *Some* of the people are very nice."

Thick eyelashes fringed eyes whose corners wrinkled with laughter. He was sharp, I had to give him that. Further reflection suggested he wasn't the sort of man who missed much that went on around him.

I wondered how he'd missed the fact that his fiancée and my brother had been involved for nearly a month before Alan's death.

"I think you'll find that most of us are very nice." He nodded at me in a meaningful way. "See you later. Brent, come over and meet the bull tonight. He's the handsomest devil around these parts. I'll bet the cows will be chewing their cuds with ecstasy once he starts plowing his way through their ranks."

Stiffening, I managed to turn an impassive face toward him as his eyes cut back. "You're welcome to come, too. Miz . . . Levee, is it?"

If that was a sample of his small talk, no wonder Tiffany had preferred Alan.

"Mrs. Levee. And I have plans." I couldn't resist adding, "As for liking it here, I do find people in Rahunta are more outspoken than what I'm accustomed to. Some to the point of being almost rude."

He reached over to lightly tap my fingers with the tips of his. "I expect that's meant for me, but I'll apologize if you will."

It took all my strength of character not to jerk away from his touch. I trembled with the effort. "Of course I'm sorry I failed to recognize you, Mr. Forrester. If you'd told me who you were to start with, we'd never have had any trouble, would we?"

His eyes widened in delight. He was laughing at me, damn him. "Mrs. Levee," he said solemnly, "I wouldn't have missed it for the world."

He left with Brent, which was just as well. I was too unsettled, too *infuriated*, to deal with his presence any longer.

Jason Forrester was not at all what I'd expected.

CHAPTER FIVE

AN ARTICLE I ONCE read theorized that people meeting for the first time know within ten minutes whether or not they are attracted to each other.

The thesis seemed sensible, and I saw no reason to question it. Not until I met Jason Forrester.

From the moment I knew who he was, I honestly didn't know what I felt about him. His cavalier laughter at my expense angered me. And I'd already half formed an opinion, not an approving opinion, of him because of Alan.

Still, as I sank into a wooden rocker that evening to watch the sun set over the gorge, I could think of nothing else. The purely physical reaction he'd evoked disturbed and at the same time excited me. Not knowing my own mind unsettled me.

Absorbed in such contemplations, I was oblivious to the sense of being spied upon that had become a common occurrence. Eventually, though, the old tingling began.

I'd invested in a good pair of binoculars for observing the wildlife and plants in the gorge and used them now, sweeping the sides and top.

As always, there was nobody in sight, spectral or human.

Was it my nerves, or was I really being watched?

While I rocked, trying to concentrate on the vista before me, a familiar figure came out of the wooded area hiding the gorge trail. As had become his habit since I'd moved in, Matt Graven made his way to my porch. The unseen spy was forgotten when he sat down in the rocker beside me. "Great walk we had last week. I thought we might take a longer hike Saturday morning."

I was agreeable. He hadn't known Alan, but he did know the gorge and I was anxious to learn it, too.

We chatted in a relaxed fashion and watched the sun set.

Matt asked about my job. "Are you still liking it?"

"Yes."

It was true. I enjoyed working with Lettie and Lois and Brent, and I was fast developing an appreciation for the local people who were in and out of the office.

Much as I wanted to avoid the subject of Brent's brother, Matt brought him up. "I hear Jason Forrester's back. You met him yet?"

"I have." I was glad Matt was gazing toward Brent's house and not at me. "He came into the office today."

"What did you think?"

I shrugged. "I've only seen him the one time."

"Don't let him push you around, Anna. You may be new up here, but you're not without friends."

He was very much in earnest and I was touched. "Why, Matt, how sweet. Thank you." I leaned over to squeeze his hand. "But I'm not an easy person to push around. And to be honest, I don't think Lettie would let anyone bully me."

Behind the thick glasses, he scowled. "Jason Forrester can get away with anything."

"I'm not dependent on this job, I assure you. I can quit anytime I want to."

"Good. That makes me feel better."

In perfect accord, we watched the sun become an orange sliver until my cell chimed. The number was unfamiliar, but it might be Charles Raite or one of Bob's sons. With an apologetic word to Matt, I answered.

To my surprise, Simone Forrester, in her pretty accent, asked me to lunch on Saturday. "The only women our age around here are so boring. I'm dying to talk about something other than canning or crocheting or babies."

There was nothing I'd like better than to have a little chat with Jason Forrester's sister-in-law, but . . .

"I wish I could, but I just made plans to go hiking in the gorge Saturday."

"With Matt Graven?"

"Yes."

"I thought so. I saw him go toward your cabin earlier. Why don't you both come?"

"I'll ask him. Hang on."

"Oh, heck, I can't." Matt's disappointment was obvious as I relayed the question. "I have a friend from Charlotte coming over Saturday afternoon. But we can plan on getting to Simone's about noon and you can eat with her, Anna. She can drive you back afterward."

Simone squealed when I told her. "I'm so glad! Brent and Jason are going off and I'd be bored to tears here by myself."

Murmuring sympathetically, I hoped she'd volunteer more but she didn't. I had to fish. "I suppose Brent will be back in time for work Monday."

"Oh, he'll be back Saturday night. They're only going over to Tennessee. Something about a job they have to redo."

"Cavalry Stables. Footings poured backwards."

I could almost see Simone's little shrug. "You'd know better than me. I don't keep up with such tedious stuff. I'll expect you and Matt about noon Saturday then."

After Matt left, I stared into space, thinking of Jason Forrester. Chill bumps on my arms made me get a sweater.

I wanted to get to know him. Because of my brother, I told myself. I wanted to pump him, find out what had happened between him and Alan.

There was an air of wickedness about Jason Forrester, but it didn't seem like the kind that leads to murder. His sins would more likely be speeding down back roads, drinking too much, sneaking out with one woman while engaged to another . . .

No, no, that was wrong. It was Tiffany who'd run around on Jason, not the other way around. And despite his golden eyes and hypnotic voice, he was a hulking mass whose brain was probably the size of a peanut.

I wondered what Tiffany was like in person, if she possessed that same irreverent air as Jason. I tried to picture the sophisticated woman in the photograph with the bearded rustic I'd met today, but couldn't.

My dreams, in abeyance for a while, returned that night, but Alan was no longer the central figure. Some sort of blurred wraith beckoned me and my feet couldn't resist its coaxing.

As I went toward it, I saw my brother off to the side, frantically beating as though on an invisible wall. I could see his lips mouthing my name along with other disjointed phrases I couldn't hear. Powerless to stop and decipher what he was trying to tell me, I could only follow that irresistible silvery figure as it lured me through shadowy forests and jutting rocks toward a forbidding fantasy castle.

Strangely, I was not desperate to discover what Alan wanted from me as I'd been in the earlier dreams.

This time I was fearful but determined, sure the truth waited for me inside.

At the threshold of the dark castle, I hung back because instinct warned that if I went in, I'd be lost. Just as my spectral guide persuaded me to open the door, I awakened with a hoarse cry. My heart pounded furiously. It took several moments to quiet the thudding in my ears.

Had my meeting with Jason Forrester engendered such fear?

* * *

ON FRIDAY, I ARRIVED at the office to follow the smell of fresh coffee to the kitchen where Brent and Jason stood. My entrance caught them unaware. Brent's head hung dejectedly as Jason talked in a low voice, one hand on his brother's shoulder. "—nearly made it up. The Louisiana sugar project should put us well in the black. It'll be okay then. You'll see."

They looked up. Jason's arm dropped and so did his gravity, replaced by the nonchalant air I'd seen before.

He looked no better than on our previous meeting, but his movements when he got up were as supple as I remembered. "Good morning, Mrs. Levee." I'd never before heard my name spoken in such a sexy way. Its intonation told me he remembered every detail of how I'd looked with my blouse gaping open and my lingerie exposed.

"Good morning." In the tiny kitchen, I had to turn sideways to keep from touching him as I went over to pour myself coffee and pick up one of Maggie Mahone's biscuits.

"You look a lot different without your glasses," he said approvingly.

"I've heard that before." My tone told him that it was a hackneyed line that didn't work anymore.

"Jace and I are about to run over to Birmingham to look at some steel siding." Brent was completely unaware of the friction. "Mom'll be here later on, but Lois is out."

"She still sick?" Jason forgot me in his concern for Lois.

"Strep throat. You know how susceptible she is."

"Poor Lois." His attention came back to me. His eyes turned soft and merry. "Kind of heartless, leaving Mrs. Levee to run the office by herself."

"I can manage." He probably looked at all women that way.

"Anna's right, she can manage. Mom did good when she hired her." Brent smiled at me. "I'm glad you're coming over to see Simone tomorrow, Anna. I hope you and she can become friends. There aren't too many people around here she feels comfortable with. She gets . . . lonesome."

I caught the curl of a bearded lip as Jason turned abruptly and went out.

Matt was right. Jason Forrester didn't care for Simone.

The kitchen seemed twice as large without his presence.

* * *

SATURDAY MORNING, CLAD IN a comfortable, lightweight athletic suit and new hiking boots from L.L. Bean, I awaited Matt. The uncompromising lines of Simone's house were obscured by light morning fog, its bubble roof dark and mysterious. A pickup truck drove down its hairpin drive and parked behind the dome. Within minutes, the same truck climbed back up and disappeared over the top of the hill.

Jason and Brent were off to Tennessee.

Promptly at eight-thirty, Matt came up. "Ready?"

He'd led me over the rim to Lettie's house the past Saturday. We set off in that direction as if we were going to walk the same route.

"We've been this way," I protested to his back. "I thought we were going down into the gorge."

"Sure." He didn't break his stride. "We're going down the old logging road. We can rest at the bottom and then climb back up to Simone's. If you don't dawdle," he added, throwing a stern glance over his shoulder, "we should get to her house right at noon."

"Lead on, MacDuff."

Ten minutes later he pointed out a path that intersected with the trail we were following. "That goes down and back up to my cottage. It's safe so long as you keep to the path. You can use it when you come to see me."

Would I be going to see him? I'd have to think that over.

A little farther, before we passed Lettie's house, the path forked again at a large oak. "That trail leads straight to Simone's house," he said. "Don't ever take it by yourself."

"Is that the way we're going?"

"No, places on it are way too rough for beginners. And we'd get there in about thirty minutes, a little early for lunch."

Passing within a hundred feet of Lettie's house, I saw no sign of movement, though her car was in the open garage. What would it be like to grow up at the edge of this awesome cleft, as Jason and Brent must have done? I could imagine the rugged Jason as a little boy, sneaking out and exploring the trails, getting himself scolded, maybe spanked.

But not Brent. The very idea of Brent doing anything he wasn't supposed to made me smile. Brent was like me: too cautious, too mindful of what was expected. If Brent was ever punished, I'd bet it would have been because of his brother.

Why couldn't I keep my mind off Jason Forrester?

Pushing back a briar, I followed Matt's intrepid figure in front of me. Without optimism I hoped my thick socks would keep the new boots from blistering my feet.

"From here you can see the Rahunta Rapids," Matt told me when I made it up to where he leaned patiently on his hiking staff. "Isn't it a glorious view?"

It was that and more.

At the bottom, a tangle of rocks and water marked all that was left of the Rahunta River, which had once boasted several raging waterfalls. The slope from here seemed gentle, but I knew in places the trail was narrow, steep and treacherous. "Lettie said there are several places where people have fallen."

Matt pointed with his staff. "One's over there on the trail to Simone's. That rocky part."

"But it looks so lovely."

"Lovely to look at, but treacherous as hell," he said with a frown. "Don't take any chances around the gorge, Anna."

"Of course not." Not cautious Annabelle.

From here I could see my cottage, look down in front of it to where my brother had died. I could feel Alan prompting me, telling me I needed to get organized and find out exactly what had happened that terrible night.

The other niggling presence was absent for a change, and I was glad.

"The logging road's back there just a bit," Matt said, "but I wanted you to see the gorge from here. Ready to start down?"

"Ready."

After we'd gone about ten yards, the way took a sharp turn. I hesitated, dizzy at the sight of the twelve hundred feet below.

Matt looked back. "What's the matter?"

"There's no railing."

"No, but if you stay on the inner edge of the path, you'll be okay." He must have seen my disbelief, for a grin lit his face. "Honest. Hey, this is one of the good trails. Trucks came in and out this way. Still do sometimes, for that matter."

"I'm glad to hear that. I feel so much better," I muttered, but quietly. I'd discovered early that Matt had very little sense of humor and understood sarcasm not at all. He took himself and everything around him very seriously.

Once we were on the old roadbed, the walking became easier. By midmorning we were at the bottom, where the walls of the gorge, looming on both sides, cut off most of the sunlight.

We picked our way through the shaded underbrush until, finding a large rock soaking up sunbeams beside a limpid pool, we stopped to rest.

The mossy seat was barely wide enough for two, but we sat side by side with our shoulders touching. Matt pulled out a bottle of water, and, after I apologized for knocking his ribs with my elbow, we drank in companionable silence.

"A lot different from Atlanta, isn't it?" he asked.

"Yep. No traffic to fight, no people arguing next door, no cruisers going up and down the streets. Just the birds and the trees and the rushing water."

A cloud went across the sun, and in that instant the conviction that someone or something was watching us returned. And not just watching. I felt spite behind the unseen eyes, and felt it strongly enough to destroy my peace of mind.

When I got up and looked around, no one was visible so I said nothing to Matt. I didn't want him to think I was crazy, though I was beginning to wonder. A large gray puff rose above the trees, distracting me. "Smoke?"

"From the Underwoods' chimney. They have a hundred acres over beyond the trees." He paused, his mood changing. "By now you've probably heard Tiffany Underwood was engaged to Jason Forrester."

"Yes." I went on encouragingly, "Although after meeting him, I can't imagine why she wanted him."

He laughed. "She's too young to know better. She won't graduate from college until this spring and he's thirty-two or three."

"I heard she jilted him."

He looked away, his discomfort obvious.

"Come on, Matt," I coaxed. "Let's have all the unsavory details."

"Well, I don't know personally, of course, but I've heard . . ." Matt lowered his voice confidentially and in a few moments I'd wormed out of him everything he knew about Jason and Tiffany and Alan.

Jason and Tiffany had become engaged at Christmas nearly two years before. The following spring, when she was home on break, Tiffany had met Alan for the first time. Gossip said they'd immediately entered into a passionate and clandestine relationship. When Jason found out, he shot my brother in a jealous rage and took Alan's wallet to make it look like a robbery.

"Then he threw McKenzie into the gorge. Nothing was ever proved, though," Matt hastened to add. "The gun was never found, and without it, there was no way Jason could be tied to it."

"So Tiffany called off the engagement."

"Uh huh. She never believed his story."

"She and most of the county, I understand." I could not help but think of those soft golden eyes. Would a murderer's eyes look like that?

"Most people around here think he was justified," Matt said. "This is a peculiar region, Anna. Wild. Savage. People have their own set of values. They don't always think the way you or I would."

"Do you think Jason murdered him?" I shivered and moved a little closer. Maybe Matt's nearness would dispel that encroaching presence.

"I don't know. But I made friends with Tiffany this last summer, and she says Jason nearly killed a man one time before. When he was engaged to another girl ten or twelve years ago. And you know why?"

He leaned over to emphasize his words. "Because this guy was running around with his fiancée."

"Really?" Now that was something I had not heard. I nearly forgot the malicious eyes observing us. "Did the authorities know about this when they were searching for—for the teacher's murderer?"

Our heads were so close, I could see the dissatisfaction mirrored through his lenses. "Tiffany told them. She says it didn't make any difference, that the cops in this county are all controlled by the Forresters, that there's no use trying to pin anything on one of them."

I grunted, cold from the resurgence of the mysterious presence. Why did it only dog me whenever I was near the gorge? And why did it seem so, so angry today?

Picking up a stone, I fingered its smooth surface, all the while wondering if the apprehensions that seemed to come out of the blue were a sign that I needed to go back to Dr. Brunweld. Maybe my coming here hadn't been such a good idea.

"Listen, you won't repeat any of what I told you, will you?" Matt, belatedly remembering that I was in the camp of the enemy, turned anxious after unburdening himself. "The Forresters finance the school, and I'd hate to get on the bad side of them. Not that everybody doesn't already know all this."

I threw the stone into the placid water. "My lips are sealed. As a matter of fact, I'd already heard most of it." All of it except that Jason Forrester had nearly killed a man. A man who had stolen his fiancée.

Glancing around, I leaned back on the rock, hooked my hands around a knee and held my face up to the autumn sun. There was no one sinister in sight, tourist or local. "You're right about the people here backing Jason. The woman who cut my hair yesterday said that he never killed anyone. She said she'd believe Jason over Tiffany Underwood any time."

What Janie had said was that Tiffany was a spoiled brat who, when she had a man like Jace Forrester on the line, deserved what she got when she started casting in another pond.

"Jace made her give his ring back, he did, when she broke the engagement," Janie had said with smug satisfaction. "She slandered Jason, and then didn't want to return that flashy big diamond of his grandmother's. But Jace has backbone. He went over there and took it off her hand."

"The story I heard was that she was buck naked," the older woman next to me having her hair permed chimed in. "I heard Jason didn't pay her any more mind than if she'd had on a nun's habit. He just went up to her bedroom and pulled the ring off her finger, and didn't pay a bit more attention to her screaming and carrying on than he would to the man in the moon."

Janie had smiled as her quick hands clipped at my hair, a secretive knowing smile tinged with admiration. "That's Jace for you. Makes up his mind that something needs to be done and does it. Come hell or high water. You can always depend on Jace when something needs doing."

If he made up his mind to kill a man, would he go about it the same way?

My repeating Janie's insinuations irritated Matt. "Tiffany wouldn't hurt a fly. She's smart and pretty, so it stands to reason people are jealous of her, Anna. Just like they're jealous of Simone for marrying a Forrester." He added bitterly, "Jason Forrester thinks he can get away with anything."

Oho. Matt's quick defense of Tiffany might arise from dislike of Jason Forrester. Or not.

He got up. "Shall we go?"

I took the hand he offered and dusted off my running suit pants, wondering what Jason had done to earn Matt's resentment. Matt didn't strike me as the kind of person who'd harbor a grudge for no reason.

The hovering spirit receded as we climbed. Simone lived only a short distance above, but, with the curving, uneasy trail, it was noon before we emerged from the woods beside her house.

Confronting it brought on a revulsion so strong that I hung back when Matt strode confidently up to the entrance. My reaction baffled me until I realized that this house before was similar to the castle of my dreams. In them, it had appeared dark and ominous, hanging out on a shelf of the gorge. In reality, it was starkly modern, with the gray dome curving over one half and a flat roof emphasizing the straight concrete sides of the other.

Perhaps I had subconsciously incorporated the house into my nightmares after seeing it.

Or perhaps Alan was back to his old tricks.

CHAPTER SIX

"HI, JENNY," MATT GREETED the unsmiling young woman in jeans and an Atlanta Falcons' sweatshirt who opened the door and showed us to the living room.

This was a dramatic area at the beginning of the dome. There, beneath the shaded glass, Brent's wife sat cross-legged on an Oriental carpet looking at a magazine. A toddler tried to climb over her shoulder. Simone, artless with her light hair pulled back and minimal makeup on her flawless features, looked about twelve. She might have been baby-sitting for a younger brother.

Matt bumped into me as I stopped in midstep to exclaim, "How adorable. The two of you make a perfect picture."

"With me in these old things?" Despite her disparaging remark about her appearance, Simone seemed pleased at my admiration. "Never. But I can't wear my good clothes with Christopher, for he either spits or makes poopoo on them." She saw Matt behind me and her face lit up, making her lovelier than ever. "Matt, how nice to see you again."

The baby was tearing pages from the magazine, but Simone didn't notice as she got to her feet.

Matt's voice was warm. "It's good to see you, too, Simone. I enjoyed hiking over with Anna."

I added my appreciation. "The hike was great, Matt. Thanks for bringing me."

Simone went over to put her hand on Matt's arm. "Are you sure you can't stay and have lunch with us?"

They were obviously good friends, but for some reason the scene seemed out of kilter.

"Thanks, Simone. I wish I could." Matt put up a hand to press hers. "Lew's coming up to see the gorge and I need to get back to meet him." He glanced at his watch. "In fact, he's due anytime now. I'd better go." He reluctantly released her to wave at me. "See you later, Anna."

Simone pouted. "You'd rather eat with some boring old school-teacher than with Anna and me?"

He seemed more distraught than the occasion warranted. "No, no, I swear I wouldn't. If I hadn't told Lewis—"

"I forgive you." She took his arm. "I'll even walk you to the door.

I'll be right back, Anna," she called over her shoulder. "Christopher will entertain you."

As they went out, I heard her teasing voice coaxing answering laughter from Matt.

They seemed to know each other quite well. In fact, she'd held onto his arm in a familiar way that . . .

I shrugged my suspicions away. I was as bad as the townspeople Matt complained of. Simone was a beautiful woman who enjoyed flirting. Lots of beautiful women enjoyed flirting.

Everything and everyone was beginning to take on sinister undertones. Those cursed dreams were ruining my life, and now they were taking over my days as well as my nights.

Damn them. And damn Alan for causing them.

I watched the baby tear the magazine pages for a few minutes, then knelt down beside him as he waved a fistful of paper. "What educational material are you reading, little one?"

"*Vogue*, but he only wants to eat the pictures." Simone had slipped in behind me. She looked breathless, like a woman who'd just been kissed.

I firmly kept my imagination in place.

"See, Anna, how he likes only the pretty ones." She giggled as Christopher, on cue, put a brightly colored page into his mouth.

"He'll choke," I told her. I'd had lots of experience babysitting when I was a teenager plus Bob had small grandchildren we sometimes kept. I held Christopher's dimpled chin and took the paper out. The boy, who had his mother's clear blue eyes, looked at me reproachfully.

"Oh, but he'll cry," Simone told me disapprovingly. Even as she spoke, the baby was puckering up his mouth. "See?"

"Better have him cry a bit than let him choke. Here, perhaps he'd like a rattle." I gave him the toy lying on the edge of the rug and helped him sound it.

"He'll not play with anything for long." Simone shrugged. "Anyway, it's time for his nap. Jenny! Jenny!"

The woman who'd admitted us must have been right outside the door, for she stuck her head in immediately.

"Jenny, take Christopher and put him down." Simone gave her a brilliant smile. "Anna and I wish to visit a bit. We'll have out lunch when you get him to bed."

"Sure, Simone." Jenny, poker face never breaking, picked up the baby with practiced ease. "Come on, runt. I'll bet you're getting hungry."

"He's a darling baby," I said with sincerity. "And he favors you so much."

Simone waved a hand modestly. "Oh, no, not at all. It's his father he takes most after. Everyone says he looks just like Brent."

"I think he looks just like you."

She laughed, a silvery gurgle of music. "For heaven's sake, let's not talk baby talk. I am so sick of it I could die. Tell me about you. Are you liking it here?"

"Yes. Very much." I thought about Jason Forrester and averted my eyes, afraid Simone would read my doubts. "Most of the time, anyway." I pretended to look around. The setting, only now fully perceived, was an interior designer's dream. "Simone, this house is wonderful."

The living area where we were, housed a traditional sofa group set casually about a freestanding fireplace with various tables scattered within strategic distance from each seat. On the left wall stood a desk, over which hung a glass case displaying rifles and handguns. The other wall boasted a gorgeous mural, its cleverly painted trees and sky continuing until the picture merged with, and was lost in, the outside view brought in by the transparent dome.

Beyond us, a macadam walkway wove its way among huge palms and banana trees and other smaller plants that formed a conservatory. A statue of some muse or other stood in its center, while smaller sculptures nestled in secluded corners.

The huge dome, thirty feet or more at its highest point in the garden, started in the middle of the living area overhead and curved outward over the true focus at the far end.

Through the palm fronds, a miniature waterfall cascaded invitingly into a shimmering pool disguised as a natural rock formation. Its area was defined by a decorative wrought-iron banister and gate, barely glimpsed through the plants and greenery.

"We had to add the fence when the baby was born," Simone said, following my gaze. "It detracts from the appearance, but Brent was afraid he would fall in." Dismay clouded her features. "I should've told you to bring your bathing suit. I have extra ones if you care to swim. Do you?"

I told her it sounded like heaven. "But not today. Next time I'll come prepared. May I see the rest of the house?"

She brightened instantly. "We'll go on the grand tour. Everyone admires our house. It's much in demand socially, let me tell you." Her ingenuous pleasure took away any sign of boasting. "The school takes yearbook pictures here and it's always on the Tour of Homes. The garden club uses it, too."

"I'm sure it's not just the house. You and Brent must be very cordial hosts."

Simone was every bit as enchanting as her first impression had suggested, resembling nothing so much as the fairy princesses one reads about. With silken hair falling about her graceful shoulders, she could have stepped right out of Grimm.

She took me through the kitchen with its center island and top-line appliances, chattering all the while. "I wanted everything to be modern. I hate these new old-fashioned styles."

She barely gave me time to glance at the amethyst marble counters and enameled lavender cabinets before hustling me down a long hall. We peeked into a lavender and pale blue nursery where Jenny, giving the baby a bottle, frowned at us.

Simone put a finger to her lip and cast me a conspiratorial glance. "Baby's going to sleep," she murmured and led me on down the hall.

An open door caught my eye. Sunlight poured through skylights to bounce off pristine white walls and varnished hardwood. Hanging on and leaning against the wall, and stacked up on the floor in untidy piles, I saw painting after painting, each an unexpected explosion of color.

Simone grimaced when she saw what had caught my attention. "Brent's studio. We dare not touch it to clean, you can see. He doesn't like anything to be moved."

Stepping inside, I looked at the canvas nearest me. "I didn't know Brent painted."

"Oh, yes, it's his hobby."

I surprised her look of disdain.

She saw the question in my expression and gave a little Gallic moue. "He does not do so much now as when we were first married. Now that we have the baby."

There was something out of the ordinary in her manner. Surely it wasn't resentment. Jealousy?

I examined the paintings.

Though all Brent's work showed talent, a series of his wife was brilliant. Simone at her dressing table in a filmy nightgown; outside in torn jeans and clinging T-shirt; against snow with a fuzzy sweater and ski pants; beside the pool, her legs and arms bare and honeyed against the briefest of bikinis.

Most arresting was a pastel on one of the easels, unfinished, looking as though it had been abandoned for some time.

In it an obviously pregnant Simone was dressed as if for a garden party. Shapely arms emerged from a sleeveless dress while her neck was crossed with choker pearls. A wide-brimmed hat, its crown wrapped with a purple scarf, shaded her forehead.

Brent had chosen to portray his wife with a pouting mouth and a blank stare. The likeness was good, the features perfect, but a disturbing quality stood out, as if the artist had reached inside the woman and brought out the nerve ends. Nerve ends that were raw.

Simone peered around my shoulder. "That's awful. I hate it. I'm glad Brent never finished it. I was pregnant, so fat and ugly."

"You could never be ugly."

She drew me away, pushing me past an immaculate guest room into the master bedroom suite crammed with furniture. It included a dressing room, a reading area, a tiny kitchenette and a whirlpool bath in its own garden alcove.

I oohed and aahed at the proper places and was rewarded by Simone's smile. "I decorated it myself." She proudly indicated the heavy velvet draperies and lacy accessories, all in varying shades of purple. "I am fond of purple."

I looked at the lavender tiles and fixtures of the master bathroom, the grapes and wisteria in the expensive wallpaper, the lavender chandeliers over the mirror and tried my best to summon enthusiasm. "Yes, I can tell. What unusual paper. Wherever did you find it?"

French doors led to a long deck that overlooked the gorge and brought us back to the living area. The gold of flooding sunlight was a welcome contrast to the cloying purples and lavenders.

"Ah, isn't it wonderful?" Simone saw me basking in its warmth. "I tried to tell Brent to put these roofs into his boring little buildings, but if I have suggestions, he says they are ridiculous and costly. Let him come up with something, though, and it's innovative and imaginative and exactly what people want." She flung her hands out in a mock serious gesture. "Do you think that's fair? Are all men like that, or is it just in Brent Forrester's blood? His papa was very strong-minded, you know. And his mama."

She paused for breath, giving me the opening I unconsciously awaited. "His brother, too?"

Her face changed. She looked away as one fragile hand twined in the silvery hair. Her voice was muffled when she spoke. "Jason is . . . He is stubborn, too." She looked back at me almost slyly. "And more. You've met him, then. Didn't you feel something?"

"Feel something? Only annoyance, I'm afraid."

"Ah, you see it, too."

"See what?"

She bent toward me. "Jason is a bad man, Anna."

This was such a strange choice of words that I had no idea how I should answer. "Is he? Lettie seems to depend on him a great deal."

Simone twisted her hair in a childlike manner. "Letitia thinks both her sons are perfect."

"I've heard rumors about Jason." How far dared I go?

"Oh, Jenny, there you are!" Simone abandoned the subject with relief, as if afraid she'd said too much. "We're hungry. Was it hard to get Baby down?" Her face was innocent and untroubled.

"Not hard at all. Little fella went like a lamb." The laconic Jenny set down a tray from which she took appetizing cold plates and tall glasses of iced tea. "He always does. Christopher's a good baby."

"Yes, he is." Simone got up to dance over to the table. "Jenny, the salad looks so good. Though Anna doesn't need a salad, slim as she is."

I got up, too. "I hope you don't worry about your weight, Simone. Your figure's ideal."

She preened but gestured modestly. "I'm fine up here." She put both hands to her chest. "But if I'm not careful, I get too fat down here." She put a hand on her stomach. "Babies are hard on a woman."

"Yes, but they're worth it."

"Ah, that just goes to show you've never had one," Simone retorted, watching as the silent Jenny set the table and left. "Wait till you do. Men won't look at you, you're fat, and you get stretch marks. Oh, you'll change your tune then."

"That's a long while off." Thoughts of Alan and the children he should have had roughened my voice. "Maybe never."

"Well, they *are* a lot of trouble. Oh, Anna, I'm so glad you're here! I've needed a friend, someone to talk to."

"I'll try my best to be your friend." As much as I could be a friend to any of these people, I told myself, salving my conscience. I couldn't look Simone in the eye and to hide my discomfort, I picked at my salad. "Isn't Jenny your friend?"

Her ebullience fled. "Jenny looks after the baby and the house," Simone said carefully. "Jason hired her for us."

"Jason?" I stared.

"She's wonderful with Christopher. We are very fortunate to have her." Her voice was wooden, the words rehearsed. Her expression gave away nothing.

If I pried too much, she might retreat again. "Lettie says you're from Canada." The tuna salad presented in split tomatoes over lettuce was delicious. "How did you and Brent meet?"

"I'm French, but my father died when I was young, and my mama and I moved over to Quebec to live with her brother. Brent came up to build a plant, and one of the men took him to a shooting match where my uncle was competing. That's where we met. We fell in love immediately, and when he finished the plant, we eloped and I came back with him."

"How romantic. You must have been swept off your feet."

"I think this must be true. I hadn't known him even two weeks when we married. It was all very fast. Sometimes I think it was too fast." She smiled wistfully.

I would certainly never risk marriage after a two-week courtship. Simone was much more impetuous than I. "Brent seems like a very nice man."

"Oh, he is, he is. Only occasionally, I wish I had waited. Perhaps traveled a bit, saw some of the world." She grimaced. "Now I do nothing but stay in this, this rural backwater. It is very hard sometimes."

"I'm sure it is." I felt sorry for her, in spite of thinking any woman worth her salt would do something for herself if she was so unhappy.

Brent's voice came from the entrance foyer, and he entered a second later.

"Brent! I thought you were to be gone till this afternoon." There was nothing but pleasure in the greeting Simone gave her husband.

He planted a kiss on her forehead. "Jace and I got through early. How're you, Anna?" He smiled but looked tired as he shrugged out of his jacket.

"Fine, thanks."

"I asked Jace to come in for a bite before he went on home, hon," he said to Simone. At her movement, he added, "No, don't get up. I've already told Jenny."

And *he* came into the room at Brent's words, as if he had been waiting on his cue.

I almost fell out of my chair.

The long hair was smoothly cut off and the stubble of beard was gone, leaving only a neatly trimmed mustache. To my amazement, without the concealing whiskers, he was, in a totally different way, as arresting as his brother.

Brent was a proud Viking seafarer, while Jason's swarthy skin and high cheekbones made him a Spanish buccaneer. All he lacked was a gold earring.

Instead, he wore a striped polo shirt with sleeves that outlined the heavy muscles of his shoulders and upper arms. His faded Levi's fit snugly around the hips and left no doubt that a man wore them.

"Hello, Simone. Hello, Anna. Good to see you again."

I flushed as I realized exactly where he had caught me staring.

"You look a lot different without your beard," I said.

He grinned, surveying my running suit from top to bottom. He was patently wondering if what lay beneath the knit fabric would satisfy his tastes and if it would be possible for him to find out. I knew without being told that he was debating whether he *cared* enough to find out.

My blush deepened as a quickening in my own body made me aware I was thinking exactly the same thing about him.

Turning away to hide confusion, I caught a glimpse of Simone as she pushed back her chair.

A good thing I was the only one in a position to see her face, because there was stark hatred written there. A second later, she was composed and turning toward her husband.

"I didn't expect you for lunch, since you said you'd be gone all day, Brent. We would have waited to eat. But we'll have coffee with you and Jason. And guess what? Anna enjoys swimming. She's going to come and swim with me one day soon. Isn't that nice?"

"Yes, it is," her husband said, with an inattentiveness I noted and filed away for later reference. He rolled up his shirtsleeves before he sat down at the table.

"Very nice," his brother drawled. "Brent's dome is great for private sunbathing. You can wear a bikini or nothing at all if you like, the way it's designed."

I caught myself squirming and forced myself to be still. There was no doubt in my mind that he was picturing me laid out in the buff, his for the taking.

"Sun's bad for the skin, but swimming is good exercise." I pointedly discouraged such imaginings. "I love your pool, Brent. I suppose you designed it yourself?"

We embarked on the subject of architecture, where Jason joined in enthusiastically. "—but there's nothing like seeing the final project. After months of drawing and redrawing, watching the foundations go in and then the framework . . . Seeing everything happening like you planned it is more satisfying than you'd ever believe."

"The Kumpher Building near Lenox is one of Forrest Lands, isn't it?" Bob had pointed it out to me years ago. "I remember my husband telling me it went against the trend at that time in using beauty as one of the basics."

Brent and Jason both looked gratified, but it was Jason who answered. "Your husband was pretty smart. That was Dad's design. His feeling was that if a building isn't aesthetically pleasing, no one's going to want to live or work in it."

"And you carry on the tradition?"

His eyes smiled into mine. "As best we can. Brent's the artist. He imagines what a building should look like. I'm mainly the engineer. I see his ideas to completion."

Brent was quick to demur. "Don't let him fool you, Anna. Jason's as good a designer as me."

Jason attempted to look modest. "What can I say?"

"That without Mom we'd be nothing?" Brent countered.

Jason's vehement denial led to a good-natured argument on who contributed more to Forrest Land Company, allowing the conversation to flow smoothly for the rest of the meal.

Except that Simone no longer chattered.

And except that whenever I glanced over toward Jason Forrester, he met my eyes with a look that sent a frisson up my back. He was the type of man used to taking what he wanted, and I had the strangest urge to give it to him.

My calm responses should send out the right signals, that I was not available for the taking. *His* taking, in any event, even if he was my boss.

I had no intention of entangling myself with Jason Forrester. It would be idiotic to encourage him. Besides the fact he might be tied to Alan's death, I refused to be another woman like Lois, fawning all over him.

As he chatted with Brent, I stole one more glance at him. I'd always been drawn to men with strong facial bones, and his were unforgettable. As was his gorgeous body. It was a shame his personality didn't match his appearance.

On the other hand, he was being very careful today. He sat there making small talk like he was enjoying himself. One could almost forget the underlying arrogance.

I felt myself mellowing.

After lunch, he took me back to my cabin. I'm not sure how that came about. I certainly never intended to ride with him.

One moment Simone was saying she'd drive me back, while I protested it wasn't that long a walk, and the next I found myself being herded out to Jason's truck.

"I can walk home," I said emphatically. "Thank you anyway."

"No, ma'am, it's four or five miles if you go around by the road. And Lettie'd have my hair if I let you take that trail," he said just as emphatically. "You're be bound to fall and she'd blame me."

Before I could refute him, he had taken my arm. Before I could escape his unsettling touch, he'd forced me into his truck.

Well, perhaps *forced* is a bit strong. Perhaps I wanted, a little bit, to get into it.

He climbed in behind the wheel. "It's dangerous for a big-city lady like you to be going off by yourself around the gorge. Never know what might happen."

"I've not been by myself. I had a guide."

"Oh?" He put his truck into reverse. "Who?"

"A friend."

We started to climb up the asphalt drive. "You can't have met that many people up here," he said meditatively.

"I've met enough. Maybe even a few too many."

He laughed, and suddenly, without my understanding how he'd managed it, he turned into the most engaging man I'd ever known.

Perhaps it was the gold of his eyes, reminding me of the sunlight streaming through Simone's domed roof. Perhaps it was the husky timbre of his voice, which turned almost musical when he loosed it over me. "Do I have to get down on my knees and apologize for the other day?"

"I don't know what you're talking about." I would not fall victim to his looks or his charm. I told myself that and believed it.

We came to the highway and he stopped, checking right and left before turning. "I don't mind apologizing if that'll make you forgive me. I'm sorry, Anna. It was pure cussedness that made me do it. I was in a hurry and there you were,"—he diplomatically said nothing about my unbuttoned blouse although, according to the provocative curve playing round his lips, he was remembering it—"determined to keep me out. At first I wanted to shake some of that high-hat manner out of you, and then I got kind of tickled."

"I don't want to discuss it." I felt as If I were smothering.

"All right, Mrs. Levee. But just remember, I did apologize." He was laughing at me, flirting with me, sneaking a sidelong look to gauge my reaction.

"And I've accepted. There's really no more to be said. I suggest we forget the whole matter."

"Okay. I'm game if you are." He attacked from another front. "I guess your being a widow makes you standoffish. How long has it been?"

"Since Bob died?" My voice didn't break. "A year this month."

"Still grieving? Is that why you're giving me the cold shoulder?"

"The cold—?" I had to remain aloof, but I couldn't tell him why. "I'm sorry you think that. It's just that I've always chosen my friends carefully."

He was looking at the road, but I thought I heard him chuckle. "That's probably a good idea. I hope you remember it when it comes to Simone."

"Simone?" His warning came out of the blue.

"She isn't like you. Believe me, you don't want to get mixed up with Simone."

What was he insinuating? "She's very charming."

"When she wants to be." His words were final. "Underneath, she's a bitch, Anna. Nothing like you."

"You don't know anything about me." I'd made sure of that.

He looked at me for a split second, and I saw he *was* laughing. "Lady, everything you think is written on your face, so plain a first-grader could read it. I bet you couldn't lie if your life depended on it."

Angry with him—or with myself—I looked straight ahead.

We drove in silence after that, but I couldn't keep my gaze away. At first I fastened on his feet, still in work boots, relaxed and confident as they moved, pressing and releasing the accelerator or clutch.

Then my secret examination grew bolder, following the line of muscled calf and thigh encased in denim up to the big hand resting on the stick shift. His other hand casually controlled the wheel as he drove with easy competence, braking and changing gears with the same smoothness I'd noticed in his walk.

There was none of Brent's dreamy indecisiveness about this man. He was a pusher, a doer, with lusty appetites not to be denied.

"Here we are," he said, stopping the truck in front of my cottage after about ten minutes in which neither of us spoke. "Safe and sound. No charge for the transportation, no charge for the conversation and most especially, no charge for the frustration. Nosirree, I insist. I wouldn't hear of it."

I tried not to smile. My rebuffs hadn't dampened his good humor. Was the man always so cheerful?

As I started to get out, he caught my wrist and leaned over. My skin beneath his fingers jumped to life. He had to be aware of my racing pulse.

"If you want to go hiking, let me know." His breath blew warm against my cheek. "I'll take you." His voice turned low and intimate. "Anytime."

He released me, and I got out hastily, my throat too tight to speak. A slam of the door, a flash of teeth, a friendly wave and he was off.

I found my hand in the air, responding, the skin still burning from his touch.

Why did Simone hate him?

Why didn't he like Simone?

As his truck disappeared, my hand fell slowly to my side.

And what could he tell me about my brother's death?

CHAPTER SEVEN

I SUPPOSE IT WAS that afternoon that marked the beginning of my softening toward Jason Forrester. Or perhaps from the moment I'd met him, my prejudice had begun to melt. He was too candid to be a murderer, but he was also the only thread sticking out in the tangled web that surrounded Alan's death.

And I longed to pierce that web and discover the truth.

My dreams were again becoming a nuisance. They were as frequent as before, and more diverse. In them I sometimes fled to a dark castle where terror awaited, sometimes to a different place that I knew was forbidden. Sometimes a shadowy figure pursued me while at other times I was compelled to follow a gray wraith.

Always there was this feeling of something left undone, something seen but not comprehended.

Alan was generally present in the dreams, sad but never despairing. He seemed to be reassuring me, at the same time urging me on.

If only I could figure out why, what he wanted me to do.

The dreams had to be related to Rahunta and the Forrester family. If Jason Forrester could help decipher them, I would use him without remorse.

Not that there wasn't a certain fascination about the man. I'd never known anyone like him. My father, my brother and my husband had been kind and sensitive; but all had been totally lacking in the enthusiasm for life that was such an integral part of Jason.

Yes, our first meeting had been unfortunate, but when he was on his best behavior, Jason was as delightful a man as I'd ever met. Working with him had convinced me he was just what he seemed— honest but blunt—and that rumors had distorted his character. He was dangerous only because of his candor.

And his charm.

"He's sure a lot of bull," Jason Forrester told his mother and me as we watched a large and cumbersome animal supposedly worth $100,000 approach an unsuspecting cow. With a Western hat and pull-on boots, Jason might have been a cowboy leaning on the fence. Only his loud yellow jacket spoiled the picture. "Yep, Lochinvar's going to be quite a stud."

"I don't know about the stud part, but there does seem to be an awful lot of bull around here," I muttered.

Lochinvar didn't impress me. Neither did the manly sight of Jason, profiled against the light gray sky with his old Australian shepherd snuffling around his feet. Sexy enough for a woman's calendar he might be, but I was above such emotions.

Besides, I'd planned something else for this overcast November morning.

The local paper wasn't online, so hitting the Internet turned up nothing about Jason's earlier engagement. My lunch hour should have been spent in the library, with old newspapers from that period. I could have been reading in a cozy room at this very moment, except Lettie had asked me to help with the annual inventory.

Thus I was exposed to Jason Forrester's forthright method of flirtation. If he hoped to impress me by talk of studs and breeding practices, he would be sorely disappointed.

I was being unfair.

After all, getting out of the office was nice. And hadn't I wanted to get to know Jason Forrester better? If only he wasn't so, so earthy.

I thought my needling remark had gone unheard until Jason, leaning on the fence, lazily turned his head. "You're slap on the money there, Anna. Lochinvar might be the biggest bull around here, but he's not the only one, as you so aptly observed. He may not even be the best."

Although the brim of his hat shadowed his face, I could see the glint in his eyes. He'd understood me perfectly, but was pretending to take my words at face value. "There's one bull, Julius, who's serviced over a thousand cows since we first got him. Now Julius isn't big, but he sure is popular. The herd can't seem to get enough of him."

He paused, shifting his narrow hips so that he could hook his thumbs through the belt loops in his jeans. Assuming a pedantic air, he went on. "Theoretically, all bulls have the same equipment. The truth of the matter is, some just naturally know what to do with it."

I kept my composure with an effort.

He was no more discussing bulls than the man in the moon. If I hadn't become fond of Lettie, I would've given Jason Forrester a piece of my mind. But since that would have distressed her, I held my tongue.

That didn't mean I had to turn the other cheek.

"Goodness, poor Julius must be quite worn out, if you've been working him that hard," I said sweetly. "No wonder you had to bring in a new bull. Perhaps you ought to be a little more careful with this one. You wouldn't want to wear *him* out before he's middle-aged." I looked pointedly at Jason. "Like a lot of men I know."

"You must know the wrong men!" He straightened so abruptly

that his hat fell off and he had to bend over to retrieve it. "Nobody ever got worn out by a good scr—"

"Jace!" His mother was horrified. "For pity's sake, don't be so crass. Why you feel the need to be so vulgar is beyond me. You've been so much better lately, too."

I smirked. He was as touchy as any other male about his sexual abilities.

He opened his mouth, fire in his eye.

"Good gracious," Lettie went on, putting an end to the juvenile bickering by ostentatiously holding up her watch.

As usual, she was dressed in polyester pants and a blouse sporting a large bow that had come undone. With her seamed face and wild hair, she looked like a farmer's wife, completely at home in the autumn meadow. No one would have guessed she was one of the wealthiest women in the state.

She didn't give Jason a chance to speak. "We don't need to hang around here just to watch Lochinvar rutting, Jace. Let's go on over to the stables. I'm planning on leaving the Sunday after Thanksgiving, whether we're done with inventory or not."

Some days earlier she had informed us that she was going to Palm Beach with a friend for a few weeks of relaxation.

"You ought to wait until after Christmas to go, Lettie." Jason swung a booted foot up on the bottom board of the fence and leaned back in a distinctly masculine pose. "What are you and Cousin Sue going to do in Palm Beach, cooped up in some little house with each other?"

"I've put Sue off for ten years, but this time I'm really going. Don't worry. I'll be home before Christmas, Jace, in plenty of time to put up the tree and the stockings. And get your presents wrapped."

He might have blushed, but his skin was so dark it was hard to tell. "Aw, Ma, you know I'm going to miss you. I'm not worried about any old Christmas presents." He spoiled his disavowal of avarice by an anxious: "You did remember to order me those speakers for the '64 Mustang, didn't you?"

Lettie ignored him, after flashing one of those maternal smiles that said she knew he was trying to be cute but that it was out of place. "Anna, you've caught on real quick to things around the office. I don't feel a bit bad about going off with you here. I reckon we never mentioned it, but our trial period's been up awhile. If you care to stay on, we'll be happy to keep you for as long as you want. I know Brent and Jason here would agree."

"I'd love to keep working with you." At least until they found out who I was.

"Oh, we couldn't get along without you, Anna." Jason abandoned his attempts to get a rise out of his mother and smiled his sleepy smile which made me forget everything I hated about him: blunt opinions, cocky attitude and that sheer masculine ambience. "I don't know about Brent, but I couldn't stand the thought of you leaving."

At that moment I felt as low and deceitful as I ever had in my life. These people were nothing like I'd imagined, none of them. For a bare second, I thought about resigning and going back home. Then common sense took over.

I wasn't doing anything wrong. I was simply withholding the fact that I was Alan McKenzie's sister. Surely that wasn't a crime.

But my secret was beginning to weigh heavier with each passing day. What would happen when they did a background check that turned up my maiden name? What would happen when I had to admit who I was?

Those worries were for later. Right now I had to help finish counting cows. Afterward we counted the horses and colts. Then it was hogs. By the time we got back to Lettie's house for lunch, I had seen so many cows and horses and pigs, I felt like Old MacDonald.

Lettie's kitchen, which we entered directly by going around the porch to the back door, was large and bright. Though boasting appliances as modern as Simone's glossy magazine kitchen, it was the exact opposite. Cheerful curtains and Windsor chairs around a scarred, hardrock-maple table gave a homey, lived-in look.

Lettie's taste showed up everywhere. Dried rushes in a tall pottery jar stood beside the kitchen door, while an old churn sat beside an arched opening that led into a formal dining room. Through the arc, I could see Duncan Phyfe furniture, its gleaming mahogany elegant against blue draperies and carpet.

The housekeeper, an old woman who looked as if a strong wind would push her over, whipped up grilled-cheese-and-tomato sandwiches, and fresh onion soup on a stove overhung by iron pots and skillets. Her face was set in disapproving lines and she complained all the while about being grossly overworked.

Neither Lettie nor Jason paid any attention to her, other than to make sympathetic noises.

She laid out crockery on bright patchwork placemats and, leaving us to serve ourselves, disappeared with a mumbled, "Them front curtains need to be taken down and washed."

"Didn't she do them last month?" Jason asked his mother, helping himself to soup from the steaming tureen.

Lettie unfolded her napkin with a tired sigh. "You know how particular Maggie is. Her schedule says every six weeks they're to be taken down and by George, nothing'll do but to take them down and wash them."

"Maggie's the boss of this household," she added to me with a twinkle. "No matter how much she gripes. And don't think I'm a slave driver. Maggie does exactly as she pleases. We wouldn't dare try to suggest she do anything else."

"We'll have to one of these days." Jason sucked his thumb, where he'd accidentally stuck it into his soup. "She can't go on acting like she's twenty years old indefinitely."

His mother shook her head in rueful acknowledgment.

"Has she worked for you a long time?" I sampled a glass of iced tea, my stomach giddy from the sight of those pliable lips on the blunt thumb.

"Since before my marriage," Lettie said cheerfully. "She came to us from old Mrs. Forrester when Moss and I married. She's quit a few times for family reasons, but she always comes back. Thank goodness."

"Yeah, we're pretty fond of the old gal." Jace smiled at me in a conspiratorial way. "And we have a habit of hanging on to people we like."

I hastily took a bite of my sandwich. It was perfectly browned, with the tomato tasting like summer and the cheese melting in my mouth.

We ate congenially, until Simone interrupted in the middle of freshly baked apple pie. Her arrival put an end to the interesting conversation about artificial insemination versus active participation.

Cattle, again, of course.

The familiar, slight figure in vibrant rose sweater and slacks rushed in, perspiring, a leaf tangled in pale hair. Flushed cheeks made her more bewitching than ever, but the kitchen door slammed as she stopped short before Jason. "You! You! This is all your doing, isn't it?"

I remembered the look of hatred on Simone's face the previous Saturday, and the way she'd been so quiet, like she was trying to avoid Jason's notice. Today she was too angry to care.

"What in the world?" Lettie was bewildered.

Jason knew.

I could tell he knew by the way he leaned back in his chair with a patronizing smile. Gone was the geniality he'd exuded all morning.

Lettie took in Simone's appearance. "Don't tell me you ran all the way over here by the trail."

"He's talked Brent out of taking me with him to New Orleans in January! After Brent promised I could go!" Simone, wild-eyed and near exploding, confronted Jason. "You did, didn't you?"

"Why, Simone, I'm sure that's between you and Brent." Lettie shot a questioning glance toward her son, her anxiety reminding me of Brent's. "That's none of Jace's business."

Simone glared. "No? Then why did my husband say this morning when he left for work that we could go by Las Vegas while we were out that way, then when I talked to him a few minutes ago, he told me the trip was off? It was because he'd seen Jason this morning and Jason made him change his mind!"

She covered her face with her hands.

Lettie and I were mute, neither knowing what to say.

In a mercurial about-face, Simone's anger switched to despair, tears making her eyes look like rain-drenched pansies. "Oh, Lettie, I must go. I'm a caged bird, rotting away here in these godforsaken hills."

"You've been to Atlanta, San Diego and Baltimore this past year," Lettie pointed out, kindly but reasonably.

"Bah!" Simone threw up her hands in disgust. "Please, please speak to Brent and make him let me go. He'll listen to you, Lettie."

Lettie was sympathetic but gruff. "Now, hon, don't carry on so. You probably wouldn't enjoy the trip anyway." She got up from the table to put an arm around Simone's shoulders. "They'll only be in New Orleans for a night or two 'cause the project's way outside the city. Don't cry, Simone."

Jason, who had been quite companionable over the luncheon table, showed his true colors. "Mother's right, Simone. We'll barely be in New Orleans long enough to visit Bourbon Street and make a few stops in some cathouses along the way. We won't be there near long enough for you to hit the stores so you might as well stop your caterwauling."

"Jace," his mother protested over Simone's head.

Simone turned livid. "You animal! Brent won't go with you. I won't have it, I won't!"

"Stop being so stupid, Simone." He didn't try to hide his impatience. "You know the only thing Brent thinks about when he's out of town is doing his job. He doesn't have time for playing around or sightseeing. He doesn't have time to pamper you and follow you shopping, either. If you went, we'd be wasting time dealing with your histrionics, and you'd be out spending money that Brent doesn't have. Go home and give him hell if you're unhappy about it, but leave Lettie alone."

From the safety of Lettie's arm, Simone quivered with rage. "You! You care nothing for the needs of the soul. You are an insensitive boor, a, a tyrant."

"I've been called worse," he said dryly, never losing his temper.

"You, you—"

I thought for one long minute she was going to say something too awful to forgive, but she curbed herself. With a smothered cry, she buried smoldering eyes in Lettie's shoulder. "How I hate you. If it were not for Brent and Lettie, I'd—"

"What would you do?" He didn't bother to hide his scorn. "You've never let thoughts of them stop you before. By all means, don't let them stop you now." He laughed mirthlessly. "Go ahead and do whatever it is you'd do, Simone."

"You bastard!" She lunged out of Lettie's arms toward where he sat, but he fended her off easily by catching both fragile wrists in one huge hand and holding her away from him.

"You're upsetting Lettie, Simone. And what's this? A new ring?" His voice turned flat as the amethyst-and-diamond ring caught his eye. The lines of his face became as hard as his voice. "Just where'd you get the money for this little trinket?"

She pulled away from him. "It—it's one Brent bought me the other day, when we went to see the aquarium in Chattanooga." She put her hands behind her back, suddenly nervous, tears forgotten.

"Brent's barely had money to get his car tuned since he married you." His narrowed eyes held hers. "I thought he'd put his foot down. He knows damned well he can't afford stuff like this."

Simone broke, turning and running out of the house.

In the silence that followed the slamming of the door, I could hear the clock over the kitchen door ticking and Maggie singing "Amazing Grace" in a cracked, tuneless rhythm from the front of the house.

Lettie sighed. She always had too much energy for me to remember her age, but now she looked every minute of her sixty-four years. The look she fastened on her oldest son was not angry. A trace of sadness interlaced the anxiety I'd noted before.

"Ignore her, Ma. She's just a selfish little ingrate." Jason's harsh features softened at Lettie's distress. He reached out to her. "She'll get over it. She always does."

"Oh, Jace, I wish you would try harder with Simone." His anxious mother squeezed his hand with both of hers. "She's such a sensitive little thing. All this fuss over a silly trip. Why shouldn't Brent take her with him?"

Jason removed his hand to sit stiffly erect at the table. "Because she's too damned expensive. You know yourself how much she went through that first year after Dad died. As for sensitive, she's about as sensitive as a rock."

His jaw set in the same uncompromising pose I remembered from the newspaper photographs, and his mouth looked as unyielding.

He was a different man altogether from the one I'd worked with all morning, the one who'd teased his mother and flirted with me. So different that a chill ran down my back. Had I been wrong about him?

Uncomfortable, I got up and took my dishes to the sink.

Lettie knit her brows. "I hope Simone's all right. She oughtn't be using the trails by herself."

"With luck, she'll fall into the gorge and break her neck."

"Jason!" His mother was stunned and so was I.

He shoved his chair back and left, little shock waves emanating from him as if anger could no longer be contained.

"Oh, that boy," Lettie muttered.

I rinsed my bowl, appalled at the sudden change in a man I had hardly begun to know.

"Don't pay any attention to Jace, Anna." Lettie started to clear the table. "He's the type thinks he's got to look out for everybody. When his daddy died, he gave up his little house on the other side of town and moved in with me. He said it was because he was tired of his own cooking, but I know he thought I needed someone to tend to me, the idiot." This was said with affection.

"I can tell he cares for you a lot." In the office, Jason bantered with his mother and never complained about running the smallest errand for her. He might be curt with others, but never with Lettie.

"He does. It just comes naturally to him to worry about anybody he cares for. He's always looked out for Brent, ever since they were little. And that's part of the problem, I think. He never felt Simone was good enough for Brent." Her forehead furrowed as she stacked dishes in the sink. "Sometimes I wish Jace'd marry, so he'd have someone to worry about besides Brent and me. Sometimes I wish—" Biting her bottom lip, she took up the placemats. "Oh, well, if wishes were horses, as the old saying goes."

Finding a dishrag, I began to wipe off the table.

Jason came back, his black mood gone. "Sorry, Ma. I guess my temper got the best of me." He leaned down and kissed the top of Lettie's head.

"Well, 'sorry don't feed the bulldog' as your grandfather was so fond of telling me when I was growing up." Lettie was back to her tart self. She kissed Jason's cheek, a gesture that he accepted without embarrassment.

I'd not known many men on such affectionate terms with their mothers. It was easy to imagine docile Brent apologizing to his mother, but to see Jason doing so was novel. What kind of man was he?

Rinsing out the dishrag, I looked out the window. "This is a wonderful view."

And it was. The set of box windows let the outside in. The leaves had lost the full autumn colors that, in the past month, had made the gorge a riotous crazy quilt as far as the eye could see. Limbs of birches, oaks, elms and poplars rose bare and graceful against the side of the gorge, while pines and cedars flaunted their evergreen dress under the cloudy sky.

"How clever of you to have the kitchen facing this way."

My remark prompted Lettie's reminiscences.

"The only thing I asked when Moss, my husband, started renovating this house thirty-five years ago was that he leave the kitchen and our bedroom facing the gorge," she said with a touch of nostalgia.

"How old is the actual house?"

"It was built in the mid-eighteen hundreds. We started fixing it up after we married and I still work on it. I'm not one who believes in keeping old houses exactly as they are for their own sake. I'm too fond of my comforts."

"Me, too." I shared her smile.

"Moss made everything the way I wanted it, much of it with his own hands." She glanced around her kitchen. "We added on the study and he laid the fieldstone for its fireplace. Jace here has hammered a few nails in his time, too, haven't you, son?"

"I started young and never stopped," he said cheerfully.

He was back to being high-spirited and outspoken, invariably making a joke of everything. The man I was beginning to know was not hard, not rancorous.

I hadn't realized it, but my stomach had turned into a knot that only now started to unwind.

"That's the truth," Lettie agreed with a nod. "Jace helped fashion this house and one day it'll be his. If the gallivanting fool ever finds some girl stupid enough to marry him, I might move over into a rental house we have on the other side of town. Let his wife pick up after him for a while."

"Now, Lettie." Jace grinned at her. "You know I'm housebroken. I put my dirty clothes in the clothes basket and everything. You oughtn't to give Anna here such a bad impression."

I liked to see him smile. "Oh, you needn't worry. Nothing your mother said could possibly change my opinion of you, Jason. I find when you work with a person day in and day out, you pretty much know everything about him there is to know."

Dark lashes narrowed but failed to hide a glinting yellow light that revealed his appreciation at the subtle dig.

No, he wasn't slow.

My heart twisted painfully, in a most unaccustomed way.

"Speaking of work, I guess we'd better get back to it," he said without rising to the bait. "Anna, do you feel up to tackling the north pastures now?"

"It's raining."

He looked out the window as if amazed. "So it is. Lettie, there's no need for you to go out in this weather. Anna's got the hang of it now, and she and I'll do just fine together," he told his mother with a gleam in his eye that I mistrusted.

"There's no need for anybody to go out in this." Lettie looked as if she was aware of that same gleam and knew more than I about what it meant. "Don't worry, Anna, we may expect a lot from you but we don't intend you to catch pneumonia. The north pasture'll keep till tomorrow. We'll go over to the warehouse and work there until the rain lets up."

"Fine." I hoped my relief at not having to be alone with Jason didn't show."

CHAPTER EIGHT

MY RESPITE WAS short-lived.

A phone call as we were leaving summoned Lettie to the garage in town. We dropped her off on the way to the warehouse, and I was left alone with Jason to finish the inventory. Despite my apprehension, we spent the afternoon together without incident. My initial vigilance faded to a grudging concession that he was going to be a perfect gentleman, intent only on the job at hand.

As he was.

Until we were nearly finished.

"And four hundred eighty-seven six-foot metal panels," Jason said, clambering down from his ladder. "That's it, Anna. We're done. I bet you're glad."

I looked up from my clipboard to see him smiling at me.

"Yes, I am." I stretched my aching shoulders. "It's been a long day, counting all these nuts and bolts and cows and things."

"Back hurt?"

Feeling quite charitable since, even without Lettie's restraining influence, he had continued to behave himself, I nodded. "A little."

He was sympathetic. "Here. Let me help."

Before I knew what was happening, he'd turned me around. His hands at my neck were big but gentle. When he started to knead my shoulders, they felt marvelous. I should have protested, but I was too exhausted and his fingers felt too good. He squeezed and massaged for at least five minutes, until all the tension was drained out of me and replaced by something I didn't want to acknowledge.

I heard his breathing, soft and even, as he worked on my shoulders. I felt the warmth of his body just behind me, almost touching me. I smelled his scent, perspiration mixed with a faint, woodsy cologne. A dull heat began to rise, emanating from my thighs and spreading upward to expand in my stomach and reach up to my nipples. I stood hypnotized, letting him work his magic on me. My body responded to his, but I was powerless to stop it.

As if he knew what I was feeling, what havoc he was wreaking, he turned me, gently, slowly, until we were face-to-face and I could look up into his eyes.

Pure gold.

Instinctively, I leaned into him, felt the muscles beneath the cotton shirt tighten as my breasts grazed his chest. The warmth of our bodies met and melded as we moved together, so that the heat between his thighs became mine and the heaviness in my body became his. I wished I could touch his bare skin.

His hand moved to the back of my neck and he bent his face down to mine.

My cheek met the roughness of his mustache. My lips trembled, parted in anticipation. My breathing constricted in longing as I waited for the inevitable.

His mouth was soft, questioning. When I made no effort to stop what was happening, his other arm went around me, drawing me fully against him. Lost in the sweetness of desire, I forgot who I was, who he was. My arms slipped around his waist, pulling him closer. My mouth opened and his tongue delved into me greedily, as if he was afraid I'd change my mind.

"Hey, Jace, you back there?"

I jumped away in confusion. Jason didn't try to hold me, nor did he display annoyance at the interruption. He simply looked at me regretfully, his hand resting on my shoulder the barest second before falling away.

"Yeah, Brent," he called, eyes still bright.

Still molten gold.

Brent was completely unaware of what he'd interrupted. "Mom called, saying you weren't answering your cell."

"Turned it off so it wouldn't spook the animals." Jason pulled it out. "Guess I forgot to turn it back on."

"Well, she needs a ride home."

Scurrying away with flaming cheeks, I clasped my clipboard to my chest as if it was a life preserver. My lips were burning, my heart racing. Whatever had I been thinking?

"Can't you pick her up, Brent? I have something I need to do." Jason's voice came from behind me.

"Sure. I've got to stop for some milk, anyway. I'll run by and get her on the way." As always, Brent was agreeable to his brother's slightest suggestion.

I threw on my sweater, knowing I couldn't remain there alone with Jason. I didn't trust him. I didn't trust myself. The thought of him taking up where he'd left off threw me into a panic. I wasn't ready for this, not with him unaware of who I was.

"If you're going back to the office, Brent, I'll ride with you so I can pick up my car. We're finished here, aren't we, Jason?"

Jason didn't answer for a second, but when he did, the note of mockery in his voice was pronounced. He knew exactly the state he'd reduced me to, and why I was running away. "I reckon we are. If you say so."

I looked up sharply, but he was unconcernedly putting on his jacket.

* * *

IN THE SAFETY OF my cabin that evening, Jason Forrester dominated my thoughts. He was too masculine for my peace of mind, and male arrogance always repulsed me, yet my knees had turned to water at his mere touch. Something about him excited me to the point where I would have lost all self-control had Brent not appeared. I'd have let Jason . . .

I resolutely refused to think about what I would have let him do. Could I be so attracted to a man if he had killed my brother?

Trying to be dispassionate, I honestly couldn't see Jason coldbloodedly shooting anyone. At least not the Jason I was learning to know, the Jason who teased his mother and deftly managed his brother and the workmen.

Perhaps if he'd found Alan and Tiffany together, he might have shot Alan in a burst of temper. Assuming he had a gun. But I was convinced that Alan's list referred to an appointment with his killer, and I was equally convinced that Jason Forrester was not a man who would plan and carry out a murder by appointment.

I told myself that as I sat on my glassed-in porch drinking hot tea and watching the clouds clear. By the time the faded sun slid behind the trees on the other side of the gorge, I'd almost convinced myself.

The intrusive presence was absent for once. Usually at this hour I felt its malevolence, but this evening nothing distracted my jumbled emotions.

As the last silver wedge dipped below the horizon, a light appeared at Brent's house. A door in the smoky bubble was thrown wide, allowing the inner brightness to spill out.

As I strained to see through the shadows, a flash of fluorescent yellow appeared.

Pleased recognition was followed by bewilderment.

Why was Jason Forrester standing on his brother's deck?

Or was it really Jason? It was hard to tell.

I reached for the binoculars beside my rocker and put them up in time to see another person, a smaller figure in vivid rose, rush out to grab his arm.

The two were locked together in a strange embrace before a sudden sweep of the yellow sleeve sent the woman stumbling away.

As I watched in disbelief, Jason pulled his arm back and threw something overhand, the way a baseball pitcher throws, swinging his shoulders and lifting his knee in one powerful, athletic motion. Simone—for in my heart I knew the other person was she before the binoculars confirmed it—rushed at him again but too late.

Something whirled in the air too quickly for me to follow. I lowered the binoculars in time to see a laggard sunbeam catch and reflect off the object for a bare second before whatever it was fell into the ravine.

Simone beat at him with her hands. I could make out the motions and raised the binoculars once more. He grabbed her shoulders and shook her. She sank to her knees. He yanked her up as if she were a rag doll and half pushed, half carried her back into the dark bubble.

I sat stunned, doubting my own eyes.

What had Simone tried to prevent Jason from throwing onto the rocks below?

They'd almost appeared to be hugging, until he had thrust her away. An old folk saying came to mind, something about people in love fighting the most.

Headlights lit the driveway behind Simone's house. Brent was home. Would she tell him what his brother had done, how Jason had pushed her away and forced her inside?

My stomach knotted up again as I looked down into the gorge. Only the dark outlines of bushes and trees and rocks, and occasional glints of water, showed up below. There couldn't possibly be any trace of whatever it was Jason had thrown away. There was no telling where it had landed.

A coldness covered me, but it was not the chill of that mysterious, malignant someone, something, looking over my shoulder.

The coldness seeping through me was from my own fears. Fears that I could be wrong about Jason Forrester.

And I didn't—oh, I didn't!—want to be wrong.

* * *

ALAN CAME BACK WITH a vengeance that night, his eagerness playing over my confusion like a brilliant light. "You must go down, Belle. You have to find it."

Down into the gorge? Was that what he meant?

In my dream, bewildered and against my will, I looked out into the gorge where Alan insistently pointed. Replaying the afternoon, an indistinct object was hurled from the dark castle.

Alan clapped his hands in delight. "That's it! Don't you see, Belle? You must get it for me."

"And exactly how am I supposed to find it?" I asked petulantly. "I don't know what it is and I don't even know where it went. And how can I get down there? Anyway, it's probably lost forever."

"Gawd, ain't you the worrywart," Alan said in his best redneck accent. "Come on, Belle. Don't be so poky. Forget you're my cautious sister. Try."

Mist began seeping across his face. "Try, Belle," he insisted. As the tendrils of wispy white continued to gather between us, he finally disappeared from view and all I could hear were wistful echoes: "Please, Belle. Try."

CHAPTER NINE

MY DREAMS LEFT ME heavy-eyed and sluggish.

I dreaded going to the office and facing Jason. I wanted to ask him. More than anything, I wanted to come right out and say, "What did you throw into the gorge and why was Simone hitting you?"

But I didn't.

"Good morning," I said instead.

"Good morning." He lingered a moment by my desk, lowering his voice so Lois wouldn't hear. "How's your back?"

"It's fine. Thanks." Remembered longing billowed before my matter-of-fact mind squelched it.

"Anytime you need a shoulder massage, let me know." His assurance irritated me. "I'm pretty good at them, if I do say so."

"Inventory's finished." I ignored his underlying message. "I shouldn't have to call on you. But thanks anyway."

He winked to show he hadn't taken offense, and went to get a biscuit before continuing on to his office. He said nothing about being at Brent's house, nor did I bring it up.

And when I saw Simone later that week, she didn't refer to it either. She did hint about her fear of Jason, but when I tried to pump her, she gave a meaningful look before lowering long lashes and changing the subject.

It was all quite exasperating, particularly since I felt I was making no progress, that I was only marking time in Rahunta.

My social life was expanding despite my consistent refusals to Jason's casual invitations for hiking or movies. Matt and I'd started playing poker with three other couples, teachers at the school. We gathered at Matt's cabin every Friday night for pizza and beer and music before settling down to the card table.

They were convivial evenings, but wasted insofar as learning anything new about Alan's death. I was hoping I'd have more luck from my growing relationship with Simone.

There were two distinct social groups in Rahunta, one comprising professional people and the other mostly locals. Since Simone didn't fit in with either group, she latched onto me eagerly. She met me in town for lunch a few times, and I visited her frequently. I noticed that whenever Matt accompanied me, we were closely chaperoned by the ever-watchful Jenny.

One Saturday I drove Simone to Helen, a quaint resort town modeled after an alpine village. Its specialty shops featured all types of merchandise, some discounted, that Simone snapped up. Our last stop was at a shoe store.

"Look at these gorgeous sandals." Simone held them up. "In Chattanooga or Atlanta, they cost twice as much. I wish I'd saved some of my money."

"I can loan you some. You can pay me back later." The running shoes I tried on felt more comfortable than hiking boots.

"Would you?" Her face lit up, only to fall. "But I won't have money to pay you back. And Brent wouldn't like it. You try them, Anna. They'd be perfect for holiday parties."

"No, thanks. I don't need sandals. Why would Brent care if I loaned you money?" Approving the running shoes, I sat down to pull them off.

She poked out her bottom lip. "It's Jason. He's convinced Brent I'm a spendaholic."

"What business is it of his?" Jason's gibes about Simone's shopping habits came to mind.

She didn't answer. "Do try these on, Anna. One of us should buy them." She pushed the sandals toward me.

"No, I have evening shoes. Besides, I can't wear straps between the toes." I pulled off my sock and stretched my toes.

She paled, her eyes and mouth opening wide.

I was used to people's expressions. "It's not a disease, silly. Webbed toes just happen to run in my family. Like blond hair and blue eyes run in yours."

"Both feet are like that?"

"I'm afraid so."

"Isn't it uncomfortable?" She couldn't tear her gaze away.

"Only when it comes to sandals like those. Buy them if you want. I'll explain to Brent."

"It isn't Brent I worry about," she said bitterly. After a last, longing look, she set the shoes aside.

Remembering Jason's reaction to her amethyst ring, I tried unsuccessfully to extract more information. She was quiet on the way home, quieter than she'd ever been with me.

Something deeper than a personality clash lay behind her animosity for Jason. On later occasions, she lamented that he was tyrannical, and that Brent and Lettie let him do just as he liked. Several times she seemed on the verge of confiding but always stopped short.

In my own relationship with Jason, I was having trouble keeping him at arm's length. He flirted with me whenever he was in the office, to the point that Lois had noticed. She thought I was crazy not to encourage him.

After witnessing the way women blatantly pursued him, I decided my aloofness, which arose from my fear of being alone with him, stoked his interest.

Still, I couldn't fault his behavior toward me. And I was not as immune to him as I preferred to believe. It was hard to refuse his invitations.

That was how things stood before Thanksgiving, when Simone, saying she had a special favor to ask, invited me for lunch the next Sunday. "Bring your swimsuit. Brent will be gone and we can enjoy the pool."

At the appointed time, I approached the dark house. The old revulsion was alive, something to be acknowledged and ignored. *It's only a bad place in my dreams*, I told myself firmly. *Brent and Simone live here, for pity's sake.*

Jenny, baby on her hip, accompanied me to the living area before returning to her chores. Simone's innuendos about her housekeeper might be the product of an overactive imagination, but it did seem Jenny always managed to stay just short of underfoot.

Simone waved at me from a diving rock, a neat figure in her swimsuit. Its deep purple color complemented her creamy complexion, while the bikini style emphasized her curvy body.

She was beside herself with excitement. "Jenny can't hear us here." She looked toward the hall, as if her maid could eavesdrop from beyond the plants and living room. "Even if she comes in to see what we're doing, she'll be too far away."

Though the hall was a good fifty feet distant, Simone's trepidation infected me. "Why don't you want Jenny to hear?" The water felt wonderful, soft and warm and caressing. The tension seeped out of my body.

"She tells Jason everything I do, everything I say." Simone lay back in the water. "She spies for him and I hate her."

Spies.

The word set my mind racing. Could Jenny be looking out toward my porch in the evenings? Could she be the cause of the uneasiness I felt? But what had I done to cause such malice on her part? Could it have something to do with Jason?

No, surely not. Jenny was plain, too plain to attract someone like Jason.

I could be considered plain, too.

"Why don't you fire her?"

Simone gave a pitying look and disappeared, emerging with water streaming down her face. "I have no control over her. I have no control over this house. No control over anything."

"You're Brent's wife—"

"Brent is a, a wimp. He will never stand up to Jason, never." Simone was angry, but I'd seen her angry before. "Do you remember the day I begged Lettie to help me go to New Orleans?" She became more heated.

"Yes."

"Do you know what Jason did afterward?"

I remembered the scene I had witnessed, when she had fought him. "What?"

"He took my ring away from me, my new ring." Her face dissolved in tears. "Oh, Anna, it was so pretty and I loved it so much, and now it's gone."

Was it the ring he'd thrown away? Whatever it was had glittered in the light.

"Simone, I'm sorry. How could he take your ring away? Surely Brent wouldn't let him."

Her face registered disgust. "Brent always listens to Jason. I'm beginning to despise him as much as I do Jason. That's why I'm telling you this." Tormented blue eyes appealed to me. "I know Jason is bewitching you."

My face heated.

"I see how he acts around you. I know what he's doing," she said, her voice rising. "He's playing with you, making you respond, making you want him. He does it with every pretty woman. Until she gives in. Then he makes her very unhappy."

"I don't care about him at all," I protested.

She paid no attention. "I don't want you to be hurt by him, Anna. He's a wicked, wicked man."

Lying back in the water, I drifted, troubled.

"I see you don't believe me, but it's true." Looking furtively toward the door, she reassured herself that we were alone. Treading water, she said, right at my face, "He's a murderer, Anna."

My heart stopped. "What do you mean?"

"He killed a man last year. A teacher at the school who was having an affair with his fiancée." She was watching, gauging my reaction. "His name was Alan McKenzie."

How I kept my face blank, I don't know.

She went on, speaking very fast, determined to get it all out before I could stop her or she changed her mind. "Alan was nice. We were friends until he met Tiffany." She shuddered. "Until Jason shot him and threw him into the gorge."

Somehow, the words coming so starkly from Simone dismayed me more than I thought possible.

"I heard the tale." I chose my words carefully. "But there's no proof, is there?"

Simone looked back over her shoulder at the door. "Jason has the gun," she whispered.

"What?" I must have misunderstood.

"The gun that killed Alan McKenzie. I heard him and Brent talking about it. Oh, please, please, don't betray me." She was obviously frightened. "If Jason knew what I'm trying to do, he'd kill me."

"I don't understand." My patience with Simone's half reality, half fantasy daydreams was wearing thin. At one time I had likened her to a fairy, but one could not live in a fairy-tale world forever. And I'd learned these past weeks that my truth was not always hers. I could believe Alan had befriended her; he'd always had a soft spot for strays with problems.

And Simone definitely had problems. Or thought she did.

"I need your help, Anna." She spelled it out, childlike, eager. "Jason hid the gun in his house. I could find it, except I'm never left alone. Jenny is always here, while every time I do manage to slip away, Jason or Lettie is home."

She stopped expectantly.

"What is it you want me to do?" My logical mind fled in the face of Simone's accusation. I couldn't think, couldn't reason.

"They trust me with you. After Thanksgiving, when Lettie leaves for Palm Beach, you and I can say we're going to Helen, like the other day. Only we'll go over to her house instead, and look for the gun."

I pulled myself together. "Simone, I'm not going to go rummage through Lettie's house."

"We don't have to. I heard Jason tell Brent it's behind some shelves in the study, in a chimney they covered during remodeling. When they were little, Jason and Brent used to leave each other messages in it."

I didn't believe her. I told myself it was because she was a flighty and fanciful creature, but I knew the truth.

If I believed her, that made Jason a murderer.

"You overheard him and Brent talking about this?" My mind began to function again. "That means Brent knows Jason killed Alan—this teacher?"

"Not till later," Simone said quickly. "Jason convinced him it was an accident." She glided toward the ladder. "Brent's gullible, Anna. He believes anything Jason tells him. He didn't know until afterward. Jason is the guilty one. Brent had nothing to do with it."

"I didn't say he did."

Simone made more sense than I wanted to admit. Brent was a talented, creative architect, but he didn't have what it took to kill anyone. He was too easygoing and too indecisive. He would never have enough nerve to plan a murder and carry it out. In his relationship with his brother, he had some input, but of the two, Jason was the driving force.

Jason with his quick mind and ability to react.

"Will you help me, Anna?" On the ladder, halfway out, Simone looked over her shoulder. "Please?"

"No." I was firm. "It's a crazy idea. If Jason's a murderer, he'd have no qualms about hurting either of us. Go to the police, Simone."

"No, no! Don't you understand? They'll never do anything where Jason Forrester is concerned." Simone became frantic. "Anna, you must help me. I don't have anyone else."

As I climbed out of the pool, she began to sniffle and stopped only when I promised to think about it. I had no intention of giving in, but that quieted her for the time being.

"Lettie's going to Palm Beach after Thanksgiving." She mapped out her plans but kept one eye cocked toward the hall doorway in case Jenny appeared. "Maggie's off weekends, too. We have only to wait until Jason goes out."

"And if he comes in while you're searching?" I asked with some aggravation. "What then?"

She wasn't listening. "He must not suspect what we are doing, Anna." She shivered, eyes dilating. "I don't know what he would do if he thought we were over there looking for that gun, but he must not discover what we are doing."

I could agree without reservations to *that*. I wouldn't want Jason to find out I was in any way connected to Simone's outrageous scheme.

In which, of course, I could not participate.

Taking the towel she offered me, I sat down on a lounge chair to soak up the glow of filtered sunlight. It might be cold outside, but inside the dome, it was cozy. There was no reason for the chill stealing over me.

"Simone, have you and Jason ever got along?"

"No." Even wet and dripping, Simone looked like a model.

"Why not? Did something happen?"

She was straightening her long hair, pulling it back from her face and behind her ears, but paused at my words. "I'll tell you why he makes my life a hell, but you must never repeat it." She slipped on dark glasses.

"You know I won't."

"Especially not to Brent. It would break his heart to think his own brother—" Her voice broke.

Dropping onto the lounge chair by me, she screwed up her face in misery. "Jason's been after me since the first week I came here as Brent's wife. But I won't give in to him. I'd rather die." She put a hand up to her mouth as if nauseated.

"You mean he tried to seduce you?"

Simone gave a bitter laugh. "He almost raped me. And because I fought him, he tells Brent terrible things about me—that I spend too much money and that I can't care for my baby. He made Brent hire Jenny to spy on me, and I despise him with all my heart."

It sounded only too logical. Simone would turn any man's head, despite her flightiness.

"Why does he need Jenny to spy on you?"

"He jumps on every mistake I make," she said, engrossed in listing her grievances. "And I do make some, Anna. Me, I don't claim to be perfect. But he goes to Brent when I do something a little wrong, and says, 'Yes, I told you so. You should get rid of her.' Oh, I know what he tells Brent behind my back."

She seemed only then to hear my question. "You ask why he sets Jenny to spy on me?"

"Simone." I glanced uneasily toward the living area.

Each word came out more impassioned. "So that he can know every little thing I do. So that he can tell Brent and undermine my marriage. And it's just because I won't let him do it to me. Oh, Anna, I am so unhappy."

Dismayed, I comforted her as best I could.

The worst part was that her story could well be true. I could see Jason wanting a woman and doing everything in his power to take her. The one thing I couldn't picture him doing was seducing his brother's wife. I'd thought he disliked her.

Simone was childlike and imaginative. She could be mistaken. Still, I wondered if my own reaction to Jason was responsible for distorting my view. Jenny's presence was a fact, however discreet she tried to be.

And Jason had made a really big deal out of Simone not going to New Orleans with Brent, when even I could see she craved the lights and shopping and excitement of a city. Our simple outing to Helen had done wonders for her.

Then that look on Jason's face at the mention of Simone. I'd thought it contempt, but suppose it wasn't? How would a man look when he had been rebuffed and still wanted a woman?

God knows Simone would be any man's bedroom fantasy, with her exquisite figure and delicate features.

We sat up, me drying off thoughtfully while Simone pulled a voluminous cotton caftan over her head. "I have no choice, Anna. Unless I can find that gun to prove Jason is a murderer, he will destroy my marriage, maybe even me."

Without voicing any doubts, I slipped on my canvas clogs and walked over to drape my towel across a wrought-iron chair. Hanging from its arm was a pair of binoculars while past the sliding door lay an excellent view of my own porch directly above the gorge. Anyone might have sat here in the evenings while I watched the sun set.

Anyone. Jenny?

Sinking down onto a large floor cushion at Simone's feet, I fished for more. "Simone, do you know what happened the night Al—the night of the murder?"

"Yes. Jason found out Alan and Tiffany were lovers. He went down the trail and shot him in a rage." The words rolled off her tongue without hesitation.

"How do you know?"

"I overheard Jason telling Brent." She looked up at me from beneath long lashes, trying to see if I believed her.

I wasn't sure I did.

"Was that when you found out about the gun?"

"No-o." She was reluctant. "It was just recently that I . . . If I'd known then, I'd have found some way to get it before now. Anna, will you help me look for it?"

The more I mulled it over, the more difficult I found it to imagine Jason as a murderer, no matter what Simone thought, no matter what she'd overheard.

Perhaps I was being foolish. Men had deceived women before. According to Simone, Jason did it all the time. My judgment wasn't infallible. Perhaps I ought to help Simone in her mad scheme. If she was right and Jason had the gun, then at least I would know. If not . . .

I ridiculed the thought almost before it formed.

A sensible woman would never break the law. A sensible woman would never search for some questionable gun in some unknown hiding place in someone else's house. The idea of Annabelle Levee doing such a thing was ludicrous.

"Hello, ladies."

I froze where I sat cross-legged on my cushion. My fingers, combing my hair, checked convulsively. Despite all my resolutions, happiness surged through me at that voice.

CHAPTER TEN

GOLDEN EYES ABOVE A hawklike nose and black mustache surveyed me warmly from across the large room. Far too warmly for my peace of mind. The old whispers of longing unfurled despite my best efforts to restrain them.

As I tried to bring my hand away, my fingers inexplicably caught in my hair. It took me a moment to free them, and Jason examined me the whole while. My swimsuit was modest, though the French-cut legs revealed more of my hips that I preferred in front of those damnably observant eyes. But the top was plain and the straps wide, cut in one piece from the bodice so that cleavage barely showed. There was nothing in my appearance to make me ashamed.

From the way Jason Forrester was staring, however, I might as well have worn no clothes at all.

I grabbed my cover-up as he opened the child-proof gate and came toward us.

Brent trailed in behind him. "I've asked Jace to lunch." He kissed Simone and put an arm around her waist. "With Mother out today, there's no sense in him eating alone."

There might have been a hint of truculence in his tone, but I was too distracted to pay much attention. The distracting influence himself sauntered over to me, so close I could smell his aroma. The woodsy aftershave mingled with an earthier, masculine scent that made me dizzy.

I fumbled with my shirt, trying to get my arm into the sleeve and hoping I wasn't blushing.

"Allow me." He was very near.

"I can get it." Belatedly hearing the coolness in my voice, I softened it. "Thanks, anyway."

Manners were unnecessary. In his highhanded fashion, he'd taken my shirt and was helping me into it whether I wanted help or not. "A lady could catch a cold, soaking wet like this." The intimate voice and the slight contact as his fingers brushed my back sent fire up and down my spine.

"Thanks." I turned slightly away and looked over my shoulder at him, not wanting to reveal how my fingers trembled on the buttons.

The feeble gesture was as useless as my protesting his wrapping me in my shirt.

His tiny smile told me that he knew exactly what effect he had on me and that he intended to enjoy every minute of my discomfort.

He was incorrigible.

That didn't mean he was a murderer, did it?

Throughout lunch, I ate and made small talk, acutely aware of his every word and movement. The large palms outside the dining alcove provided a tropical background against which he looked more like a pirate than ever.

Simone was unnaturally quiet. I knew why, now.

If she was telling the truth.

Jason was loquacious as always, talking with Brent about the new project in Louisiana they were about to undertake, and explaining to me what all was involved. "Brent and I'll go out to get it started, about the middle of January. Then we'll take turns staying there until it's finished."

"How do you manage with local building codes and things like that?" I wasn't really curious, but steering the conversation away from controversial subjects seemed the easiest way to keep peace.

"We hire local builders. Our job is planning and using our expertise to oversee large projects." Brent looked as though his day had been disagreeable. He picked at his food, though his iced-tea glass containing Jack Daniels and water was nearly empty.

"We furnish most of the capital, too." Jason glanced at his brother's drink. "Money's the main thing. No matter how beautiful or creative or lasting buildings are, they can't go up without money. Speaking of which, Anna, you ought to go with us in January. You and I could fly out to Vegas before we start the job. See a few shows. Hit some of the casinos. I can see you now, standing there cranking the handles on the slot machines." He made several quick motions with his hand, as if he were playing one.

"I'm not a gambler," I stated, making the mistake of looking across the table at him.

One corner of his mouth turned up at the same time one brow twitched, as if he knew something I didn't. "You're probably wise. If you were, you'd be a lamb for the fleecing."

Simone glared at him; when she'd begged to go, he'd laughed.

"You should take Simone, Brent," I said. "She'd enjoy getting away."

Brent roused from his meditation. "I would, Anna, except that I'm probably going to be stuck in a roach-bag motel in the middle of nowhere, with just a truck for transportation. Simone can come on one of the other trips, where there're places to shop and go out at night."

"You would take me except for Jace!" Simone could no longer restrain herself. "I am sick to death of Jace deciding what I can do and what I cannot do and where I can go and where I cannot go."

"That's not fair." Brent's discomfiture showed.

"No, it isn't," she flashed back. "In fact, it's *extremely* unfair." She started to say more, but suddenly desisted. "Oh, what's the use?"

Alternating between pity and embarrassment, I stole a glance at Jason. His face was unreadable. I couldn't tell if his expression signified contempt or unrequited passion.

After her outburst, Simone clamped her lips together and refused to look at either Jason or her husband.

Her lowered eyes made her lashes seem longer and darker. Her tiny mouth curved into a pout, delectable enough to make a man forget she was his brother's wife. A certain kind of man might find it exciting to play cat and mouse with a woman who didn't want him. The chase would merely whet his appetite.

If Jason Forrester went after a woman, he wouldn't stop until he possessed her.

"Brent's right," I heard him say to Simone. "You wouldn't enjoy this trip."

"You're disgusting." She spoke with loathing. "Lettie may believe you spent all your time at the auction in September, but I know better. I know that sleazy woman from town went with you. You're low and contemptible, and I'm glad that Anna knows it."

"Simone." Brent tried to soothe her. "Jace didn't mean anything. Anna didn't take him seriously. Did you, Anna?"

"No." I was curt. "I'm not in the habit of going off with men to Las Vegas or anywhere else. I still think you should take Simone, Brent. She might enjoy it more than you realize."

Simone's face lit up. She sent a grateful mile toward me "See, Brent? Anna knows how dreary it is here. Please take me. We could go by Las Vegas like Jason said."

"Simone . . ." Brent wavered, on the verge of giving in. The weary lines in his face were more pronounced as he looked at his brother. His eyes were blue orbs sunk in leather.

"When you went to Atlantic City last year, you lost twenty thousand dollars." Jason's voice was mild, but that didn't keep it from sounding sinister.

My mouth wanted to drop open. Only determination kept it closed. Twenty thousand dollars!

"And that was just one trip to the tables. Since you married Brent, you've gone through God knows how much. There's no way he can afford to take you anywhere, Simone, until you get rid of this strange notion that money grows on trees. Why don't you quit whining and grow up?"

"We *are* going up to Richmond before I leave," Brent said before Simone could reply. His eyes pleaded with her. "And you and Lettie are going to Atlanta soon. Maybe you can come to New Orleans later. Please, darling, try to understand."

I could see her inner struggle, but her glance darted toward Jason rather than her husband. Biting her lip, she gave a small nod. "All right. I'll be good. I'll do my Christmas shopping in Atlanta."

Brent relaxed. "That's my sweetheart."

Jason ignored the smoldering hatred aimed his way and went back to his sandwich. There was a slight curl to his top lip, as if contempt warred with satisfaction and won.

The food engrossed me while Simone lapsed back into a moody silence.

Only Brent remained oblivious of all the undercurrents around the glass-topped table. Beneath the unlighted bronze-and-crystal chandelier, he drew Jason into a discussion of the design for a new hotel. Each detail of their vision for the completed project was examined, while the lines of exhaustion in Brent's face grew more pronounced.

I hoped he wasn't ill, though the liquor he downed during lunch made me wonder if the illness was something other than a simple cold. Unlike Jason, Brent was sensitive and caring and just plain nice.

At last Jason became blunt about the frequently refilled glass. "Taking to drink, Brent?"

Brent laughed it off, but drank no more.

As soon as we finished eating, I pleaded grocery shopping to do for the Thanksgiving holidays and rose to leave.

"Stay," Brent urged. "Jenny'll bring Christopher out in a few minutes so we can play with him before he takes his nap." The lines of worry lifted when he spoke of his son.

"Yeah, the little devil's scooting around everywhere now, fast as anything. You should see him go." Jason was unembarrassed at displaying avuncular pride.

Brent was open, but Jason was the most unselfconscious person I'd ever met. If it wasn't for that one lapse in Lettie's kitchen, I'd think him refreshing.

"Actually—" I began, not anxious to prolong the afternoon in his company.

"Anna's tired," Simone put in quickly. "Don't make her stay, Brent. I'll walk her to her car."

Jason tossed his napkin down. "No need to do that, Simone. I'll walk out with Anna."

"There's no need for anyone to go with me," I said. "My car's right outside."

"I'm leaving anyway." The offhand voice masked unshakable intent as he stood up.

Further objection would seem rude, so, presenting a calm face, I said my goodbyes.

Simone called to me as I started out. "Oh, your swimsuit! One moment, Anna."

She darted out of the dining area and came back with my damp suit and towel in a plastic bag. "You won't forget?" she whispered as she handed it to me. "You'll help me, won't you? I can't live like this much longer."

Her composure had fallen away, leaving a haunted shell. She might look like a child, but the innocence was giving way to the ravaged countenance of someone who'd been witness to some unbearable tragedy. "You must help me."

The simple declaration elicited my pity. Even so, what she wanted was beyond my capabilities. "I'll see, Simone." I squeezed her hand.

She smiled wanly. "I can't do it alone."

Jason waited at the door. "Anna, it's kind of late. I'd better follow you home."

"It's two o'clock in the afternoon."

"Well, that's late for up here," he said with laughing eyes. "I just want to make sure you get home safe and sound. I wouldn't want anything to happen to you."

"Don't bother." Tossing the bag with my damp things across the seat, I climbed into my car. "I think the only thing I need worry about is standing right here beside me."

"Me?" Undecided as to whether to be astonished or offended, he ended up looking reproachful. "You're not talking about me, are you?"

I gave him a tight smile as I slammed my door in his face.

He knocked on my window. "Ma thinks you're coming over to eat with us on Thanksgiving."

I let my window down. "She thinks what?"

He repeated what he'd said.

Had I forgotten an invitation? No. "Why would she think that?"

"I guess because I told her you'd be eating a turkey TV dinner alone." He looked immensely pleased with himself. "She's really counting on having you come."

"Oh you . . ." I was annoyed. Never mind I had nowhere to go. He infuriated me by assuming I'd fall in with whatever he wanted. "I'm sorry. I have other plans."

His face mirrored disappointment. "C'mon, Anna, I heard you tell Lois you were just going to stay in. And Lettie's looking forward to your coming so she'll have somebody to talk to during the football games. She got Maggie to buy an extra big turkey and told her to double the dressing recipe. They're washing up the good china and planning on having this special salad. She and Maggie have gone to a lot of trouble for you." He gave me a practiced, hurt look, making it all my fault they'd be disappointed.

"I'm sorry. It's just . . ." I tried not to let him see I was weakening.

His voice deepened, becoming throatier, more intimate. "I'd like to have you, too. My Thanksgiving would be perfect if you were there. Won't you come?"

"Well . . ." I wasn't proof against that devastating smile. "All right."

"Great."

"I've got to go."

He leaned toward my window as if to stop me from leaving, but I hastily let it up and sped away, spinning my wheels in the process.

Half-afraid he would follow me, I looked in my rearview mirror nearly as much as I watched the road before me.

There was no sign of his truck, and I was strangely let down.

What was wrong with me? I'd never before been so indecisive nor had so much trouble standing up for myself. This man was wrecking my complacency. I had no mind of my own where he was concerned. Every time he came near me, I was thrown into confusion.

When I got ready for bed that night, I explored the unfamiliar sensations Jason Forrester had persuaded to grow from somewhere in the uncharted depths of me.

Lust, I told myself. That's all it was. The physical longing he evoked made me ache clear to the pit of my stomach. But worse than that were the jealous pangs brought on by hearing about a woman he'd taken to Las Vegas. He couldn't be in love with her, not and flirt with me the way he did.

Unless he was an accomplished liar.

Which he could very well be.

I didn't want to believe he was as cold-blooded as Simone painted him, yet his treatment of her bordered on the callous. If he'd truly tried to seduce her, he had no morals whatever.

But Simone was, sadly, not very reliable. Though possessed of a woman's body, her mind was in some respects lacking the necessary development to keep pace with those feminine curves. She could have misunderstood Jason's motives.

That thought made me pause.

I turned down the covers on my bed and stared at the white linens unseeingly.

A woman like Simone misunderstand a man? Any man?

Ha!

"Tell us another fairy tale, Auntie Annabelle," I murmured to myself as I hopped between the sheets of my virginal bed. The sheets were cold, and I was glad of my flannel pajamas. A wistful remembrance of my husband's warm body made me, for one long moment, wish another person was beside me.

I refused any conjectures on who I wanted that other person to be.

No, there was no possible way a man like Jason Forrester and a woman like Simone could misunderstand each other.

Turning off the lamp, the welcoming darkness lay over me awhile before I went to sleep. A light wind blew, causing the leaves outside my window to rustle as if they were whispering about me among themselves. *Silly*, they murmured, *silly, silly woman. Eyes of gold, teasing you, hands so bold, pleasing you* . . .

I smiled at my clumsy rhyme before I finally fell asleep.

The dreams returned with renewed strength.

I was being propelled by some unseen force, being carried into a large white palace half-hidden by smoky clouds of fog. I wanted to go inside, but I wanted to go on my own terms. I kept saying, "No, I want to walk by myself, let me walk by myself," but I had no control over my body.

Then I was inside, thrust into deathly silence. I waited in breathless anticipation, knowing what was coming but unable to flee. I saw the shadowy figure gliding toward me.

Closer, closer it came while I stood frozen.

Hide. Hide. Don't let it see you.

But in my dream the form stopped, reaching out a long, black, shapeless arm as I screamed and covered my eyes.

And that was how I awoke, sitting up in bed with a hoarse "No!" hanging on the air, my hands in front of my face.

It took a moment to believe I was alone, that the scream that had awakened me had come from my own lips.

There was no way I could get back to sleep.

CHAPTER ELEVEN

THANKSGIVING DAY WAS CRYSTAL clear, its brisk air permeated with that peculiar scent given off from dried leaves crackling underfoot.

Anticipation filled me as I climbed up the sunny steps of Lettie's house. Despite my pretense otherwise, I knew deep within me why I was so happy.

I would see Jason.

His old dog barked at me halfheartedly until Lettie, dressed in her usual knit pants and top, opened the door. "Hush up, Digger," she chided, and the dog's tail wagged once before he lay back down. "Well, don't you look nice," Lettie went on, approving my russet sweater and slacks in her forthright manner. "Come on back to the kitchen. Jace and I are finishing up, and Brent and Simone ought to be here shortly."

In the kitchen, Jason, neat in starched khakis and crewneck sweater, bent over the oven.

I couldn't resist. "How domestic. But do you know what you're doing?"

He grinned at me over his shoulder, and my heart flip-flopped. Settle down, I admonished myself. It's only a smile.

"Jason always cooks the turkey," Lettie said. "And our Christmas ham, too."

"Jason?" My face must have shown my astonishment.

Lettie burst out laughing. "Wouldn't have thought it, eh?"

"No, I certainly can't see Jason as a cook."

"I'll have you know I roast a pretty mean turkey," Jason defended himself as he pulled the rack out. "And my brown-sugar baked ham is probably the best you'll ever eat."

"Sure." I rolled my eyes. "I bet."

"This bird's ready." He ignored my skepticism by wiggling a drumstick. "We'll eat—" he cast an eye at the clock above the door "—at one o'clock, with or without Brent and Simone."

Lettie snorted. "Pay no mind, Anna. He talks a good game, but it all depends on Maggie's dressing." She went over to pick up a long pan filled with batter, and popped it into the open oven. "Sometimes it takes thirty minutes and sometimes forty-five. We'll eat whenever this dressing gets done."

She shook her head at her son, but he just grinned, licking his fingers where he'd pinched off some crusty meat.

"Want a bite?" he asked me.

The aroma was inviting, and the turkey was a beautiful brown. "Smells great."

He used a knife to cut off a morsel, but when I reached for it, he held it away. "It's hot. Let it cool a minute."

When it had cooled, he offered it to me. I made the mistake of letting his hand brush mine.

And felt the same reaction as before, stronger than ever. Fire, hot and sweet, surged from him and through me. I almost gasped aloud.

He didn't release the turkey but instead lifted it up to my mouth, which opened of its own accord to take it from his fingers. They lingered a little too long on my lips, but I didn't protest. His golden eyes were muted and a little puzzled, as though he felt the same current and, like me, didn't know what to make of it.

"Let's see." Lettie frowned at the dishwasher, completely unaware of what was passing between her son and her guest. "Anna, if you'll help me, we'll take this china in and set the table. I rinsed the dust off yesterday so the plates are dry."

"Right." I pulled away from Jason with an effort, and began to make myself useful. His gaze followed me, still holding that bemused expression.

When Simone, Brent and the baby arrived, dinner went off without incident. Afterward, everyone helped clear the table except for Simone. She pleaded a headache and lay down with Christopher for a nap. Jason and Brent took their beers into the family room to watch football while, in the time-honored tradition, Lettie and I finished up in the kitchen.

From the box windows, the gorge looked pristine and lovely and I said as much. "It's hard to believe it's so dangerous."

Lettie grunted. "It is, though. In more ways than one."

I hesitated, but plunged ahead. "The teacher who died here . . . I understand Jason found him."

Lettie was matter-of-fact. "I'll never forget that night. Brent came rushing up to the house yelling for Jason. They went down, but it was too late. You've heard the gossip?"

"Well, yes. Some of it. I didn't realize Brent was there."

"Jason spent the evening with me, helping me sort old photographs. He was telling me why he and Tiffany weren't going to get married." She gave me a sidelong look as if to see if I doubted her. "I'm sure you've heard about that, too."

Embarrassed, I mumbled an acknowledgement.

Lettie shrugged. "I know most people don't believe he was here. They think I'd lie to protect him. And maybe I would. But that night he really was with me. We didn't know anything about what happened till Brent came shouting that a man had fallen. And when I found out it was Alan McKenzie, it was like a bad dream, like—"

She stopped abruptly. "Water under the bridge now. Jace is strong. Talk's never bothered him. But Brent . . ." She bit her lip. "He's my sensitive one. Takes things too much to heart. Seeing Alan McKenzie fall did something to him, it seems to me."

"I'm sure it was hard on him." So Brent had been there when Alan fell. And Jason had been with his mother. My heart felt unreasonably light. Why couldn't the F on Alan's list have stood for Brent Forrester instead of his brother?

"Jason and I, we've always kind of looked out for Brent, tried to protect him from the hard facts of life. When his father died, Brent went to pieces. It was Jason who talked him into getting counseling. He'd barely got back to normal when that happened. He insisted on going down with Jason, and then . . . Oh, yes, it was hard on him."

She put the silver platter that had held the turkey into its protective covering and turned to me. "I know Jason kind of grates on you, Anna—"

I murmured polite denials. Lettie didn't have the slightest idea about how her son affected me.

She didn't listen. "—But he's as good-hearted as they come. When Moss was dying, Jason took turns with me sitting in the hospital. One or the other of us was there all the time the last few weeks. And I told you how he moved back in with me afterward, telling me he reckoned he'd be more comfortable with me to look after him."

She laughed. "Course it was the other way round. It was awful after Moss died. Jason being here made it bearable."

Why was I not surprised? Hadn't I seen for myself the way he treated his mother and brother? I couldn't have liked him half so well had he been as thoughtless and indifferent as he sometimes made himself out to be.

"He's not an easy man, Anna," Lettie went on. "He's a lot like his father, wanting to look after those he loves, and with some of my stubbornness thrown in to boot."

"That can't be all bad," I said.

"No, I suppose it could be worse."

I helped her put her china away, in the built-in cabinets on either side of the fireplace in the dining room, and then we joined Brent and Jason in front of the television.

It was nearly dark when I got ready to leave.

When Jason got up to escort me home, I demurred politely; but he insisted, and Lettie, not knowing what she was encouraging, backed him up. "The trail looks different in the dark, Anna. It's real confusing. Jace knows every turn."

He didn't try to touch me as we walked over the lip of the gorge toward my cabin. He was much too crafty for that. Instead, he aimed a flashlight in front of us and talked about football and recipes and, inevitably, his family's business.

"We have blueprints for a project in midtown Atlanta I'm anxious to start. Hopefully we can line up some investors and pull it off the drawing board in the next five years."

"Will it be expensive?"

"Yes." The word was clipped. "We could've financed the whole project ourselves except we had to dip into capital to get Simone out of hock. We're just now getting out of the red.'

In the dark, I couldn't see his face.

"I know you think I'm hard on Simone, Anna, but she came damn close to ruining us with her little jaunts to Atlantic City and Vegas. If I hadn't discovered how she was financing them, the company would have been bankrupt. As it is, we've had a time staying solvent."

"The business seems to be doing fine now," I said, thinking of the set of books I sometimes worked on and wondering how much truth there was in what he said.

"Yeah. And I intend to see it stays that way. After all, I might get married one of these days, have to support a wife."

"You haven't given up on women then?" I tried to be light.

"Hell, no. I've just become a lot more choosy. Glamor's all right, but I've learned integrity's better. Give me a woman who says what she means and I'll be happy as a clam. When I marry, I want somebody I can trust. Somebody like you, Anna."

Acutely aware of my duplicity, I couldn't say a word.

Thankfully, we approached my porch, so no answer was required. The security light threw a yellow glow around us, making his flashlight unnecessary.

At the bottom of my steps, he seemed big and solid under the artificial illumination. I could understand how Brent and Lettie would lean on him.

"Damn, Anna. You're too easy to talk to," he said. "I tell you things I oughtn't. Don't you go repeating them, especially about what nearly happened because of Simone's gambling. Lettie'd blame herself if she knew, because she trusted Simone to do the accounting then."

"No." I turned. "I won't say anything. Thanks for walking me home, Jason." I held out my hand in hopes of fending off an advance

I knew without a doubt was coming. "And for the turkey and dressing. It was great."

He looked down at my hand with a faint smile, and as I had expected, took it only to use in pulling me toward him. I held him off for a moment, my hands spread against his chest. But looking up into his rugged face, I was lost, as lost as I'd been that day in the warehouse, except that now there was no Brent to interrupt.

He realized he had won and bent over, a small triumphant smile coming closer and closer.

His tongue, sure of its welcome, made short work in parting my acquiescent lips. It moved slowly, provocatively around my mouth, exploring each tooth, caressing my tongue, leaving a trail of fire so liquid I thought I was drowning in flame. I lifted my hand to push him away, but ended by tangling my fingers in his hair and pulling him closer. Our bodies, two separate entities, seemed to lose their identities and merge into one as we stood in embrace. I felt him tightening, hardening, and shifted, parting my thighs to enclose him as much as was possible in our fully clothed state.

He let out a strangled noise, one hand coming down against my hips to press me against him while the other held my neck so that I couldn't escape his lips.

As if I wanted to escape his lips. They were marvelous portals of delight, opening the way to a cavern of wonders never before imagined.

Jason was the first to pull away. "Do you know what you do to me?" he murmured hoarsely, eyes glassy. His hand was pulling up my sweater as he spoke, lifting it in a delicious erotic fashion that indicated his intent.

"I think so." My voice was as hoarse as his. When his hand slid under the sweater and cupped my breast, I strained against his touch. Not until his fingers slipped inside my bra and touched my bare nipple did I regain some sanity. With a gasp, I slid out of his reach.

Spell broken, the old feeling returned with a vengeance, that of being surrounded by hostile spirits waiting to pounce. In spite of my arousal, the animosity frightened me. And it wasn't emanating from Jason because of my rejection. It came from the other, that dark unknown phantom who dogged me with such determination, such rancor.

"We're moving too fast." Breathless, I couldn't make my words as assertive as I intended. An uneasy glance toward the dark gorge revealed nobody, nothing. "I'm not ready for this yet, Jason."

"You act damn ready to me." He didn't move toward me. His voice was throaty. "Every time I get within five feet of you I can feel the electricity. And I think you feel the same thing."

"Maybe I do. But I'm still not ready."

Any frustration or anger he felt at my retreat was concealed. "All right. That's up to you. But I know where we're heading, Anna. And so do you." He sounded indulgent, willing to let me choose the pace at which we progressed.

"Please. I think you'd better go now."

He nodded slowly, a grin starting and then widening. "All right, Mrs. Levee. I'll back off. For a while." He sounded cocky, very sure of himself. "I just hope you don't take too damned long making up your mind."

Annoyance made me forget for a moment those watching demons. "I'll take as long as I like."

He laughed. "I've got to go over to South Carolina tomorrow for a wedding, and I won't be back till late Saturday night. I wouldn't go except I'm an usher. Why don't we do something Sunday afternoon, after I get Lettie off on her trip?"

"I'm going over to a friend's house Sunday to watch football." I was uncertain whether to be glad or not. Jason needed the put-down, but I longed to be with him.

"Your schoolteacher friend?" Was that a hint of jealousy? If so, it was well contained.

I nodded.

"I should have known. I guess I'll see you Monday, then."

"Yes." It took me a second to realize he was waiting for me to leave him.

As I went up my steps, I was afraid. I don't know if my fear arose from the emotions he induced each time we were alone, or if it came from that aura of unseen malevolence. At the door, I looked back. "Good night. Thanks for walking me home."

"Goodnight, Anna." My name was a caress. "Sleep well."

Sleep was long in coming as I lay and remembered his body against mine. But when sleep did come, it was deep and dreamless, almost as if his parting words were a benediction to keep the demons at bay.

CHAPTER TWELVE

FRIDAY MORNING, I AWOKE refreshed, Jason on my mind. Why did I like him so much? Surely it was against my prudent nature to fall for a man right off the bat like this.

When my cell rang, it was Charles Raite, my attorney.

"Just a couple of things I'm sending for you to sign. The lease renewal for the Lenox Square shop Bob left you, and a quitclaim deed for the half acre behind the factory where the new employee day-care center is going."

"Fine." I should have been happy, since I'd pushed for that facility for years, but that was a part of my other life. Fleeting satisfaction was all it merited today.

Charles revealed the main reason he'd called. "An agent from the Georgia Bureau of Investigation came up to see me a few days ago, Annabelle. It seems that something belonging to Alan has turned up. A rather valuable coin."

Anguish choked me.

Charles hesitated and went on. "It was traced back to a Chattanooga pawn shop."

"His eagle," I whispered when the lump in my throat went away. A 1798 eagle with six stars that he'd had since he graduated from the university.

Bob had been frantic when the gold coin with its protective metal rim fell into a crevice in our house. We were about to take up the hardwood flooring to retrieve it, but Alan, only sixteen, came in with a magnet strong enough to pull it up. Bob had been impressed with Alan's common sense, so impressed that he'd given it to my brother for a graduation gift.

"It was valuable." Charles cut short my emotional reminiscences. "Worth several thousand dollars."

"Alan wore it on a chain round his neck. For good luck." I came back from the past reluctantly, dreading to ask but needing to find out. "Do they know who pawned it?"

"A young woman got twelve hundred dollars for it."

"A woman!" Relief, sweet and enervating, flooded me. I hadn't realized how much I wanted Jason Forrester to have no connection with Alan's death.

Charles must have been baffled at my reaction. "Er, yes."

"Could they identify her?"

"No. All the clerk remembered was that she had long red hair. He said, at the time, he didn't think to check his list of stolen items. The GBI man didn't act like he believed it." Charles's tone said he didn't believe it, either. "A dealer recognized what it was and alerted the GBI. Bob's social security number engraved under the rim led them to me."

I barely heard the last part. A lot of people from Rahunta shopped in Chattanooga, since it was the nearest city. That was where Simone had got her ill-fated ring. A redheaded woman . . .

A woman with a cloud of red hair like Tiffany Underwood.

But Tiffany had no reason to kill Alan.

Unless they'd quarreled. Would she shoot her lover and leave him to be discovered by the Forresters?

Charles was still talking, and I hadn't heard a word in several minutes. "—turned over to me. When they do, I'll keep it for you, Annabelle. I suppose you'll be home soon?"

I stuttered and stammered and hemmed and hawed, and moved quickly on to something I'd asked him to do. "Charles, did you have a chance to get a copy of Moss Forrester's will as I asked?"

"Ye-es." He was trying to hide his curiosity. We'd always gotten along well. He was a modest man, prudent and careful like me.

Like I had once been.

I pushed guilt aside. "Did Moss Forrester leave any of his money to his sons?"

Charles's reply was prompt. "He left everything to them."

"Everything! What about Let—his wife?"

"Letitia Forrester is quite well off in her own right. Her father was a wealthy property owner in Atlanta and she was an only child. Evidently Moss felt she was adequately provided for and that the boys should inherit whatever he left."

"Was it a lot?"

"It depends on what you consider a lot."

I was getting tired of his lawyer's caution. "A million?"

He paused. "I imagine you can safely multiply that by ten." His voice was very dry. "Moss was an astute businessman."

Brent had millions and Jason was quibbling about Simone's expensive habits? I was first outraged, but then curious as to how much she'd gambled away if she had left the company nearly insolvent.

Of course, I had only Jason's word for that.

"Did what Moss leave consist only of the business or was there more?"

"The business was separate and left to the boys outright, but he had various other holdings. Income from that, plus interest from the stocks and bonds he held, was divided into a trust for each."

"So they can't get at the principal?"

"Brent Forrester has taken control of his."

But not Jason? I asked why.

Charles was happy to explain. "Moss's will specified that the trust would revert to each son upon the birth of his first child. Jason Forrester has never had a child."

What a ridiculous requirement, as if siring a child could make a man worthy of handling money. "That's pretty antiquated."

"Moss felt that a family was the most settling influence a young man could have. I'd normally agree, but according to my sources, Brent Forrester has been dipping into his capital pretty heavily. In fact, except for the business, his inheritance is all but gone. Moss Forrester may have suspected his sons would be extravagant, thus the trusts."

So Jason had been telling me the truth.

That pleased me, yet I was shaken by the discovery of Alan's talisman. It made me aware of how desperately I wanted Jason to be innocent of my brother's death.

And who the devil was the woman with the red hair?

That night, my dreams of misty rocks and muted voices returned with a new twist. This time there was a baby. He held a golden coin, his hand turning it over and over in the careful way babies have. He sat on a trail of the gorge, and was perilously close to the edge. My heart was in my throat as I watched him rocking closer, but I couldn't seem to get near him. I could only follow the trail I was on and hope it would lead to him in time to save him from going over into the gorge.

Off to the side was Alan, behind his glass wall where I couldn't reach him, his face obscured by clouds. "Hurry, hurry," he kept calling as I struggled along a trail in the gorge, slipping and sliding and straining to see through the mist. "You have to go faster, Belle. You'll be too late. Can't you try harder?"

When I awoke, a sense of urgency left my heart thumping.

Alan wanted me to do something, but what?

* * *

SUNDAY, I STARTED TO Matt's, using the trail that forked off directly under the lip of the gorge in front of my cabin. Since I'd had to forgo a day with Jason because of my previous commitment, I was out of sorts. Television football would be much more fun with him than with our poker group.

Busy brooding and halfway to Matt's cottage, I ran into Simone.

She jumped at seeing me. "Anna! Hello." She looked very young and very happy. Her mouth, which always looked as if it had just been kissed, seemed softer than usual.

I was as surprised as she. The only place this trail led was to Matt's house, but I didn't like thinking what I was thinking. "Hello, Simone. Where're you going?"

"To Lettie's. What about you?"

I explained about Matt's party, inviting her to join us, but she refused with a shake of her head. "I don't like football."

It struck me, as I walked on, that she hadn't asked me again to search Jason's house. Perhaps she'd given up the idea.

Surely, she hadn't talked Matt into helping her with her scheme. Matt was one of her few friends. I hated to believe he was anything more than that, but Simone, with her flirtatious ways, certainly encouraged him. It would take a more upright man than Matt, I was afraid, to withstand her pleas.

None of our fellow card-players had arrived at Matt's, so I said point-blank, "I met Simone as I was coming over."

Matt met my eyes steadily, but a faint flush showed around his collar and he took a long time to answer. "Brent offered to loan me a book on the academy, and Simone brought it over."

There was nothing more to say, but I was beginning to feel sorry for Brent. And Matt.

* * *

WHEN I ARRIVED AT the office on Monday, Jason was there.

I said a civil "Good morning," ignoring the joy spreading over me when his smile reflected mine. As I went to my desk, he came to the front and sat down in one of the reception chairs facing me. He stretched out his long legs, balancing his cup so as not to spill any of his coffee. A few drops splashed onto his jeans anyway, and I watched the big fingers brush them off.

"Enjoy the football games yesterday?" he asked.

"Yes, thank you."

"Saw you going down the trail toward Graven's place."

I eyed him with caution, wondering what he was getting at.

"You ought not to go out alone."

"I'm always very careful." I put my purse away.

"The gorge is dangerous if you don't know it." He took a sip as though his coffee were scalding.

"So I've been warned." I closed the desk drawer.

"I don't like to see you going off by yourself. Anytime you want to hike, I'll be glad to go with you." One big hand held the bottom of the cup while the fingers of the other traced the lip. "You don't need to wait for your friend."

He was jealous. Despite his effort to hide it, he was jealous and I could not deny my elation. Nor could I push away the unbidden surge of longing unfolding at the sight of that fingertip leisurely stroking the cup. I picked up a ballpoint pen, to have something to do, and turned it back and forth. "Thank you very much, Jason, but Matt wouldn't take me any place that was dangerous."

"Maybe so. But he's not from here. He doesn't know all the ins and outs. You think about it."

I knew what he was really asking, and I didn't want to think about it. I wanted to jump up and shout, "Yes, yes! I'd love to go with you! How about tomorrow? Just you and me, and I'll bring the loaf of bread and jug of wine and a blanket."

"Thank you." Such a struggle I went through to remain demure. "That's very kind of you. I'll remember that."

"I'm not kind." He was blunt as always. "You'd have more fun with me than you do with Graven. And I know I'd have a better time with you than Graven does."

My brows shot up. "Kind and conceited, I see."

He got up, smiling a lazy grin that made my knees turn to water. "The trouble with you, Anna, is that you've let our first meeting prejudice you. You've been taking everything I say the wrong way. I keep telling you I'm sorry, so can't we start over?"

I swallowed. Hard. "I thought we had."

On my lunch hour, I ran an errand I'd been putting off. Old issues of the local newspaper were on antiquated microfiche at the library. The article I sought had been written thirteen years previously. I would have missed it except for the picture.

Jason, very young and without the mustache, looked truculent as he stared out. He seemed vulnerable, with his generous mouth revealing none of the harshness seen in more recent newspaper pictures. A middle-aged, attractive Lettie was on one side of him while a man with a lantern jaw, identified as Moss Forrester, was on the other.

The report said that Jason had jumped on another man. The victim was hospitalized but in stable condition. Three weeks later, a short item reported that both men had been fined for fighting.

There was no mention of why the two had fought, but in an issue three days after the report of the fight, there was a brief notice that the Jennings-Forrester engagement announced previously had been canceled "by mutual consent."

For a long while I sat there and imagined a young Jason discovering his fiancée had been cheating. At twenty, there might be some excuse for hitting out and trying to hurt the man who had stolen his girl. At thirty-three, there was none.

I couldn't believe the older Jason would have been that easily provoked, not unless he had unexpectedly come upon Alan and Tiffany in bed.

Not even then, I decided.

When I got back to the office at two, Jason was there, tapping a rolled-up sheet of paper on his open palm. "You're late," he told me brusquely. "I've been waiting for you. We need this contract right away."

I took off my coat and hung it up, sat down at my desk and put my purse away. Swiveling in my chair, I put on my glasses, met his eyes squarely and put out my hand for the paperwork.

He gazed at my outstretched hand and burst out laughing. "If you don't beat all I've ever seen. What does it take to upset you, Anna Levee?"

He didn't know it, but I was already upset. Every time I got within ten feet him, my heart did strange things.

My purpose in Rahunta was no longer simply to find out why Alan had died or what he was trying to tell me.

I now wanted to prove to my own satisfaction that Jason had had nothing to do with Alan's murder. Until then, I'd have to keep my distance. It wouldn't do to fall in love with a man who might be involved in my brother's death.

I refused to believe it was too late.

CHAPTER THIRTEEN

DESPITE JASON'S TEMPTING OFFER, I didn't go with him into the gorge. Being alone with him wouldn't be prudent, since the effect he had on me was such that my own body might betray me. It would be ill-advised to put myself into a situation where he might overwhelm me by sheer physical appeal.

Instead, on the first weekend in December, Matt and I and one of his friends from North Carolina descended into the ravine. The day was beautiful, with mild temperatures, blue skies, high fleecy clouds and a brilliant sun that made it seem like July—an altogether perfect day for hiking.

Matt deeming me sufficiently experienced, we took the difficult path to Brent and Simone's house that forked off the main trail between my cottage and Lettie's home. Not only did we have to scramble over a fallen tree at one point, but the trail was uncomfortably close to the edge at times.

One particularly nasty section marked where several hikers had fallen in past years. The ledge beneath our feet was barely a yard wide, and one wrong step would send us plummeting into the gorge. I turned sideways, glad of a convenient sapling to hold on to and even gladder of the safety line Matt had brought to secure me.

At the bottom, Matt and Lew decided to do a simple climb up a different slope. Citing fatigue, I chose to walk among the rocks dotting the riverbed.

"I don't know." Matt hesitated about leaving me alone. "It isn't as safe as it looks. Some of those pools are deep. If you fall in—"

"I'll be fine. I don't intend to get in the water."

He didn't like it, but I insisted and Lew sided with me. We arranged to meet where the trail led back up to Simone's house.

At one time there'd been a series of waterfalls roaring down the gorge, but once the dam was built, they'd ceased to exist. The deep, rapidly moving river they'd fallen into was now a collection of placid, boulder-strewn water holes.

It was hard walking on the rocks, but so long as I took care not to step on one that was unstable, I managed all right. At least here at the bottom, there was no danger of falling any distance.

Somewhere in this vicinity, my brother had met his death. I turned to look up and saw the fading sumac bushes that marked the point where, beyond the curve of the gorge's edge, the trail we'd just trekked began, about halfway between my cottage and Lettie's house.

Alan had fallen, or been thrown, from that fork. That meant he would have landed within fifty feet of where I stood. He would have fallen and—

I was no longer alone in the gorge. The ugly sensation was back, as if cruel eyes bored into the back of my neck.

There was no movement overhead, no sound except that of my own ragged breathing and the water somnolently trickling among the rocks at my feet.

Was Alan trying to tell me something? Was I not deciphering the dreams fast enough to suit him?

No, Alan's shade would never come back to torment me like this. This was a hateful spirit, one that had died on the gallows or been shot in the back or knifed during a brawl. Not being fanciful by nature, I scolded myself for allowing my imagination to get the better of me. After all, spirits were simply emotional manifestations, with no physical power to harm the living. The thing watching me might make me uneasy, but it couldn't hurt me.

Not unless I got so upset I tripped and hit my head on the rocks. *Forget about whatever it is and do what you came for.*

So I searched the gorge bottom.

I didn't know what I expected to find: bloodstains, perhaps, or a bit of Alan's favorite Georgia football jersey, which he'd worn so often.

In any case, there was nothing to mark the exact spot where Alan, my witty, tenderhearted, high-spirited, darling brother, had lain until his lifeblood flowed out of him.

When I touched my face, it was wet with tears. *Oh, Alan, who would have thought it would end like this?*

Somber, I retraced my steps to where I was to meet Matt and Lew, but it was impossible to rid myself of the notion that unseen eyes watched my every movement. If only the bottom were not so open. There was no place to duck under cover, to sit back and wait for whatever was stalking me to show itself.

My back fairly prickled.

It's nerves, I told myself. Walking the rocks where Alan had died was more upsetting than I admitted.

Stop thinking about it and go on.

At the trail leading up toward Simone's house, I bent down at a tranquil pool to wash the dirt from my face and hands.

The water was cold and refreshing. As I stood, something glinted in its depths. Mildly curious, I peered down, shading my eyes from the bright sunshine to see better.

And forgot my sense of being spied upon.

At the bottom of that crystal-clean pool, so distinct that I could almost reach down and touch it, rested something solid. A clear plastic bag? Whatever it was gave off a dull, metallic gleam in the diffused sunlight.

A gun?

Unbidden memories invaded my mind. Jason's form, rearing back to throw something into the ravine . . .

No, no, the suspicious was ridiculous. My imagination was running riot again.

Kneeling down, I tried to gauge the depth of the pool. I first rolled up my sleeve and stuck my hand in the water, logically aware that I couldn't touch the object, but trying anyway.

When reaching down didn't work, I looked around for something to use as a hook. It took several minutes to make my way to the trees at the side and find a dead sapling with a protruding branch that might serve.

Leaning down at the edge of the pool, I lowered my stick into the water. It seemed near to touching the object.

Suddenly a bee buzzed past my ear. I flinched. A faint dull thud came from the rocks behind me.

The next thing I knew, I was sliding on the moss, scrambling to save myself. To no avail. I fell in headfirst.

A mountain stream in December, even on a warm, sunny day, is not a nice place to swim. The plunge was like jumping into a tub of ice water.

My heavy hiking boots hindered my surfacing, but I had to get out before the cold made it impossible for me to move. Pushing my head above water, I gasped for air and got my bearings.

Wet clothes and heavy boots pulled me down again, but I didn't fight it. Instead, I propelled myself toward the side as I sank. Banging my head, I bobbed up again at the edge of the pool.

The first rock I grabbed was unstable and fell into the pool beside me. The next one was set firmly in place, but was slippery with moss. Gripping it was impossible.

After two or three tries, I literally threw myself out of the water like a jumping dolphin, and lay gasping on the rocks, my legs still in the cold water and my cheek resting on a ledge of solid rock. Safely secured, I took a thankful moment to recover, then crawled the rest of the way out of that innocent-appearing, treacherous pool and collapsed.

Only then did I allow myself the luxury of reflection. No bee ever whizzed into the dirt at such speed.

Someone had shot at me.

Whoever had fired might try again. If they did, there was no place to hide here on the bottom of the gorge. I didn't even know where the shot had come from.

As I lay there with pounding heart and face scraping the granite ledge, two boots came into view. Cowboy boots. Not the usual work boots.

I turned my head with difficulty to look up at Jason Forrester, grinning down at me. There was no weapon in his hand. Could . . . ?

No. Impossible. I didn't believe it.

"What are you smiling about?" I found my breath. "Give me a hand."

To his credit, he leaned down, caught me by the collar of the sodden jacket and lifted me up bodily before setting me on my feet a safe distance from the slippery rocks. He then wrapped his jacket around my shoulders, the ugly yellow jacket that I had laughed at.

No laughing today.

"It's mighty cold weather to go swimming." His concern was evident despite his amusement. "Don't you know better than to go traipsing off down here by yourself?"

Fear of a watery grave subsided with the reality of cold, wet clothing. A shudder racked me. "I wasn't by myself. Matt and Lew are around here somewhere."

He shook his head. "They shouldn't have left you alone. I told you, you ought to go hiking with somebody experienced in gorge climbing, like me. It can be very dangerous for city girls who don't know what they're doing."

"Especially when the natives start shooting." My teeth started to chatter, either from cold or fear.

"Shooting?" His grin vanished. "What are you talking about?"

I looked beyond him, toward where the bullet would have hit. There was no sign of any disturbance, nothing to corroborate my story. I'd never find a tiny bullet among the expanse of dirt and rocks.

Jason was either a good actor or he really didn't know what had happened.

"I thought it was a bee," I said slowly, staring straight at him. "But now I don't. You saw me fall in. Why didn't you come help me?"

His eyes narrowed. "I did come. Just as fast as I could from back there." He gestured toward the trees higher up the side of the gorge. "Took me awhile to work my way down. I thought you were a goner till I saw you kind of lunge over the edge of the pool." A smile lurked. "Never saw anything like it."

Still a distance away, two other figures were hurriedly picking their way down over the rocks toward us. Matt and his friend Lew.

"What were you doing spying on me, anyway?" Was Jason the source of the malevolence? "Shouldn't you be up watching your bulls assaulting the cows or something?"

"I saw you down here alone. I figured you needed someone to keep an eye on you. Why the hell didn't Graven stay with you? Didn't anybody warn you exploring the gorge is dangerous?"

As if everybody and his brother hadn't warned me. I shivered from anger and cold.

"Was it here?" He stepped away to examine the ground where I'd heard the thud.

My temper erupted, hindered by the audible chattering of my teeth. "Your keeping an eye on me doesn't seem to have helped, does it?"

He gave up inspecting the ground and moved over to look into the pool where I'd fallen. He froze, shoulders rigid.

I'd forgotten the reason for my being soaking wet. Better keep quiet about the thing in the water for now. I spoke to his back to draw him away. "I'm freezing after pulling *myself* out of the water. Without any aid or assistance, I might add, until it was too late to matter. If—"

"If you don't get some dry clothes on, you're going to have hypothermia." He came back and took my arm in a way that brooked no protest. "My truck's over at the old logging road. Save your breath for walking."

He half carried, half dragged my shaking body over the rocks, his steps sure when mine faltered.

Matt and Lew cut across to meet us.

Matt was agitated. "Are you all right?" Assured that I was basically fine, he relaxed. "We saw you fall in, but we were way up there." He pointed vaguely behind him. "What in heaven's name were you thinking, getting so close to the water like that? Lucky Forrester drove down when he did," he added grudgingly.

When I opened my mouth to protest that I had saved myself, I closed it again. What did it matter? I was cold and, the aftershock hitting me, scared. All I wanted was to get home.

"We'll talk about it later." Jason never broke stride as he propelled me on. "Right now Anna needs to get out of those wet clothes."

Jason had been raised on the edge of the gorge, learning all the rocky ledges and danger points. He would know that a man pushed off from above would have little chance of survival, especially a man with a bullet in him.

And he'd also know a gun thrown into one of the myriad pools on the bottom could lie undisturbed for years.

But Jason Forrester was not a murderer.

He was not.

CHAPTER FOURTEEN

BY THE TIME WE GOT to Jason's four-wheel-drive truck, my hands were blue. He turned the heater up full blast and set off up the rutted road much too fast.

Hanging onto the armrest to keep from jouncing toward him made it impossible to talk. I didn't realize where he was heading until he stopped the truck, and Digger, his Australian shepherd, gave a joyous bark.

"Oh, no!" I said. "I'm not getting out here. No way. Take me home right now." Lettie was in Palm Beach, nor would Maggie Mahone be there on a weekend to offer protection. The last thing in the world I needed was to end up in a house alone with Jason Forrester.

He turned off the motor. "It's a twenty-minute drive to your cabin. You need to get out of those clothes." He sounded stern, but his mouth twitched.

"It's only fifteen minutes." I got out and slammed the door. "Never mind. I can walk from here."

He got out, too. "Suit yourself, but in your condition, I'm not sure you'll make it."

I almost threw prudence to the winds and marched off. But one step and the wind changed my mind. The excellent heater in the truck had done little to dispel the icy chill from my bones. Already, I was shivering again.

Clenching my teeth to keep from cursing him, I swung around and followed Jason Forrester meekly up the steps, past Digger's amused eyes and wagging tail, and into the kitchen.

"There's a bathroom right here." He herded me through the dining room and the study into a back bedroom. "The best thing you can do is hop into a warm shower while I find you some dry clothes."

Rather than admit I didn't want to take off my clothes while alone with him in this house, I said coolly, "If you'll just get me a t-towel, I'll b-be fine." Unfortunately, my chattering teeth spoiled the effect.

"Don't be stupid. You're going to catch pneumonia." A thought struck him. "Worried about me?" He grinned. "Don't be. I promise I won't force my attentions on you. Not that I don't want to. I don't usually go for skinny women with mouse-colored hair. I've always preferred 'em a little more rounded and blonde. But you've really put the whammy on me. Yes, sir, you bring out all my best instincts."

"I—You—" The recollection of his lips on mine, and my own acknowledged fascination for the man, added to my wrath.

"You'll be perfectly safe." He added masterfully, "Now let's get you in the shower."

I found my tongue. "I don't give a damn about the kind of woman you prefer."

He nudged my back. "This way, please."

With considerable restraint I allowed myself to be pushed into an airy bathroom that was blessed with a wall heater. Jason turned it on as I was still trying to think of a fitting rejoinder, but all that I could dredge up was: "In fact, Jace Forrester, I doubt you even *possess* any good instincts." I wasn't satisfied, but I could think of nothing worse on the spur of the moment.

He grinned provocatively, but spoke only about the heater. "There. It's making heat already. It'll be real cozy in a couple of minutes. Look, there's a nice modern lock on the door. Be a good girl and stay under the hot water at least ten minutes, okay?"

He left me speechless and fuming.

But he was right about the hot shower.

While basking in its warmth, I thought about what I'd seen in the pool. The glittery thing was too large to be Simone's ring. And it might not be a gun. But then again, what if it was? I didn't wholly believe Simone's and Matt's contention that the authorities of the county were bought and paid for by the Forresters, but it might be better to go to someone else. Just in case.

It wouldn't hurt to call Bob's nephew in the FBI and see if there was any way he could investigate the presence of a suspicious object in the bottom of the gorge. If it wasn't a gun, I'd look pretty silly. But time enough to worry about that afterward.

Remembering the sight of Jason on Brent's deck, arm pulled back to throw, I hoped it wasn't a gun. Despite my annoyance, my opinion of Jason hadn't changed. He was too candid to be a murderer.

But what if he was helping cover up for someone? Maybe Simone had the story backwards. Maybe it was Brent who'd killed Alan, and Jason was protecting him. The facts fit. Kind of.

I felt wonderful when I emerged from the stall. The upbeat mood remained until, rubbing myself with a thick towel, I spotted a white robe hanging on a bathroom hook.

It had not been there when I locked the door. I would've noticed.

What's more, the sweater, jeans and underwear I'd carefully draped around the bathroom were gone.

Jason Forrester had come in while I was showering. A look back at the transparent shower panel and I could have died.

A moment later, in the study off the hall, I confronted him. "You said the door locked, you liar!" I hauled my fist back to let him have it, except he twisted slightly and caught my arm before any damage was done.

"Lady!" he said, shocked. "Watch where you aim. You could've made me a soprano."

"I meant to make you a soprano! How dare you come into that bathroom while I was in the shower? You knew I locked that door expressly to keep you out."

He shook his head piously. "You wrong me, you really do. I admit I came into the bathroom, but only to get your clothes and throw them in the dryer and leave you my robe so you wouldn't be left naked."

When I took a step toward him with my fist clenched, he danced back, keeping a wary eye on it. "You may not be averse to jaunting around other people's houses in the buff, Anna, but let me tell you here and now, I don't allow anybody to do it in Lettie's house. She'd really disapprove."

"You—you liar! You pulled a low-down, sneaky trick on me, telling me that door locked, knowing the only way I would've taken off my clothes with you in the same vicinity was from behind a locked door."

"I didn't say the door locked. Although it does, in case you're interested." He put on a virtuous expression that wouldn't have fooled a child. "What I said was that there was a nice modern lock on the door, which there is. True, I didn't say I've been able to open it since I was eight and Brent locked himself in and I had to get him out, but if you'd asked if I could open that locked door, I would have told you—"

"Oh, stop it." I was tired of the conversation, tired of him, tired of my whole charade. "Get me my clothes so I can go."

He gave me a hurt look, but a tiny twinkle spoiled the effect. "They'll be dry in a moment. Sit down there by the fire that I was kind enough to build for you. If you can bring yourself to talk real sweet, I may even fix you a cup of hot chocolate."

The tempting offer gave me pause.

He might intend to poison me, but after he'd taken the trouble to put my clothes in the dryer—I heard it tumbling from somewhere beyond the dining room—it seemed unlikely.

On the other hand, if seduction was what he had in mind . . .

My foolish body was already transmitting weird signals from being this close to him.

Reluctantly surrendering, I sat down on a cushioned stool by the fire. When he brought the promised hot chocolate, I made him set it on the table beside me before picking it up and sipping greedily.

"Now," he said, standing in front of the fire and watching me drink. "Isn't this better?"

I had to agree.

He leaned against the mantel. "Good. Since you're all comfy and cozy, why don't you tell me what you were trying to fish out of the water."

The question was not unexpected, but I'd hoped to evade it.

"I thought I saw something, but it was probably just another rock." I went so far as to bat my eyelashes in hopes he would drop the subject.

My effort distracted him, but not for long. "Those holes are anywhere from two to fifty feet deep. That particular one is about ten. The stick you had didn't reach anywhere near the bottom."

I didn't believe him. The glimmering object had been very clear. Small but plain in the sunlight.

I forced a docile smile. "I'm sure you're right."

"Just exactly what was it you thought you saw?" One boot propped casually on the hearth.

I shrugged in my best helpless-little-woman manner. "It's hard to tell. Let's not talk about it, Jason."

"All right. We'll skip it for a moment. You said you were shot at. Is that true, or are you just taking up Simone's habits?"

The mug in my hand trembled. Looking at him, I saw he was still watching me and had assumed a mocking air. He was an arrogant man. If he'd got away with murder, or even with covering up murder, he had cause to be arrogant. A great sadness swept through me at the thought, a pressure building on my rib cage and squeezing my heart.

"Is that what you think I'm doing?" Looking up from beneath my lashes, I adjusted the neck of the robe to show more skin, and crossed my ankles enticingly. Simple diversionary tactics, I told myself. I didn't want him to take me up on my unspoken offer. Goodness, no.

He would not be diverted. "You're a funny little thing, Anna. What did you see in that water?"

The renewed attack threw me off balance. I abandoned my pathetic attempts to sidetrack him. "A bag. It looked like a plastic bag. One of those clear ones. I saw its reflection in the sun."

"Why were you so anxious to fish it out?"

There was no point in lying. Once I left, he was capable of getting to it before the authorities. If he knew what I'd seen, perhaps he'd realize he couldn't hide it.

"I thought it looked like it had a gun inside it," I said slowly.

"A gun?" Beyond a slow blinking of his eyelids, he showed absolutely no emotion at all. "You saw a gun in the water?"

"Maybe."

He hooked a wooden chair with his toe, bringing it close to the fire, and sat down to survey me from shuttered eyes.

When the silence stretched out until I could no longer bear it, I said, "I know there was a man killed near there last year. What if it's the gun that killed him?" The pressure in my chest was so intense I could hardly breathe.

"If you know that, I imagine you also know some people think I killed him."

His coming out with it shook my resolve, but I had to ask. "Did you?"

He smiled, shaking his head ruefully. When he spoke, his voice was relaxed, no longer probing. Almost as if he'd come to a decision of some sort. "Anna, Anna. Just because you think you see a gun doesn't mean it is one. And if it is, that doesn't mean it's a murder weapon."

He was not being honest with me. I could feel it. What was he hiding?

We watched each other warily. I had the strangest feeling that he was playing with me, that he knew what I'd seen and didn't care in the least.

"You're right. They never found the gun that killed the teacher." His stare didn't waver. He smiled slightly with his lips, but those hawklike eyes remained serious. "They thought it might be in one of those old river holes. Maybe they were right and maybe you've found it. But you shouldn't try to fish things out by yourself, Anna. It isn't safe, as you found out today."

"Yes." Was that a warning?

"Let the authorities take care of things like that." His eyes narrowed, and the smile was gone. He seemed for a moment like a very hard, very dangerous man to cross.

I had to look down into the dregs of my hot chocolate. "Do you think I should let someone know about it?"

For answer he went to the phone, dialed and spoke. When he hung up, he confirmed what I'd overheard.

"Our sheriff is rounding up a diver to go down and recover whatever it was you saw. Satisfied?"

"Thank you." I wondered why he was taking the trouble.

"I know you won't be happy till you find out what it is," he said as if reading my mind. "And I don't want you going back down there. Those holes really are deep. I wasn't lying. People drown in them regularly. You could have been one more statistic."

Those thick muscular shoulders and powerful thighs could do a great deal of damage in a fight. His hands were large, too. They were relaxed now, but if doubled up into fists, they could hurt someone badly.

I remembered how they'd felt kneading my shoulders and took a tight grip on my mug. Using guns didn't take muscles, I reminded myself. One finger on the trigger would do the trick. But not his finger—no, not Jason's.

I gulped down my chocolate. "Do you think my clothes are dry?"

"No." He threw a stick of wood onto the fire.

The big hands had square fingers with blunt tips. They would be as capable of controlling a gun as they would be of building up the fire or beating in a man's face. Of kneading a woman's body until all the tension dissolved in a culmination of bliss and fireworks . . .

What in heaven's name was coming over me?

He sat down again, this time on the elevated hearth beside my low stool, so close to me that our knees were almost touching.

I readjusted my legs. So long as I didn't allow him to touch me, I'd be safe.

The pressure in my chest subsided to leave a strange lassitude. I became conscious of how I was dressed, in his robe with nothing underneath. Until he sat down beside me, I'd almost forgotten our situation. Even when I'd simpered and flirted with him to deflect him from my discovery, I'd felt fully protected, fully clothed.

Now as he sat so near to me, almost but not quite touching, I realized I was alone with him—a reported would-be despoiler of his brother's wife and perhaps an accomplice in my brother's death—and all I could think about was how desirable he was, and how I was all but nude. More incomprehensible was the recognition that I was still drawn to him and hadn't the strength to resist.

How striking he was, with that pirate's complexion and solid, fit body. He was only inches away, directing at me that inexplicable expression that could be so sexy. I couldn't control my physical response to the knowledge that he wanted me, that the softness in his eyes was a prelude to intimacy.

My whole body tingled. A cautious woman should have been repelled by his frank manifestation of desire, not anticipating and responding.

My reaction was unexpected, unexplainable, and it took my breath away.

He smiled, the most seductive smile I'd ever seen on a man in my life. The edges of his mouth barely curved up under the dark mustache. I was close enough to see the yellow flecks in the brown irises, turning his gaze golden with tender mockery.

He knew exactly what I was thinking and the exact moment when

I began to think it. Dazed, I wondered if he hadn't intended it to happen just that way, but I couldn't care.

When he reached over for the edge of the white robe lying over my enervated legs, I didn't try to stop him.

"You're letting the cold air in," he said, still with that erotic smile. He draped a fold of the robe precisely to cover my exposed knee, careful not to touch my skin.

"I'm warm now." I sounded like a schoolgirl.

"Good." His husky tone sent splinters of fire throughout my body. "But let's keep you wrapped up anyway." As if my stillness implied assent, his fingers slipped under the thick terrycloth. His hand curved about my knee, leaving a current of warmth behind as it traced its way down my calf, briefly cupped my ankle, caressed my heel and came to rest on the bottom of my instep. He picked up my foot, the robe he'd arranged slipping aside so the bare skin of my thigh and calf rested against him.

I couldn't move. The leg trapped against the fabric of his shirt was on fire, devoured by an inferno that raced upward to combust. The pit of my stomach fell into a great void that begged for fulfillment.

He must have put something in the hot chocolate. Some sort of aphrodisiac.

"Your feet aren't warm," he chided. "Give me your other one, and I'll hold them up to the fire."

It didn't matter whether or not he'd doctored my drink. Without a single protest, I lifted my foot. He shifted as he placed it beside the other foot on his knee, turning my soles to the warmth of the flames so the delicious heat had access to every single cell.

My robe was gaping, the dark triangle between my legs all but revealed. He affected not to notice my squirming, which settled the seat of my craving squarely against his hipbone.

My heart was in my throat as I put the tiniest bit of pressure against him. The rough robe separating my bare bottom from his blue-jeaned hip rubbed against me, made me frantic.

Jason would make love to me here, today, and there wasn't a thing I could do to stop him. I didn't want to stop him. I'd never wanted a man so much in my life.

He ignored my movements but continued to massage my left foot in that lazy, intimate way that had effectively demolished my defenses. "What lovely feet. Here's a blister. From all the hiking you've been doing lately, no doubt. And what's this?"

He was gazing at my toes, the seductive smile remaining but unfocused, as though he had forgotten its purpose.

I jumped.

In the flush of passion, I had forgotten my feet.

To be reminded of my deformity at this particular moment was doubly vexatious. I was embarrassed to have him see them, and I didn't want him to stop touching me.

I scrunched them up tightly, and then resignedly relaxed them, letting him spread them gently and rub an inquisitive finger along the webbing.

"It's a family thing." If he found my feet repulsive, it would put an abrupt end to this attraction he held for me. Pride would prevent me from wanting a man who didn't want me. "I was born that way."

"Were you now?" He didn't put my feet down, but the heavy sexual vibrations emanating from him for the past ten minutes had vanished. I tried to pull my feet away, but he held them tightly, conjecture written all over him.

Finally, he said, "Lucky little feet, to belong to you." He brought one and then the other up to his lips, kissing each toe lingeringly.

I sat like a statue, with my head in a whirl and each toe where his lips touched it scorching hot. After contemplating them for another long moment, he put my feet down. One hand hesitated above where the robe parted below my pubic hair, and then picked up its edge.

I waited in agony, wanting him and yet afraid.

He looked into my eyes and with a little sigh, pulled the white robe firmly together. "Anna, Anna. Did you know how revealing your face is? Sooner or later you'll have to come to terms with us."

"The—the dryer has stopped."

His look told me he knew what I was afraid of, but that he would humor me until another time. "All right, Mrs. Levee, let's see if we can put you back together."

I wasn't sure that anyone could put me back together ever again.

CHAPTER FIFTEEN

THE NEXT DAY, I watched through binoculars as a team arrived with equipment to brave the icy water of the pool.

Simone called, sounding unlike herself. "Brent says you saw a gun in the water, Anna. Is it true?"

I was cautious. "I don't know what it was."

There was no reason to tell her I'd seen Jason throw something off her deck toward the pool.

"If you saw a gun, it wasn't the gun that killed Alan McKenzie," Simone whispered.

"What?" I thought at first I'd misunderstood. "Why do you say that?"

Her laughter rang bitter over the line. "I told you, Anna. That gun is safely hidden in Jason Forrester's house. What you saw may be connected, but it isn't the gun."

"Simone—"

My cell showed the call ended.

I grabbed a jacket and drove over to her house.

Jenny, dour as usual, let me in, the baby toddling along behind. She picked him up despite his protests, holding on to him as she led me through the living area and past the pool to the deck. Even with the activity down in the gorge, she wore her normal bored expression.

The deck had benches built into the railing. Simone sat on one of these with a knee folded under her, looking down with binoculars.

At my approach, she put them down and turned her head listlessly. Her hair was pulled back into a ponytail and she wore no makeup. She looked like a child recovering from an illness.

"Simone."

"Hello, Anna."

I sat down beside her. Several of the figures on the gorge bottom wore brown uniforms, while a few were in civilian dress. One in a bright yellow jacket was taller than the rest. Joy flooded me but was shoved hastily aside.

I could hardly wait for Jenny to get out of earshot. "What did you mean, Simone?"

Her hands bunched into fists at my question. A slyness about her reminded me of a child who knows things she shouldn't. "I saw you down in the gorge yesterday, Anna. I saw you fall into the water. It was a long time before Jason brought you home." She fixed accusing eyes on me. "You're falling for him, aren't you? Even after I warned you."

"Not at all." I had a plausible excuse for being with Jason Forrester. "If he hadn't been there, I would have had hypothermia or at least caught cold. It would have been stupid not to accept his help and hospitality."

I had quarreled with him, anyway, about the bathroom door, but Simone didn't have to know that.

She looked back at the figures in the gorge. "He has a woman in the northern part of town. He goes with other women sometimes, but he always comes back to Crystal."

I felt as if I'd been kicked in the gut. "There's no need to tell me anything about Jason, Simone. He's not my type."

The smile she gave me was cynical, oddly at variance with her childish face. "Jason is every woman's type." She was scornful. "He can be fascinating when he tries. I've seen how women behave when he starts to hit on them."

"Don't be ridiculous, Simone. I know what he is." Did I? How could I tell Simone what I felt about Jason when I hardly knew myself?

She reached over to catch my sleeve. Jason's face flashed into my mind, laughing as he said he used to like blondes.

Would he really try to seduce his brother's wife?

Why should I believe Simone? I knew how fanciful she was.

"Don't be angry, Anna," Simone said wistfully. "I'm afraid for you. You are the only friend I have here. I don't want to see you hurt."

"I have no intention of being hurt, I assure you. Simone, what did you mean when you said whatever's in that pool is connected to Alan McKenzie's death?"

She shrugged but refused to answer my question.

I tried a new topic. "You said you saw me fall yesterday, Simone. I think someone shot at me. Was there anybody else down there? Besides me and Jason and Matt and Lewis?"

Her mouth grew round. "Shot at you? What do you mean?"

I felt foolish repeating my story. Simone got up to pace the deck with knitted brows. "Why would anyone shoot you?" She whirled, her mouth agape. "Unless Jason did it. He was there. And on that side. Maybe he thought you'd found something incriminating him."

"No. Matt happened to be watching him when it happened." I had questioned Matt thoroughly about that last night. "Besides," I added wryly, "you can't have it both ways. He either wants to seduce me or kill me."

"I would believe either of him." Simone shivered, turning toward the gorge. "Look." Her tone shifted, the loathing disappearing and something else taking its place. I couldn't tell if it was hope or fear.

Below us, a diver in a wet suit was being pulled out. It was hard to tell, but he seemed to be handing something over to another man. Equipment was packed up, and people started climbing into the several vehicles.

Jason's truck was one of the last to leave.

I was back at my cottage before he called to tell me.

They didn't find a gun in the pool, but they did find a plastic bag.

It contained a leather wallet with no money, a worn money clip with no money, a class ring from the University of Georgia and a silver watch with a silver band. "You probably saw the reflection of the watch," Jason said. His voice was subdued. "The things belonged to Alan McKenzie. I thought you ought to know."

I clutched the cell, remembering the arc of his arm and shoulder. "How did they get there?"

"Your guess is as good as anyone's."

Items belonging to my brother.

And Simone had known.

* * *

IN MY DREAM, I pleaded with Alan. "It isn't him, Alan. Jason wouldn't kill you."

"Gawd, Belle, Sometimes you're so dense!" He would have sounded angry except that Alan never got angry.

"Tell me, Alan," I begged.

But he wouldn't. He shook his head sorrowfully, patience undercut by a frantic urgency. "There isn't time for your lovelorn meanderings, Belle. I need help and need it soon. Don't you understand?"

"No," I wept. "I don't understand, Alan, and I can't go on like this. Tell me and be done with it."

When I woke up with my face wet, I wondered what it was I'd wanted him to tell me. I pulled the sheet over my head and closed my eyes and tried to remember what it was I'd needed to know. It was so important, and I was so lost . . .

* * *

"HERE'S THAT NEW CHAIR, Lois." Jason Forrester held a desk chair as the office supply man carried in the rest of our order.

"Good. The old one nearly fell apart last week." Lois was young, not too many years out of high school. She prattled constantly about a social life that seemed to consist of juggling various boyfriends on one side, along with shopping expeditions to Chattanooga and Atlanta on the other.

In awe of Lettie and mildly contemptuous of Brent, she positively doted on Jason.

He, of course, did nothing to discourage her adoration though to be fair, he never did anything to encourage it either.

Rolling the new chair over, he whirled it around in front of her with an extra flourish.

Simone's description of him was wrong. He was not sadistic or insensitive or depraved. I didn't want him to be the way she portrayed him. I wanted him to be tender and caring and steady, the way I saw him.

He looked through some papers. "Lois, do you think you could file these for me and then find the folders on this list? I've got to have them to take to Atlanta."

"Oh, sure, Jace." She took it and looked at it. "Lord, there must be twenty-five of these."

"Right now, if you don't mind," he said, turning on the high-voltage charm. "They're all in Lettie's office."

Hopping up, Lois left the computer. That was technically the correct thing to do, since he was the boss, but in my opinion it wouldn't have hurt her or Jason if she'd lingered a few more minutes to finish inputting the construction data.

Since she wasn't my employee, I began checking off my office-supply order, to be abruptly interrupted by a hard male body settling itself on the corner of my desk.

"Chair's more comfortable," I told him without looking up, hoping the surge of blood through my veins was not visible to the naked eye. The faded blue of his jeans clung to his hip and thigh beside me. I could have reached out and touched it.

"There's a Christmas party at the American Legion Hall Saturday night." He put his outspread hand down flat over the paper I was studying. I could see nothing but his big square fingers, the few hairs black against browned skin.

Looking up reluctantly, I hoped he couldn't read what was going on inside me. "Yes, I know."

He had on a Braves' baseball cap, tipped back so the bill peeked over his dark curls. His horrible yellow jacket hung open, the collar standing up around his neck. Its padding made his shoulders seem four feet wide. "It's a formal affair, with lots of food and dancing. I hoped you might go with me."

He was smiling that sexy know-what-you're-thinking smile that made the goose bumps rise on my arms. I hesitated, torn between two courses for not the first time since the same circumstances had originally arisen in the tenth grade.

"I can't go with you," I said at last. Refusal was the morally correct decision, but that didn't keep me from being miserable. "I'm going with Matt Graven."

His expression didn't change, though one brow did seem to be on the verge of rising. "The teacher that let you fall in the river the other day?"

"He didn't let me fall!"

"Well, he sure didn't keep you from it. I don't think you realize just how close you came to drowning."

His concern warmed me. "I realize it, but I'm not going to dwell on it."

He shifted restlessly on my desk. "Was your husband like Graven?"

"Bob?" I was cautious. "Why do you ask?"

"I just wondered if that's why you're fighting me. Whether I'm not bookish enough for you."

I floundered. "I'm not—You're not—"

He leaned over, his throaty voice next to my ear. "You'd have more fun at the dance with me."

There needed to be more distance between us. "Maybe so, but I've already told Matt I'd go with him."

"And Mrs. Anna Levee never goes back on her word." His voice had an edge. "Mrs. Anna Levee means everything she says."

For a panicky moment, I thought that he was being sarcastic, that he knew about my lies.

Then he smiled ruefully, and I relaxed. How could he know?

Jerking my supply invoice out from under his hand, I held it up. "I haven't time for this." I pretended to be looking over the list of supplies carefully, but his lean presence on the corner of my desk was impossible to ignore.

Okay." To my relief he got up and dusted off the jeans that hugged his narrow hips. "Say, Anna, what kind of glasses are those?"

I looked up suspiciously. "What do you mean?"

"I never knew any kind of glasses would let you read upside down."

I flushed and flung the invoice down. "Get out. Get out and let me do my work."

"Sure." He pulled his baseball cap snug on the back of his head. "Save me a dance, okay?"

He left without waiting for the folders he had asked Lois to find for him, the folders he'd absolutely had to have.

I was in a bad mood the rest of the day, wishing I hadn't been quite so curt.

Wishing even more that I was going to the Christmas dance with him instead of Matt.

CHAPTER SIXTEEN

LIFE IS STRANGE.

I never thought a few months would find me without husband, brother and mother. I never thought I'd end up living in a small backwoods town where everyone knew everyone else's business. I never thought I'd be perilously close to falling in love with a man so converse to my own ideal.

And I never, ever thought I'd believe in ghosts.

But Alan's spirit—I'd accepted that my dreams were exactly that—continued to haunt me.

After his personal belongings turned up, it was clear that he had led me to find them. Why else would I have come to that particular pool of water at that particular time? Alan was maneuvering me toward some unknown destination and I could but blindly comply.

We learned from one of Lois's boyfriends in the sheriff's office that the plastic bag they'd recovered hadn't been immersed very long. Tests showed it had lain in the water from two to six weeks. And Alan had been dead a year and a half.

Depressed, I faced facts.

Jason had to be responsible for Alan's valuables being in the water. No matter how I tried, I couldn't banish the image of his arm pulled back, then arcing to fling something into the gorge.

Nor could I worm anything out of Simone. I was frustrated on all fronts.

Friday before the Christmas dance was busy at the office. Not until nearly eleven-thirty could I get away to take a deposit to the bank.

When I returned, piles and piles of long metal strips lined our parking area, taking up all the available space in the side and front lots, and forcing me to park a block away.

Brent, thumbs hooked in his jean pockets, was outside, ruefully surveying the mess. That particular pose reminded me of his brother, and yearning swept over me. In spite of what I'd witnessed, I couldn't believe anything bad of Jason. If he'd tossed Alan's things away, there was a reason. There had to be.

I nodded at the stacks. "What's going on?"

"Cavalry Stables siding. Somehow the truck got our address mixed up with theirs. Lois thought maybe we wanted it left here for some reason and let them unload it."

"You're kidding."

He shook his head. "Nope. I came up just as the driver put out the last bundle."

How annoying. "Why didn't you make him reload it?"

"I tried." Placid Brent was unaware of my irritation at his inability to deal with anything out of the ordinary. "He said regulations prohibited him from picking up a load once it was dumped. Don't worry. I've called some of the crew from Cavalry to come get it."

"They'd better get here soon."

A big truck rumbled down the road. "Looks like them now. By the way, Simone rode in with me so she can get her hair cut at two. She hoped you'd eat with her. You don't have a lunch date, do you?"

"Sure don't. I'll go on inside." I looked at the metal with misgivings. "If you're sure you have everything under control?"

"Oh, yeah. We'll have this out of here in a jiffy. Just see to Simone, will you?" He hesitated. "She really enjoys your company, Anna. I've not seen her so content in a long while. It's good for her to have a woman friend."

"She has Lettie." I strongly suspected Simone's contentment arose from a male friend, namely Matt Grave.

He waved a hand. "Mom's older, a little out of touch. Simone needs someone closer to her own age. Anyway, I appreciate your, you know, spending time with her and all."

The phrasing was awkward, but I understood. "No problem." Not for the world would I disillusion Brent.

His quick smile didn't hide the worry in the back of his eyes that I had noted the first time I met him.

Perhaps he knew.

Or perhaps there was another reason.

Could Simone be telling me the truth about the gun? Could Brent be to blame for Alan's death?

If that was the case, Jason would have hidden the gun to keep Brent from going to jail. And if Simone knew Brent had killed him, she might be anxious to find the gun. Having it would give her a hold over Jason.

But why would Brent have wanted to kill Alan?

It was fruitless to speculate though I wondered what Brent would say if he found out about Simone's hair-brained scheme to search Jason's house.

The office was empty. Lois was at lunch, but Simone should be there. As I laid my purse in my desk drawer, voices came from behind Jason's half-closed door.

When I went by it to hang up my coat, I heard him speaking in low, level tones. "—But I know you. You won't be happy till someone gets hurt. I won't put up with it, Simone."

I stopped, coat in hand, shamelessly eavesdropping.

Simone's accented, little-girl's voice sounded stubborn. "I won't be treated this way. You're going too far, Jason, and you'd better stop."

"You know how to stop it."

"You'll never be satisfied, will you? You're going to plague me for the rest of my life. If I had that gun, I'd make you sorry, Jason. You can't keep it hidden away forever."

My heart constricted. I almost didn't hear the response, his voice was so low.

"Long enough for my purposes." Then he laughed.

A jeering laugh that turned me cold.

"Long enough, Simone," he repeated clearly. "I know what you're up to with Matt Graven. I'm tempted to tell Brent the truth now and be damned to the consequences."

"What truth? That his brother is a sadist who enjoys making me suffer?"

"I'll tell him about Christopher."

"Christopher?" The cry was followed by silence. When next she spoke, her antagonism had given way to caution. "What do you mean?"

"Don't play dumb with me. You know exactly what I mean."

"No. No, I don't. Are you threatening to take my baby away from me?" Some of her earlier spunk returned, but it was restrained. "That's exactly what a horrible beast like you would think of doing."

"Always casting me as the beast. With yourself as the beauty in distress?" Jace mocked. "I'm not threatening anything, Simone. I don't know why I never saw what was under my nose, but now that I have, I think Brent deserves to know. I've been debating whether or not to tell, but since it's your affair—"

"You bastard!"

I held my breath and stared blindly at the door.

At her last words, Simone hurtled herself against him and knocked him backwards into my field of vision. Her fists ineffectively beat at him until he caught them both in one hand and pulled her toward him. She struggled briefly before he shoved her against a filing cabinet.

His profile was toward me, his jaw bleeding where she'd clawed him. I watched, fascinated, as his lips parted in a wolfish grin.

In one quick movement, he took her exposed neck in one big hand and held her there at his mercy as he lowered his face nearly to hers. "Don't you ever do that again. I could snap your neck like a matchstick, Simone, and the next time, I will."

He was cold and menacing, no one that I knew.

She struggled, fumbling at his hand but unable to free her neck from that viselike grip. Her face, rage replaced by fear, turned red.

Horror left me unable to move.

"I could snap your neck and get away with it when I explained the tragic circumstances." He released her so savagely that she stumbled to her knees. "All I'd have to say was that my unstable sister-in-law attacked me and broke her neck when I pushed her away."

She put both hands to her throat. A hoarse, rasping sound escaped her as she labored for breath.

He stood over her, intimidating. "Remember that when you're hatching your next plot."

I must have made a noise, for he whirled. His eyes were black, his face that of a pirate, hardened from years of marauding and plundering.

The next moment I thought I'd imagined it, so magically did it clear. "Hello, Anna. Simone rode in with Brent today just to see you. Isn't that nice?"

Simone came out, rubbing her neck and casting a sideways glance at Jason as she passed him. She was careful to keep her distance until she reached me, when she looked back sullenly. "This isn't finished, Jason."

He grunted. The pirate was gone, fled as if he had never been. "You can finish it anytime you choose, Simone. You know how." With a shrug, he dismissed us both and turned to the computer beside his drafting table.

Finish it by going to bed with him? Was that what he meant?

He'd all but admitted he had a gun hidden away. Was it the gun that had killed Alan?

Hiding my turmoil, I hurried Simone out of the office and to lunch.

Jason hadn't denied her charge of having the gun. Indeed, he had taunted her with leaving it hidden "long enough for my purposes" before he'd threatened her. I had seen him with my own eyes, heard him with my own ears.

"Oh, my neck," Simone moaned as I drove us down to the one nice restaurant in Rahunta. She pulled out a compact and examined her throat. "Am I bruised, Anna? Can you tell where he choked me? I thought he was going to strangle me. Did you see?"

"Yes, I saw." I gave her a quick glance. "And no, nothing shows, Simone. There aren't any marks that I can see."

"You heard what he said." She snapped the compact shut. In spite of her fright, she was regaining her sparkle. "He does have the gun. He admitted it."

"I heard him." I was reserved, unable yet to sort out all the admissions and accusations exchanged in the office.

"And you saw what he did to me." Her face twisted in a spasm of remembrance as she rubbed her neck. "He almost killed me. I think if you hadn't been there, he would have."

"I saw," I repeated dully.

"He showed himself, didn't he? You're going to help me now, aren't you?" She looked forlorn. One small hand reached over to touch my shoulder as I drove. "You are, aren't you?"

"I don't know. We'll see." I understood for the first time why my mother had always used the term "we'll see" whenever she intended to say no. If I'd refused outright, Simone would continue to beg until I caved in out of sheer weariness.

But what if she was right? What if Jason did have the gun that killed my brother?

I didn't want to think about it. I wouldn't think about it.

Simone sighed and sat back in the seat. "You may be afraid to help me, after what you witnessed today. He's dangerous, Anna. Maybe insane. At least now you can understand why you must never fall in love with him. He can be charming, but he's a wicked, wicked man."

"I can look out for myself," I said curtly, not wanting to admit even to myself my feelings about Jason. "What did he mean about Christopher, Simone? What is there about Christopher that he could use to hurt you?"

"Oh. You heard that." Long-lashed lids drooped. "I am not always a good mother, Anna. I try, but it's new to me, and I have no one to help me. I forgot to close the pool gate one time. Christopher got in, but Jenny came before he more than wet his feet. Later she told Jason about it, and he accused me of trying to drown Christopher." She added indignantly, "As if I would drown my own baby son."

"Why would he think that?"

"He didn't!" Simone was incensed. "He uses it as an excuse to make my life a living hell. When he threatens me, he says he will tell Brent that I tried to drown Christopher.

"I should have gone ahead and told Brent when it happened," she added after a sidelong glance at me, "but there was no harm done, and I didn't want to worry him."

She ran the tip of one finger around the edge of her compact. "Maybe I wasn't proud to be so careless, either."

I drove in silence, trying to fit the pieces together.

After a bit, she asked, "*You* don't think I am such a bad mother, do you, Anna? I couldn't bear it if you thought I was awful."

"Don't be silly, Simone." Brent should know better than to leave a child to guard a child. Simone couldn't help the way she was. She might be flighty, but she would never intentionally harm Christopher.

Simone gave a high sigh of relief. "You're the only one I can talk to, Anna. I don't have anyone else, not even Brent."

"Or Matt?" It slipped out.

"Matt?" She was incredulous. "Matt's nice, but he's almost as stuffy as Brent. You're the only one I trust, Anna. I don't know what I'd do if I lost you."

While we ate, I got the feeling that she was debating whether or not to confide something else. She made her decision after we'd finished, as we got back in the car so that I could drop her off at the hairdresser's.

"The bag they found," she began, and then stopped.

My heart leaped but I cranked the car, trying not to reveal too much interest. Once alarmed, Simone would clam up like she'd done other times. "What about it?"

She took a deep breath. "Jason put it in the water."

"Jason?" My surprise was at her telling me. "Why?"

"Because he'd given it to Brent to hide. I found it by accident. I was going to take it to the police." She shrugged eloquently. "But he got to it first."

"When did he put it in the water?" I don't know why I insisted on turning the screws tighter, but the question came out before I could stop it.

"He threw it off my deck a week or so ago. I tried to stop him, but . . ." She shrugged again. "You saw how strong he is."

So that explained that. Or did it? Couldn't there be another, innocent explanation? If Alan's valuables were hidden in Brent's house, Brent seemed more likely than Jason to have stolen them. What if Brent had killed Alan and got Jason to hide the murder weapon? If Jason didn't know Brent had kept the valuables, wouldn't he react as he had when he found out?

But why would Brent kill Alan? And who was the red-haired woman who'd pawned Alan's coin?

Common sense told me I was grasping at straws.

My heart told me anything was possible, anything so long as it exonerated Jason.

Back at work, Jason came out of his office as I closed the door. Rolling up some plans, he swaggered over to the reception area. His jeans rode low and fit tight on his hips, while the casual plaid shirt was open at the neck, its sleeves rolled up to reveal muscular arms.

The gaze that had seemed so black when it fastened on Simone was gold dust washing over me.

I didn't want to see him. I wished he'd not been there.

In the next instant, seeing him buttoning his sleeves as he got ready to leave, I was bereft.

Damn the man.

He had driven me into absolute chaos. Always before, I'd known exactly where I stood and where I was going. My life was drawn out just so, a blueprint where I carefully followed every circumspect line.

After meeting this one man, it was as if I wandered around a maze in which there was no opening. No. I couldn't find my way out because, I suspected, I didn't want to find my way out. Was that why I couldn't interpret the dreams? Was I afraid of what they would tell me? Did I unconsciously fear that if I let Alan speak, he'd accuse Jason?

"I have to run up to Tennessee," he informed me. "By the way"—he shrugged into his horrific yellow jacket—"I brought you something."

"Me? You brought me something?"

"Yes, ma'am. Let me go get it." He went back into his office while I waited with trepidation.

He emerged carrying a heavy bag, which he dropped on my desk.

"Cat litter?" I looked at it blankly. "What's this for? I don't have a cat."

His roguish grin started and spread. "No? What d'you call this?"

A tiny head poked its way out from the front of his half-zipped parka. It emitted a pitiful meow. Yellow eyes looked out at me from tawny fur.

"Oh, Jace!" I put out a hand reflexively.

"Maggie's granddaughter's cat had kittens and she got rid of all of 'em but this one. I told her you'd take it."

As quickly as I'd put my hand out, I snatched it back. "I can't possibly take it. Thanks, but you'll have to keep it yourself."

"Oh, it isn't really for you," he contradicted himself blithely. "Weren't you and Lois complaining about all the crickets in the storage room? I thought the office could use a good cat to get rid of them."

I frowned. "That was a month ago. Since then the exterminator's been in and the weather's turned cold. Your mother will never let you keep a kitten here."

He tickled the kitten's ears. "Sure she will. Once I explain how the crickets are trying to ravish our ravishing employees, Lettie'll be happy to have a fine cat like this one in the office." He looked at it with pride.

I blushed and couldn't think of a word to say.

"I bought a tray for the litter, too," he went on, ignoring my discomfort. "You can set it up in the storage room."

"Me? *I* can set it up?" I forgot the embarrassing cricket episode. "It's your cat. *You* set its litter box up."

"I would, but I haven't got time," he said with a sanctimonious air. "I've got to get up to Cavalry Stables and make sure that the siding gets there and that they're putting it up right. No, you'll have to look after it, Anna."

He rubbed the scrap of fur against my face, ignoring its cries. "See, it likes you. It'll be right at home in no time."

Thrusting the warm little ball into my hands, he gave me an encouraging grin. "Listen to that. Purring already. There's some dry food on the counter for it, and its bowl's down by the sink. There're some cans in the cabinet, too, for later."

He waved cheerfully and took off.

Fuming impotently, I put the kitten down on my desk near its litter.

It and I stared at each other, its unblinking eyes reminding me of another golden set.

It gave a tentative squeak and its tail stuck straight up. Growing more daring, it meowed plaintively.

"Chauvinistic male," I muttered as I heard Jason's truck race away. "Well." I raised my brows, contemplating the small creature. Still meowing, it was sniffing at the bag of litter. "First things first, eh? Let's set up your bathroom."

How could the man who cuddled this kitten be the same man who had manhandled Simone?

What he'd said to her about the gun kept replaying in my mind.

I didn't believe all that Simone told me, but it was hard to overlook what I'd heard. And the way Jason had acted was out of character for the man I knew. Reconciling the hard buccaneer with the concerned friend was difficult.

As I showed the new office resident its toilet facilities and gave it some of the food Jason had so thoughtfully provided, I wasn't happy.

What exactly had he said? That he could keep the gun hidden "long enough."

Long enough for what?

CHAPTER SEVENTEEN

A REDHEADED WOMAN DOMINATED my dreams that night.

Her hair was so long and flowing as to be unreal. It fell forward, shielding her face as she knelt over my prostrate brother and took something from his breast. He was not dead, but he lay still, bound by invisible cords. When the woman stood up, her hair whipped around her face in a red fury fanned by supernatural winds. She held a gun, and she lifted it up high, as if making an offering to the gods.

Alan's eyes moved—no other part of him could because of his unseen bonds—and looked directly at me. *Don't let her do it, Belle,* and while his mouth did not move, I realized he was speaking directly to my mind from his, desperation making his thoughts audible. *You have to stop her, Belle.*

Because his commands were so urgent, I followed the woman. Never once did she reveal her face.

We went over craggy boulders and through clawlike trees and between rocky ledges that cut off the light. The red strands of her hair flickered like a flaming brand as she darted and danced in and out of the shadows, always a few feet ahead, always out of reach.

We climbed higher and higher into the clouds, and then we were inside them, and they surrounded me, and I couldn't see her form or her hair or anything except the thick white fog. I put out my hands into nothing, feeling the horror spreading as I took a tentative step and felt myself plunging, falling . . .

"Alan!" I shrieked his name, my voice jarring me awake. My pillow was wet with tears, my heart pounding. Only the quiet of the hills pervaded my bedroom.

"Alan," I whispered in despair.

* * *

THE NEXT DAY I met Tiffany Underwood.

She came into the beauty shop where I was having my hair done for the Christmas party that night. I recognized her instantly—a stunning redhead who walked into the shop as though she owned the place.

Her magnificent hair was like that of the woman in my dream.

"I just got in from school today, Kay." Her voice was low and husky, her porcelain complexion and curvaceous frame reminiscent of Simone. "You can fit me in, can't you?"

The woman finishing up a man in the chair next to mine was effusive. "Sure, Tiffany. No problem at all. Right now, as a matter of fact. Just let me take George's money and sweep this hair up."

My mother, meeting her after my brother died, related how Tiffany had fallen to pieces. "Poor child." My mother's own eyes had been red and swollen. "From what Alan had said, I was afraid it was all on his side. After all, they'd only known each other a few weeks. But after meeting her, I saw she loved him as much as he did her."

That might have been true then, but a year and a half later Tiffany Underwood looked sleek and well fed, like a cat that had been given lots of cream.

Time heals all wounds, went the old saying, so I couldn't fault Tiffany for going on with her life. She was young and beautiful, and there would be other lovers for her. Who was I to censure her for putting the past behind?

My attorney Charles said the woman who'd sold Alan's coin had not been Tiffany Underwood, but a clerk in a pawn shop probably didn't remember what a customer from last week looked like, much less last month. Perhaps Alan had given it to her before he died. That was one explanation. If she needed money and no longer cared, she might have sold it.

Poor darling Alan, who'd been cut down before he could find out what life was about, what love was about.

Janie toweled my hair dry as Tiffany's shampoo was finished. I watched in the mirror as Kay wrapped a white towel around the auburn curls.

The salon was typical of a small town beauty shop. A long mirror ran down the wall, below which each operator had a sink and tools. All six stations were in use today, two of the chairs containing men.

When Tiffany swiveled around to face the mirror, Kay said slyly, "Tiffany, this is Anna Levee. She's working for the Forresters."

Tiffany's words were direct and unvarnished. "My sympathy."

Her bluntness threw me off balance. "I'm enjoying it so far. Though I still have a lot to learn."

With a sidelong glance, she took my measure fully, lip slightly curled as if she didn't think much of what she saw.

"I'll give you some good advice, free of charge." She didn't smile. "Stay as far away from Jason Forrester as you can and don't believe anything he tells you."

The words were delivered without expression, without care for who overheard them. The noise level around us abated.

Janie, intent on combing my hair, tightened her lips.

Kay looked alarmed.

I remained cautious. "I work more with Brent and Lettie than with Jason."

Tiffany shrugged. "Oh, Brent." There was an unmistakable softening. "Brent's sweet, but he's got no spine," she said, unknowingly echoing Simone's opinion. "Everyone knows it's Jason who calls the shots. Brent does whatever his older brother says."

"I've not noticed anyone in particular calling the shots, unless it's Lettie."

"Lettie thinks the sun rises and sets in Jace," Tiffany said wearily. "If you're around here for long, you'll find out he likes to have things his own way. He can twist Lettie around his finger, and Brent . . . Well, Brent's much too trusting to see what's going on."

"Most men do like to have things their own way."

Pitying green eyes caught my image in the mirror. "Jace Forrester isn't 'most men.' 'Most men' play by some rules. Jace doesn't. He takes what he wants and runs over anybody who gets in his way."

"How do you want it fixed, Anna? Up? down?" Janie's question was abrupt.

From my earlier visit, I knew what Janie thought of Tiffany, but I was undecided. My brother wouldn't have fallen in love with a spoiled brat. "Maybe some curl on the ends. I thought I'd pull one side back"—I demonstrated—"and put a bit of holly there. Maybe some glitter. What do you think?"

"No glitter." She started pinning up my hair preparatory to cutting it. "You're lucky. Not everybody has hair thick enough to wear this way."

Tiffany still stared at my reflection. "I told you about Jason Forrester for your own good. No one else in this town will tell you the truth about him."

That wasn't so. Simone had told me. Matt had told me.

My problem was that I didn't want to believe any of them.

"Weren't you engaged to him once?" I asked.

She was tough. She didn't flush or stammer, though she must have been aware how most of the town felt about her and Jason and my brother.

I met her eyes squarely in the glass and was shocked to find absolutely nothing there—no anger, no hate, no passion.

Nothing. Had losing Alan done that to her?

"Until he murdered the man I loved." She was as blunt as Jason.

"You know, Tiffany," Janie drawled, "you could've just called off the engagement."

"Come on, Janie." Tiffany wasn't offended, just listless. "You know Jace. You remember that other time when he beat up Tommy Berrell. And Alan was so kind, he'd never . . ."

She looked down, but not before I saw the shine in her eyes. "I didn't tell Jace because I knew Alan was no match for him. And it turned out I was right, wasn't I?"

Janie's expression said plainly that she wouldn't believe a word against Jason.

When I finally paid at the front, Janie said in a confidential tone, "Don't pay any attention to what she says." She gave a little nod back toward Tiffany. "She's always been a big flirt, playing one man against another."

Maybe so, but the eager girl in Alan's photograph had learned a harsh lesson, it seemed. After meeting her, I was as convinced as my mother that Tiffany had loved Alan.

I stopped by the drug store to pick up some mascara and hose for the Christmas party and was in the store longer than I intended. By the time I made one last detour on the way to the checkout—going by the card racks to choose an appropriate card for one of Bob's grandsons about to turn four—the sun was low and nearly hidden behind a fluffy wintry cloud.

That was why I almost missed the couple two stores down, standing in the shadows of a convenient doorway.

Tiffany did not see me. Nor did the man with her. They were too engrossed in what looked like earnest conversation. Their hands were joined thoughtlessly, as if they knew each other well. Before they parted, she rose up on her toes and kissed him on the cheek before saying something I couldn't hear.

The man answered in as low a tone.

She left him then, to watch her as she walked down the street to the beauty shop where her car was parked. When he finally turned away, his movements were slow, as if his mind was on something other than his surroundings.

Or as if he dreaded going home.

I hastily closed my mouth and turned to look into a shop window, so that Brent Forrester wouldn't see me as he went across the street to get into his dark blue BMW.

CHAPTER EIGHTEEN

OUR POKER GROUP PLANNED to attend the Christmas party together.

For the occasion, I'd bought a simple red velveteen gown from one of the specialty shops in Helen. The color heightened my complexion and brought a sparkle to my gray eyes, while the pointed bodice accentuated my narrow waist. With a cheerful spring of holly tucked behind one emerald-studded ear, I was ready to have fun.

Maybe the fun might not be with the man of my choice—I wasn't sure if I could even trust him—but I could still enjoy myself. I didn't admit that any real enjoyment hinged on my prospects of meeting Jason.

Rain was forecast for later that night, but waiting to be picked up, I saw no signs of it. The air was mild, while the moon, large and white, was a luminous ghost floating majestically across the darkening sky.

From my cottage, there on the lip of the gorge with the moon hovering, I looked into that lovely dangerous divide that had become such a big part of my life the past few weeks. If only it could speak, tell about all the human dramas that had taken place on its ledges and in its depths. If only it could give me back my brother.

In the magic of twilight it was as awesome as ever, with flickering shadows reminding me of spirits who resided on its sloping sides, shades of the people who had lost their lives in its belly. I thought of my brother, but with a lingering melancholy rather than wrenching sorrow.

Alan was gone. I couldn't bring him back. My coming to Rahunta had accomplished that acceptance, if nothing else. If only I could work out what it was he needed from me.

The old feeling returned as I looked over the edge, the same cold sensation. It seemed more evil than ever before, as if someone watched, intending to pounce and drag me into the dark cavernous shadows where I couldn't escape. The emanated hatred palpably spread itself over me, enveloping and asphyxiating me.

I shivered inside my warm glass porch.

Not Alan, this. Some other ghoulish specter hounded me, frightened me so that I couldn't enjoy the majestic beauty before me.

That malignant force released its hold only when Matt and the others arrived in the van borrowed from the school, to pick me up and take me down to the festivities.

There was no place for ghosts in the midst of the gaiety at the American Legion hall on the outskirts of Rahunta. A large Christmas tree towered over the lobby, where people entered and discarded their coats in eager expectancy. Sounds of music from a Nashville band brought in for the occasion floated over from the main hall.

The air was alive, but not with malevolent phantoms. Only the high spirits of partygoers filled the building. My own mood magically lightened.

Inside the auditorium, holly wreaths and candles decorated the walls, while miniature replicas graced each white-clothed table encircling the dance floor. Poinsettias framed the stage where the band played country-and-western tunes sung lustily by a Dolly Parton lookalike.

Soon we'd claimed a table, getting up almost as soon as we sat down to make our way to the sumptuous buffet. As I put barbecued shrimp and honey-baked ham on a plate and waited to get to the salads, Kathy, one of the teachers in my group, nudged me. "There's Tiffany Underwood. Her family was one of the school's original founders. Look at that gorgeous dress. It must have cost the earth."

Tiffany Underwood shimmered in a dress of gold lamé, and I forgot that I'd resolved to leave my problems at home.

Had Jason loved her? And what about that extra friendly conversation I'd witnessed this afternoon between her and Brent? Could a woman be friends with the brother of a man she publicly called a murderer? Could Brent be friends with a woman who would accuse his brother of murder?

And if not friends, what did that leave?

Lovers?

I hardly dared think it. It was too outlandish.

Still, there had been an undeniable air of intimacy about them as they stood together in the doorway, in the way they'd touched.

Could Simone have turned to Matt because she suspected Brent of having an affair with Tiffany Underwood?

I wouldn't have thought it of Brent, but I was old enough not to be shocked. People—and what they did or didn't do—no longer surprised me. I wasn't as naïve at thirty as I'd been at eighteen.

Kathy disdained the macaroni salad and went directly to the broccoli casserole. I took a small helping of both as Tiffany and her escort made their way to the far side of the auditorium.

"I wonder if the Forresters are here." Kathy, one long braid entwined with silver ribbons, looked over the room with avid eyes. "I want to be around if Tiffany and Jason Forrester come face-to-face."

"I'm sure they're both civilized enough to take it in stride," I said, trying not to be sharp.

Kathy groaned. "Oh, come on. Don't play dumb. Maybe you don't know the story."

Returning to our table, Matt and the other men went to get our drinks. Kathy and I were left with Pauline and Lindy, the other two women in our party.

The conversation centered on the Forresters, and in particular Jason Forrester.

"He's such a hunk," Lindy said. "It must be heaven to work with him every day."

My answers were short. When they discovered they knew more about Jason than I did, they were eager to fill me in.

"He's practically a legend to the people around here," Kathy said, her New England accent hardly softened by five years at Rahunta Academy.

"Really?" I murmured.

Kathy could have been attractive. Her features were nice, but she had a nervous habit of tossing her braid back and forth, kind of like a horse.

"You must have heard all the old gossip," Lindy put in. "Like how he drove a motorcycle up the gorge on a dare. And how he nearly killed himself hang gliding from the top."

"I would hope he had more sense by now." These women were as bad as Lois and her crush.

"He's considered the best rock man around," quiet Pauline put in. From our card parties, I'd learned she had more sense than the other two.

"I didn't know that." I wasn't sure what a "rock man" was and asked.

"A rock climber. Right after I came here seven years ago, the rescue team had two people injured trying to get to a fallen hiker," Pauline said. "So Jason climbed down through this narrow crevice, literally threading himself through holes inches wide, to anchor the safety lines for the others to rappel down around the rocks. The paramedic that worked with them told me about it. He's not easily impressed, but he sure was that day."

"I'm impressed just looking at him," Kathy murmured with smoldering eyes.

The others laughed.

"I work mostly with Brent." I devoutly hoped my own fascination wasn't obvious.

"Oh, Brent." Kathy flapped a hand. "He's good-looking, all right, but I prefer somebody like Jason."

"A real honest-to-god male," Lindy agreed in her no-nonsense

Midwest manner. She was probably a wonderful PE teacher, but I wished she'd get off the subject.

"Brent's plenty male." I was staunch in his defense. "And have you ever thought that those honest-to-god men might be hell to live with?"

"Honey, I don't want to live with Jason. I just want to borrow him for a night or two." Kathy took the tip of her braid and pulled it across her mouth suggestively.

"Well, it's a lucky thing he never married." I smiled widely. "If he had, he might have turned into a plain old homebody like Brent, and we wouldn't have anybody to talk about. Wouldn't that have been awful?"

She giggled, thinking I was joking. She wasn't very bright, not like some people, who would have immediately caught my drift.

A spasm of longing went through my body, so painful that it took my breath away. I didn't want to be at this party with Matt and Kathy and the others. I wanted to be with Jason.

"I can't see Jace Forrester as a homebody." Pauline looked amused at the idea.

I couldn't bear to think about him. I should be forgetting my problems tonight and enjoying myself, but the stupid man kept spoiling my evening though he wasn't even near me. He was as unsettling as my dreams of Alan.

Kathy was rattling on. "—doubt anyone'll be jumping to marry him after the scandal last year. Money or not."

"Might be just as well." Lindy looked around meaningfully. "That Canadian girl Brent married is putting him through the hoops."

"Going through money and men, I hear," Kathy agreed. She was happily unaware of my barely restrained urge to reach out and tug at her braid. Hard.

"Brent should have married Tiffany. They'd all have been better off," Pauline murmured.

I forgot Kathy's hair. "You mean Jason."

"Jason?" The three women looked at me as if I was amazingly dense.

"Jason was supposed to marry Tiffany Underwood."

"Yes, but Brent was going to marry her first," Kathy said.

"Tiffany was engaged to Brent?"

"Before he went up to Canada," Lindy corroborated. "Mr. and Mrs. Forrester were both happy about it, because they were great friends with the Underwoods."

"Brent and Tiffany were planning to get married?" I was trying to sort these new pieces out.

"Uh-huh. Only Brent came back with Simone." Lindy paused thoughtfully. "I don't know, but I've kind of wondered if that wasn't part of the reason Jason got engaged to Tiffany, kind of making up for the fact that his brother had jilted her."

My heart leapt, but I pushed aside my joy to explore more urgent possibilities. This explained the touching little scene between Brent and Tiffany this afternoon.

Or did it? Tiffany would have to be awfully forgiving if she was on such friendly terms with Brent after he'd left her high and dry.

And what about Brent? He cared for Simone, I felt, though he wasn't ostentatious about it. He was a contained individual, not the type who showed emotion easily. In that respect, he was much like Jason, who hid emotions under a cheerful smile and only occasionally gave hints of his true feelings.

I wrested my thoughts away from *that* avenue and back to Brent.

Suppose Brent found himself still in love with Tiffany after marrying Simone. Simone, while admittedly gorgeous, lacked the maturity someone like Brent would expect in his wife. It wouldn't be the first time a man became infatuated and ended up married to the wrong woman.

What if he'd accepted Tiffany's engagement to his brother because he knew Jason didn't love her, nor she him? And then what if Alan had come along, swept Tiffany off her feet, and Brent hadn't been able to stand it?

Further suppose that after he killed Alan, he went to Jason in a panic. Wouldn't that fit with what Lettie had said? Jason would do everything in his power to help his brother.

And then Simone found out.

Coming back to earth, I discovered Kathy munching on carrot sticks and discussing Jason again. And my brother.

"—surprised Jason didn't shoot Tiffany instead of Alan McKenzie. Jason's the kind of person who thinks violence solves everything." She sounded admiring.

"If he never loved Tiffany to start with, Kathy, why would he want to shoot her lover?"

She looked at me as if I were out of my mind. "Give me credit, Anna, I've been around. Jason's the dominating-male type. What's his is his, whether he wants it or not. And nobody else had better mess with it. I don't teach psychology for nothing."

Pedantic know-it-all. I bit my tongue to keep from saying pretty sharply that amateur psychiatrists were the ones who did the most harm by spreading false and malicious rumors about perfectly normal people. I'd not seen any sign of violence in Jason.

Well . . . Except for the day Simone attacked him in the office. But he was protecting himself, I argued.

"I don't care, myself." Kathy was unaware of my fingers itching to bunch up and hit her in her patronizing mouth. "Except I think he'd be better off if he'd shot Tiffany instead of Alan."

"Pass me the salt, please." I found it hard to keep a pleasant face.

When Jason's party came in, it took all my energy to pretend I wasn't the slightest bit interested.

Acting like I didn't notice them was hard. Jason and Brent were among the few men wearing tuxedos, and Jason looked marvelous. My red dress would fit perfectly against his black, and I wished I was with him.

Which was utterly illogical and inappropriate, considering my vacillating opinion of Jason Forrester. Considering I still didn't know what part he'd played in my brother's death.

With a sinking heart, I saw that he wasn't alone. Though he was with a group—including Simone and Brent, Lois and her boyfriend, and two couples I didn't recognize—the woman saying something in his ear had to be his date.

She was a dazzling redhead whose dyed hair rivaled the blazing tresses of Tiffany Underwood, though that was the only resemblance.

Tiffany had the good taste of a conservatively reared female. The person hanging on Jason's arm wore a black dress that revealed half her breasts—one tattooed—and that clung to her hips. Long earrings that looked cheap but probably weren't dangled from her ears, while red claws held Jason's sleeve possessively. She must have had on layers of green eye shadow. I could see it from where I sat, even in the dim lighting.

I wondered if she was the woman Jason had taken to Nevada, and then I wondered if she ever went to Chattanooga. Those earrings could have come from a pawn shop.

When Jason laughed at whatever she'd said, I tried to ignore the stab of jealousy.

I could have been there on Jason's arm. Had I not been so quick to accept Matt's invitation, I could have . . .

Catching my teeth clenched, I consciously relaxed. This was ridiculous. The man was driving me crazy. He was only a man, after all.

Glancing back over at Jason's group, I hoped to see him making a fool of himself.

He was helping the woman into a chair with all the courtesy in the world, smiling down and asking her something to which she responded with a little shake of the head.

Simone ignored the woman across the table. She had put her fair hair up, with the exception of a few wisps allowed to curl around her face. Diamonds sparkled on her neck and in her ears and at the décolletage of her expensive lavender dress.

It was plain what Simone thought of Jason's date.

When she saw me, though, her face lit up and she waved across the room.

I waved back and touched Matt's arm. "There're Simone and Brent."

He turned eagerly. Whatever their relationship, Matt was in love with Simone.

That was a shame because Simone would never end up with someone like Matt. He was bound to be hurt. And if she was pitching her crazy idea of searching Jason's house to Matt and trying to talk him into helping her since I wouldn't . . .

The very idea made the hair on my head rise. From the unguarded expression on his face, I could tell Matt would do anything she asked.

With a sigh, I tried to concentrate on the music. I was supposed to be enjoying myself. For this one evening, all the ghosts were supposed to be banished. But it was easier to ignore Matt's affection for Simone than it was to pretend I didn't care a whit for Jason Forrester.

Looking toward the stage, I saw Tiffany's party. Though I craned my neck to see, there was nothing—no smile, no glance, nothing—exchanged between Brent and Tiffany, who sat not twenty feet away from each other. Both acted like neither knew the other existed.

Curious, considering the touching scene I'd witnessed that afternoon. Of course, Tiffany wouldn't want to speak to Jason, but I'd have expected her to acknowledge Brent.

There was little time for conjecture, however. I reminded myself for the umpteenth time I was out to have a good time and forget my problems.

After eating, we began to dance. The floor was crowded, almost too small for so many couples rocking back and forth in time to the music. That should make it easier to keep my eyes firmly on my partner, so that I didn't stare at Jason Forrester.

CHAPTER NINETEEN

NO MATTER HOW HARD I tried, I couldn't stick to my resolution and ignore Jason Forrester. One eye would inevitably turn back toward his group, even when I was dancing on the other side of the room.

Simone was having a wonderful time. She thrived on attention, and tonight she was in her milieu. Going out on the dance floor with first one man and then another, she gained a little more radiance, a little more vivacity, every time I glimpsed her.

She and Brent should go out more often.

Brent was his usual self. When he stood, the lines of his tuxedo gave a fluid grace to his slim form, while the black color made his blond good looks stand out in sharp relief. He sat or stood, watching the dancers and talking to those around him, occasionally letting his wife or one of the other women in his party lead him onto the floor. He never once looked over at Tiffany that I could see.

Nor did Jason.

Jason's companion enthralled him. Our gazes met once, but after a breezy wave in my direction, he snubbed me for her.

Which suited me just fine. There was no reason he should tear himself away from such a fascinating creature to come over and speak to me.

I didn't expect him to, and I couldn't care less whether or not he did. He meant nothing to me.

Surely, before long I could decently plead a headache and go home. I stole a glance at Matt's watch and saw it wasn't ten o'clock. We hadn't been here two hours.

After a fast dance, Matt and I sat down with drinks. At Jason's table, the heavily made up sexpot was being led onto the dance floor by another man.

At once, Jason got up and I quickly averted my eyes. Sneaking a peek from beneath my lashes, my heart began to pound.

Yes, he was making his way toward our table.

"Dance with me?" Golden eyes smiled into mine.

He looked marvelous in his well-cut tuxedo and bow tie. His hair and mustache were freshly trimmed for the occasion, and he smelled like gardenias.

I turned politely to Matt, who had risen at Jason's approach. My normally cordial escort displayed unmistakable signs of hostility, but I ignored them. "You don't mind, do you, Matt?"

Another moment and I was in Jason's arms. He didn't allow me to keep a safe distance, but pulled me close. Both thumbs held my waist while his fingers rested on my hips in the same way they'd rested on his date's.

I was no pushover.

I put my hands against his chest. I'd rather have put them around his neck, and laid my head on one of those broad inviting shoulders, the way I'd seen her do.

But I resisted the urge and kept my head erect.

Prim, proper Annabelle. Too proud to behave like the flashy woman he'd brought with him.

When I stared him in the eye, he stared right back.

"I'm glad you got a date." I should look away from those golden pools devouring me.

His hands slipped further down my butt and tightened. I could feel his desire grow as he held me there against him, a gentle pressure impossible to ignore. A pleasant warmth pervaded me, there and wherever else he touched me.

"Oh, there's always someone around." His light tone contradicted the tender gleam in his eyes. "If one won't, another will."

I stiffened, trying to separate myself from him. He resisted, forcing our contours together. My temper, never moderate around him, began to rise. "Is that your philosophy?"

"About women?" He whirled us gently. "Why not? You had your chance."

"I—" How could I possibly be attracted to him? He was completely unlike my darling Bob, who had been as thoughtful and dependable and kind as anyone could be. "I told you I'd already promised to go with Matt."

"Why don't you admit you'd rather be here with me? I'm lots more interesting than Graven."

Such egotism left me speechless but not for long. "That's the kind of attitude that explains why you're still single."

"What? Just what do you mean by that crack?" He did not relax his grip on me.

I shrugged, the movement thrusting my breasts up into the hard wall of his chest. The unexpected contact made me gasp.

He grinned. "Ooh. Do that again."

I took out anger at myself on him. "You're revolting. Stop holding me so tight."

"I thought you liked it." He lessened his grip slightly, so that we touched but were not molded together like two hormonal adolescents. "How's that? All right?"

No, it wasn't all right. He was still close enough to make me sick with longing, but I wasn't going to give him the satisfaction of hearing me admit it. I'd die first.

We danced in silence for a moment before he asked, "What did you mean, about me still being single?"

I could be blunt, too. "Two engagements, and both broken because of other men. I'd have thought you would learn from your mistakes."

"Heard about them, did you? Well, maybe I did learn something from my mistakes."

"You sound pretty conceited."

"Just confident. I think I know how to please a woman."

"Really?" I raised a brow.

"I can give a woman whatever she wants!"

Hmm, I must have touched on a sensitive spot in his masculine pride.

He glowered. "All she has to do is be honest enough to tell me what it is."

"Maybe she has and you haven't listened." If he had, he wouldn't have brought that redheaded siren to the dance.

"No, she hasn't."

In his own way that evening, Jason was asking me to confide in him, tell me of my own accord what he already knew.

But I didn't know that. Not then.

I knew we weren't talking generalities, that he was speaking of himself and me. But I thought he wanted me to admit that I wanted him physically, while the thing I wanted most was the truth about my brother's death.

I didn't know he was asking for my trust. So I couldn't tell him what I wanted. It was easier to argue. Oh, I was out of my mind that evening. Jealousy, desire, the drinks . . .

I must have been tipsy because I couldn't stop picking at him. "Maybe she can't tell you what she wants. Maybe you don't have what it takes to satisfy her."

"I have everything it takes." Annoyed, he tugged me against him. "If she'd only give me a chance, I could prove it."

Still believing he was talking about sex, I resisted. "That's your problem, Jason. You think equipment is everything and it isn't. An intelligent woman looks for more in a man than a hard body."

"Do you think that's all I have to offer a woman?" His voice was dangerously quiet. "A hard body? A roll in the sack? Is that what you think I'm offering you?"

His bluntness was offensive. I wrenched out of his arms. "I don't know what you're offering and I don't care. I just wish you'd leave me in peace."

The moment the words were out, I could have kicked myself. All I'd wanted was to make him quit forcing me to want him. I hadn't intended to knock him down and trample his pride into the ground.

I needn't have worried. He could take care of himself. His eyes flashed like yellow lightning. "You may be surprised to hear it, Mrs. Levee, but I don't go around chasing women unless they send out signals they're interested. There's a name for women who give off come-hither vibes left and right and then, when it gets interesting, put out the Don't Touch sign."

Now *that* remark was uncalled for. "You're talking about me, I suppose." I tried to recapture my poise.

"You suppose right. Just what are you after, *Mrs.* Levee?" The sarcasm should have alerted me, but it didn't. I was too conscious of the other dancers looking at us.

"I'm not after anything. And quiet down. You're making people look at us."

Not understanding, I thought Jason was frustrated because my refusal to capitulate threatened his male ego. I was already furious because he'd brought that woman and then danced with her the same way he'd danced with me. When I tried to walk away, he blocked me, but I determined to have the last word. "I've had one successful marriage and not two would-be—"

He didn't let me finish.

Seizing my wrist, he whipped around, right in the middle of the song, and dragged me off the dance floor. The crowd parted, surprised couples shaking their heads tolerantly when they saw who it was.

He didn't stop until he'd dropped me into my chair.

"Thanks so much," he purred to an astonished Matt as I struggled for a semblance of dignity while trying not to fall out of the seat. "Your date is a lovely dancer. Perhaps when she learns to make small talk, she might be a pleasant companion."

He smirked, bowed urbanely to me, turned on his heel and left.

I couldn't remember ever being so mortified in my life.

"What—" Matt started to ask.

"I don't want to talk about it. I should have known better." Picking up my glass, I drained it in one gulp.

The curiosity and snickers died down after a few minutes, but my humiliation remained. For the rest of that night, Jason didn't come near me. He did, however, dance frequently and in an extremely familiar manner with the redheaded woman who was his date.

CHAPTER TWENTY

AT SOME POINT DURING that nightmarish evening, Tiffany Underwood and her partner danced by. She waved at Matt and raised a sympathetic brow at me before continuing to swirl round the room.

I was angry with Jason Forrester for embarrassing me on the dance floor, but I was angrier with myself for my untoward response. What on earth had come over me? I should have realized he was playing me for a fool. I fervently hoped that I'd given no one cause to suspect I'd developed an idiotic infatuation for him.

How could I have been so stupid?

I was safe now. After he had humiliated me that way, the only strong emotion he aroused was the urge to strangle him.

Sure. But if I was really over him, why did I want to go across the room and throw myself on my knees in front of him and beg his forgiveness?

I took a firm grip on myself and pretended to be having a wonderful time. Between eating and drinking, I went out on the floor with several of our builders, with the man from whom we bought office supplies, and even with Brent.

Striking in his tuxedo, he tried in his considerate way to apologize for Jason. "Jace can make an ass of himself sometimes with his quick temper, but he gets over it real fast. He'll apologize tomorrow, you wait and see."

I liked him for caring. "It doesn't matter. Jason doesn't bother me at all." Another lie added to the list but what did it matter?

We danced in silence. He held me loosely but wasn't hard to follow because he moved smoothly, flowing from step to step and drawing me with him.

My curiosity about Jason's date overcame my pride. "Jason seems to like redheads."

Brent looked back over his shoulder at where they were dancing. "Crystal's okay. They went together in high school. When she got divorced last summer, Jason helped her move back to Rahunta and get a job at the bank. He's good at looking out for people he cares about."

I was feeling ill and blamed it on Jason. Damn the man. Damn him for making me like him so much. Damn him for making a fool of me in front of all these people.

When I looked across the room, I saw his chin come down to rest on that red mop of hair. Their bodies touched as ours had.

And double damn him for dancing so close to her.

About eleven-thirty, Simone stopped at our table. "Come to the powder room with me?"

My head was starting to ache—inexplicable, since I've never been bothered with headaches. It must have been from the unaccustomed drink. Perhaps a splash of cold water would help.

Before reaching the ladies' room, Simone pulled me aside, to a secluded alcove housing candy and cigarette machines. "I saw what happened," she said in a low, angry tone. "Jason is disgusting."

"I don't want to talk about it, Simone."

She caught my arm eagerly. "You can pay him back, Anna, if we find the gun."

"Simone, I've told you I'd think about it."

She shook her head. "We can do it tonight. Listen, Anna, Jason will be here for another couple of hours before he takes that woman home. He might even spend the night with her. His house will be empty for ages."

Images swam through my mind. Jason taking Crystal home, kissing her good-night the way he'd kissed me. Taking off her clothes, touching her as he'd touched me. Nausea curdled my stomach, rose to fill my throat with bile.

Simone put her face close to mine. "I'm going over there tonight, Anna."

"Simone!" I forgot the nausea.

"I'll tell Brent I have a headache and have to go home, but I'll go there instead. Come with me, Anna. I need you."

I couldn't believe it. We were in the middle of a Christmas party and she was prating about going off on some wild-goose chase to look for a gun that might or might not be the one that had killed Alan.

"You must come," she pressed. "Otherwise, Brent'll insist on taking me home. But if you offer to go with me, he'll give us his car. I'm going, Anna, one way or the other. But it'll be so much easier with your help."

She had it all planned out.

I wanted to tell her firmly and unequivocally that I wouldn't be a part of such an outrageous and illegal scheme, but, as she waited anxiously for my reply, she looked desperate or ill.

What I said was, "Simone, I think you should wait."

Her face crumpled. "Anna, you say you're my friend. If you are, you'll help me. You have to help me. I can't do it without you."

We had been whispering furiously back and forth, unwilling to have anyone overhear us. The approach of a man buying cigarettes from the machine gave me my opportunity to take her arm and drag her into the ladies' room.

Under the fluorescent lights, she seemed frail and defenseless and near tears. Other women were putting on lipstick and combing their hair, so Simone could only look at me reproachfully before going into one of the booths.

Entering another, I sat down on the john, closed my eyes and propped my head on my hands. I couldn't deal with Simone and everything else that had happened today. As I moodily regrouped my forces for several more hours of dancing and the other rowdy entertainments these affairs were famous for, I heard the outer door open. A waft of familiar perfume came to my nose.

I knew immediately who it was. I had smelled that same gardenia scent on Jason when he'd taken me in his arms to dance.

"There's only one stall empty, but you go ahead, Laura. I want to call and make sure Timmy's okay."

Secure in my tiny booth, I hoped they wouldn't be long. Coming out and facing Crystal would be one more torture in a hellish evening.

The next stall door closed and latched before Crystal said, "Janie? Hi, it's just me checking in. Everything okay? . . . Good. Listen, I really appreciate your letting Timmy spend the night with Marty."

Silence for a moment then, "I always have a good time with Jace and yes, nosy, I *am* counting on him staying over." She giggled. "Sure, sure, take them on to the late movie. They'll love it. What time does it start, twelve? . . . That'd be great for me. Then it won't matter if I don't get any sleep. I'll plan to pick Timmy up tomorrow afternoon then . . . Great. Thanks, Janie. You're a doll."

A nearby toilet flushed and someone came out. Another voice said, "Kid okay, Crystal?"

"He's fine. Let me pee real quick and we'll go tear up the dance floor."

I seethed, so furious I could hardly breathe. He'd danced with me, held me against him, and then, after he knew perfectly well what he was doing to me, he was going to spend the night with *her*.

And what they'd do together, I couldn't bear to imagine.

Not until that moment did I learn I could be capable of violence. It took five minutes before my rage abated, leaving me drained and empty. The door opened and shut several times before there was blessed silence.

Not that I enjoyed it for long.

Simone was still in the powder room. "Anna, we're alone. Did you hear?"

"Yes." I sounded collected and calm, like I was all right. And I would be all right, once this awful, aching emptiness went away.

"Jason will be gone all night to Crystal's, Anna, *all night*. Oh, please go with me."

I put my head in my hands, stifling a groan.

When I came out, Simone was waiting. The other cubicle gates were flapped open, advertising our solitude and encouraging confidences.

"If you don't go with me, I'll go by myself," she threatened. "Will you?"

The door opened and two women came in.

"Yes."

Why did I agree?

In later years, I looked back with astonishment at how easily Simone talked me into it. But in later years, it was hard to remember how deep my disillusionment and hurt had cut. In later years, it was hard to remember the raging jealousy that blazed up and smothered all sanity.

What I did remember was my rationalizing.

Simone needs someone to look out for her, I remember telling myself. *If I don't go with her, there's no telling what might happen to her.*

And there was the gun.

If Jason had anything to do with Alan's murder, didn't I want to know it? If he had a gun hidden away, wouldn't it be best to bring it out into the open and find out why?

Despite everything, I didn't believe he was a murderer. This would be one way to prove it.

Matt was astonished to learn I was leaving with Simone. "But why?"

"She doesn't want to take Brent away from their guests."

"I'll go with you." He made as if to get up.

I put my hand on his shoulder, pressing him down. "No, stay and enjoy yourself. I'll see you tomorrow."

When he persisted, looking nettled that Simone had asked me instead of him, I leaned over. "Simone would rather have just me for company. It's a female thing, okay?"

He immediately backed off, as I knew he would. Matt was like me. Straitlaced, conscious of propriety, levelheaded.

Except that didn't describe me anymore.

Brent was alone at his table, looking up as Simone spoke at his ear. When he saw me weaving through the crowd, he got up. "I'm really sorry, Anna." He was apologetic. "I didn't realize Jason had upset you so."

"Oh, she'll be fine," Simone told him hastily, taking my arm. Her other hand clutched a set of keys. "I may stay with her a little while, Brent, so if I'm not home when you get there, don't worry about me."

Despite her admonition, Brent's harassed expression was more pronounced than ever as he watched us leave. I remembered his face later, how white and pinched it looked, how his hollow eyes followed our departure with concern approaching dread. That was after I knew the truth, when I understood the terrible stress he was under, the stress that was almost pulling him apart.

But that night I was too engrossed in my own affairs to worry about Brent's, too offended by my last sight of Crystal enfolded in Jason's arms.

"What did you tell Brent?" I picked up my cloak in the lobby and threw it over my shoulders.

"That Jason upset you so much, you developed a migraine and asked me to take you home," Simone said complacently, shrugging into her full-length mink so pretentious and out of place among the other ordinary coats. "And I told him you didn't want to have to ride with Jason's brother. That way, Brent didn't offer to drive us."

And I thought I had been clever, telling Matt it was a female problem.

Lying to poor Matt. And lying to Brent. My conscience tried its best to bring me back to my senses, but I shrugged its prickling off. That night I felt totally unlike myself. I was reckless and eager to take chances. Some impetuous sprite might have claimed my body, turning out the prudent, cautious essence that normally characterized me and filling me with a rash exuberance.

Jason Forrester might put me in the same category as his other women, but he'd be sorry. I'd show him.

Miserable, I almost hoped we did find a gun and Simone could crow over him. Deep inside, I knew we wouldn't, but I allowed my imagination to dwell on what would happen if we did. Jason Forrester would have a lot of explaining to do, and it would serve him right.

We discussed our plans on the way to my cottage, deciding to leave the car there and walk around the top of the gorge to Jason's house. Simone swore she knew where the gun was hidden, that it wouldn't take us ten minutes to find it.

By the time we parked Brent's BMW, the heady courage given me by rage and alcohol was deteriorating. I was having second thoughts. "Are you sure you want to do this, Simone?"

"Yes," she snapped. "And you promised."

I squared my shoulders and prepared to keep my word.

Simone was able to wear some of my dark gray sweats. Her feet were smaller than mine, but using two pairs of socks and stuffing some tissue in the toes, she laced my tennis shoes up tight and pronounced them wearable. I gave her my new burgundy toque to cover her silvery hair, but she used her own gloves retrieved from Brent's car.

For myself, I stripped off the beautiful red dress that had brought me so little joy, to don jeans and a thick black sweater and my new running shoes. After rummaging through drawers, I turned up an old University of Georgia stocking cap that had been Alan's.

Then, armed with a flashlight and dressed in our breaking-and-entering outfits, we set off over the ridge to Jason Forrester's house.

CHAPTER TWENTY-ONE

THE NIGHT WASN'T UNUSUALLY clear or unusually dark. It was simply a Georgia winter night, like any one of hundreds I'd seen in my lifetime.

Nerves made every tree look like a ghoulish figure frozen in flux, while every sound the wind made moaning through bare branches and pine boughs seemed to be the rustle of someone's breathing as he lay in wait for Simone and me. Low clouds, drifting in front of the moon, continuously threw unexpected shadows over our path. My imagination turned them into sorcerous spirits, dancing a nocturnal ritual dance intended to ensnare us.

Looking back in after years, I marveled that I could have gone out blithely with Simone, so unheeding of what might follow. But at the time, I was simply apprehensive of being out on the trail in the dark. I kept waiting for the evil presence that had confounded me so often to make itself known.

The moon gave enough light that we could see the path without the flashlight. We seldom spoke. There wasn't much to say.

Oh no. I'd left my cell in my evening purse. "Simone, did you bring your cell?"

"Yes. Why?"

"Just in case. I forgot mine." We shouldn't need to call for help but still . . .

She took a shuddering breath. I suspected that Simone, like me, was fearful, with her heart beating as furiously and her nerves as near to breaking as mine.

But she believed in her quest, while I . . .

I was sobering up.

As we walked, I went back over our logic.

The Christmas party would not be over until one o'clock or later. It was barely past midnight now. We'd have at least an hour to search his study. Though if Jason spent the night with Crystal—my heart twisted as I imagined them together—we would have all night.

Simone swore she knew where he'd put the gun. That finding it before he returned was a sure thing.

Everything made sense. There was no reason for the foreboding settling over me.

Perhaps I was depressed because Jason was with Crystal. The image of them together in bed was like a physical blow. Scolding myself for envying the woman didn't banish my heartache, nor did derision for my obsession with Jace Forrester.

If only I could appease Alan's spirit and leave this wretched place.

I hated it. No, I loved it. Oh, I hardly knew what I felt anymore. I was miserable and wished I'd never heard of Rahunta Gorge and Jason Forrester.

The garage adjoining the house that usually held Lettie's car and Jace's vintage Mustang was empty. I had known it would be. Lettie wasn't due back till next week, and Jason wouldn't have picked up Crystal for the dance in his beat-up truck.

The pickup stood in the shadows beside the kitchen. The place was still and quiet as death, the silence as unnerving as our trek through the woods.

We stole across the yard.

"Grrrrr."

Simone and I both jumped, but it was only Jason's old dog confronting us.

"Hello, Digger." I offered him my fingers. "Remember me?"

He immediately let out a whine of recognition. In the moonlight, I could see him grinning at me and patted his head.

"Stupid dog." Simone pressed a hand to her chest. "I nearly had a heart attack."

She followed me as I stealthily approached the porch. I was no less brave than the next person, but at the threshold of that house, I nearly turned back. Its white frame looming up before us was too much like the pale house in my dreams. "Simone—"

"There's a spare key to the back door on the ledge of the bathroom window," she said softly. The eerie silence had affected her, too. "I'll get it."

While I waited, rioting memories of the white mansion jumbled together, to be sifted through as I decided whether I should enter this house.

No, I had no choice. I'd come this far and I had to continue. In my dreams, I'd gone inside willingly so there was nothing here to harm me.

It was the black castle that terrified me, that I should beware of.

Besides, wasn't this what I had come to Rahunta for? To learn everything I could about Alan's murder? This was Alan's doing. This was another step on the path he was patiently shepherding me down, another step toward discovering whatever it was he intended me to find.

There is sometimes a moment of clarity, in even the most irrational actions, when you recognize with absolute certainty that you're doing the right thing, the only thing that you can possibly do, despite what other people or your own common sense tell you.

I'd experienced such a moment when I first decided to come to Rahunta, and I felt it again that night as I waited for Simone to find the key. Alan's presence hovered, urging me, encouraging me to continue. He was with me as surely as was his stocking cap I wore.

From that moment, I resigned myself. Whatever happened tonight was meant to be.

We went in by the back door, Simone first.

The kitchen was still, with a faint aroma of bacon lingering. Simone swiftly crossed it, me at her heels.

Going on through the house I saw the den, its worn corduroy furniture grouped around the large slim television that I'd watched Thanksgiving. There was also the formal dining room opening off the side of the kitchen, a formal living room in the front of the house beyond the den, and the study directly across from the den and in front of the dining room.

Our objective was the study, where I had sat on the stool by the fire and where Jason had held my feet. Entering it, I could almost feel his lips against my toes where he'd tenderly kissed each one.

"We'll need some light." Simone's calm couldn't hide her elation.

I passed the flashlight beam over the room. "We'd better not turn on the overhead light." There was a small banker's lamp on the desk. "How about this?"

We moved it to the floor, so that it threw its glow onto the shelves beside the fieldstone fireplace. I knew nothing about bricks or secret panels or any of that garbage that's so prevalent in gothic novels and old mysteries. I could only watch ineffectually as Simone pulled at one partition and then another.

"I can't find it," she said at length, her voice rasping with frustration. "I know it's here. One of these shelves against the fireplace pulls out and there's an opening behind it."

I got down on my knees and felt inside the cabinet. "Why did Brent tell you where it was?" The adrenaline of fear was wearing off.

She laughed, a low gurgling of pleasure. "I had this sedative the doctor gave me when I was ill, phenol-pheno-something-or-other." She was on the other side of the fireplace.

"Phenobarbital?"

"Yes, that's it. Matt told me it acted like a truth serum. I put some in Brent's drink one night."

"Simone!" What in heaven's name was she thinking? "That's dangerous, mixing drugs and alcohol."

"No, it isn't," she said blithely. "It worked just fine."

It was like speaking to a child. She didn't anymore know that she could have killed her husband than cows couldn't fly. Someone needed to talk to her, to drum into her silly head the harm she could do with stunts like that.

I resumed my search, but neither of us could find anything that even looked like an opening. By the time I climbed on a chair and worked my way to the top shelf, I was ready to give up.

"It wouldn't be up there," Simone said crossly, noticing what I was doing. "It's just a little indentation in the rocks that got covered by these shelves. Brent said he and Jason used it when they were small, so it has to be down here somewhere."

"Then where is it?" I snapped. She might not care about being jailed for unlawful entry, but I did. I already disapproved of her flirtation with Matt Graven, and after what she'd told me about fixing Brent's drink, I was beginning to wonder if she had all her marbles.

It wasn't till we'd swapped sides for the second time that unexpected headlights threw a stark glare on the far walls and drowned out the feeble beams of the lamp.

My heart thudded. "He must be bringing her back here."

"He can't be!" Simone was as panicky as I. "He wouldn't bring her to Lettie's house."

I turned off the lamp, hoping they hadn't seen its glow, and we started for the kitchen. My heart, despite racing, tightened with dread at the thought of them, together, coming back and finding us.

I should never have given in to Simone's pleadings. What in the world had come over me?

Too late to slip out unnoticed. As we approached the kitchen door, the back porch steps creaked. "Hello, Digger," I heard the familiar voice say. "How's it going, boy?"

Cursing my stupidity for failing to realize they would come to the door normally used, I pulled at Simone's arm, and we fled quietly to the living room. Our only hope was to hide until they'd gone upstairs.

I didn't allow myself to dwell on what they would do upstairs.

There were no voices.

Was he alone? That had been Jason I'd heard, hadn't it? What if it wasn't Jason, but someone else?

No, I'd know his voice anywhere.

We crouched down behind the sofa. My heart beat a frantic tattoo that must surely be audible throughout the house.

A light went on.

Sounds came from the kitchen: the refrigerator door opening and closing, water running in the sink, the clink of glass. The kitchen light went out and the hall light went on. Footsteps moved leisurely down the hallway and up the stairs, and the hall light went out again.

Downstairs settled back into darkness.

My heart pounded madly, near to bursting. I had never in my life done anything like this. If I was discovered here, I would never recover from the humiliation.

You brought it all on yourself, girl, I told myself grimly. *You didn't have to give in to Simone. You have nobody to blame but yourself.* I vowed never to take another drink of anything stronger than lemonade.

That resolve didn't help my feverish pulse, but the footsteps moving upstairs did. I calmed as silence filled the house.

After a few minutes, Simone got up from her hiding place and I followed. She crept across the room toward the front door and began to turn the knob. She pulled, but the door held fast.

I motioned for her to move aside and tried to open it myself.

The door remained unyielding. Feeling above the knob, I groped all the way to the top before discovering a sliding bolt securing it.

With Simone breathing down my neck, I tugged at it, but it was stuck. I pulled harder, trying to move it quietly, until, unexpectedly, it clanked open.

We stood like statues, holding our breath, listening, waiting to be discovered.

The house remained still.

I tried the door again. The knob turned, but now it was stuck at the bottom.

Kneeling down, I found another sliding bolt. It was while I fumbled at it that I heard Simone's quick intake of breath. Fingers brushed my head in warning before she slipped away.

A glance over my shoulder showed me the reason: a silhouette stood at the doorway leading in from the hall. With gratifying reflexes, I followed Simone's example and fled, bolting to the other side of the room where an arched opening led to the dining room and the kitchen beyond.

I made it to the dining room, that shadow on my heels, so close I could hear his breathing. From behind me came the sound of the front door opening. A rush of cold air preceded its slamming shut.

Simone had escaped. As for me . . .

If he caught me . . .

Fear lent wings to my feet.

Neither of us spoke a word as we ran. The only sound was our footsteps, muffled on the carpeted floors.

In the kitchen, I stumbled against the wooden churn, which fell over with a resounding crash, and scurried for the door. There was a clatter as he kicked the churn aside, but still neither of us spoke or cried out.

I wrenched open the kitchen door and fled across the porch and down the steps. The man behind leaped over the banister, so that when I rushed past the garage he was right on my heels. He caught me by the sweater and flung me around.

In desperation, I flailed out wildly, but he gripped my fists in his large hands and forced them back, back behind my waist, while I struggled helplessly against that merciless chest.

Only then did he speak—one word, snapping through the blackness like the lash of a whip.

"You."

There were no embarrassing questions, no accusations I had to try to explain. Not until later, when I knew the whole truth, did I find my toes had given me away long before, and that he realized when he caught me that I was Simone's cat's-paw.

But that night I could only gape as he bent his head inexorably to press his mouth against mine with a will that would not be denied.

I didn't try to deny it.

I allowed, no, I assisted, those lips to capture mine, and they complied with a bruising force that jarred my teeth against his. When his tongue snaked out to invade my mouth, it opened of its own accord, and the fiery strokes lavished were returned twofold.

I didn't recall him releasing my arms from behind my back, but somehow they were around his neck. He tugged at my cap and discarded it so he could twist my hair around his hand. For an eternity we clung together there under the night sky, unheeding of anything except each other. When he picked me up and carried me back into the house, I didn't resist.

There were many little things I recalled later that I didn't notice at the time.

He tasted of beer, yeasty and sweet, and of garlic, for some reason I didn't know.

He smelled of perspiration and lime cologne. And gardenia perfume, for a reason I understood all too well.

His face was smooth, as if he had shaved before going to the dance. His ruffled shirt was soft silk.

Inside the kitchen he put me down, but we were unable to stay apart. He found the zipper in my jeans and had it unfastened before I knew what he was about. His hand reached inside to cup my hip, squeezing it as though it were a fruit.

I wanted his hand there, fondling me, pinching me with enough discomfort to heat my blood to boiling.

His touch melted the most private places.

Another moment and he'd pushed up my sweater so that he could fumble at the hooks on my bra, and then it and my sweater were both up to my armpits. My breasts, fully uncovered by his attentions, grew turgid.

I could feel his need, throbbing every time any part of him touched me. His hands communicated by their careful strokes—sometimes harsh, sometimes gentle—the control he exercised. His lips wandering over my skin told of their longing to claim and possess. His loin biting into my hips proved he would not be held in check much longer.

Impatiently, I unfastened the studs on his shirt and dropped them on the floor. Pushing up his undershirt, I pulled his exposed chest against mine.

He drew his mouth away from my neck, gasping as if shocked at the contact of bare skin on bare skin. Another second found me triumphant over the opening of his trousers, and without that confinement, his erection forced its way out to lie eager against my hip.

He took me on the kitchen table, for neither of us could wait to find a softer couch. There was no thought of protection, no thought of consequences, no thought of right or wrong.

Later I would look back with incredulity at the magnitude of what we did, wondering what we could have been thinking of; but in truth, we were mindless savages that night, caring for nothing except the need that devoured us both.

He lifted me up and set me on the corner and somehow got my pants down enough to enter me as he half stood, half crouched in front of me.

He was large and magnificent, and I was hot and ready. With the first stroke I was halfway to the top and with the next I was there and with the third I was gliding off the mountain, shrieking out his name and sobbing as I soared and soared and soared . . .

Hands pulled at me. I came back to awareness, to the uncomfortable surface beneath my butt that belonged to Lettie's hardrock-maple tabletop where I still sat, propped up by Jason's arms. I held him closer and protested weakly as he tried to move my drained body.

He kissed my ear. "Just up the stairs, sweetheart. You can handle that, little wildcat."

"No."

I didn't want to move. I wanted to stay there with him in my arms, my head resting against the soft bed of hair matting his chest, his length filling my thighs. I wanted to listen to the thudding of his heart beneath my ear and put the tip of my tongue against his nipple. I wanted to whisper lovely things into his ear and have him whisper into mine in return.

He laughed, a low sexual laugh that made me hurt inside, my joy was so great. Picking me up bodily, he carried me out of the kitchen and down the hall, quick and sure despite the darkness.

At the top of the stairs he took me into a bedroom and laid me on the bed. "Women who are too lazy to turn down the cover get to sleep on top." The bedside lamp he flicked on revealed warm and teasing eyes.

The light brought back reality. He would ask questions I couldn't answer, say things I didn't want to hear.

"I can't stay here." My body made a lethargic effort to get up, but he pushed me back down. His big frame was a sight, with the clothes he had worn to the dance half torn off.

Looking down, I saw my own disarray: sweater and bra up under my arms and only one leg of my jeans partly on. "I can't stay," I mumbled with less assurance.

"Yes, you can." He succeeded in undoing his tie and threw it to the side before tackling his shirt. "If you want to."

It was not a question, neither was it a command. It was a simple statement, pointing out that I was in charge of my own life, and if I chose to stay, there was no reason in the world why I couldn't.

I stayed.

We made love again, properly this time, a long leisurely exploration of each other's bodies with all our clothes off. Afterwards, I lay with him beneath the covers, curled up in the curve of his body, enjoying his warmth and his distinct masculine odor, which, combined with the scents of our coupling, had nearly eradicated the gardenia perfume.

I had to ask. "Did you do this with her tonight?"

"What?" He was nearly asleep. "Who?"

"That redheaded woman you brought to the party. Did you do this with her tonight?"

"Crystal?" There was a smile in his voice, perhaps a little of the old smugness, too. "That's a silly question. Do you think I could be doing all this with you if I'd just done it with her Who do you think I am? Super Stud?"

"She thought you would spend the night with her."

"Three months ago she'd have been right. Then I met you."

"Did you—?"

He silenced my stupid, jealous questions with a kiss that left me breathless. When he had thoroughly scotched that subject, he spoke again. "I have one for you now."

"One what?" It was my turn to be sleepy and content. I wished I could stay in his bed forever and feel his long length stretched out against me every night, every morning.

"Question. You asked yours. Now it's my turn."

I grew still. "Ask away." What would I tell him? How could I explain my being here in his house?

"Did you mean it? What you said when we made love tonight?" His whisper beside my ear was husky and inconceivably sexy. His fingers barely touched my nipples before I could feel them stiffening, budding with fresh longing.

"I don't know. I don't remember what I said. Do you remember what you said?" I was as hoarse as he. And relieved to postpone the inevitable.

"Oh, yes. I remember everything I said." The smile in his voice warmed me. "But I'm asking about you. You called out my name. Do you remember that?"

"Um, I guess so." I was more interested in his body than in his questions. Beneath my examining fingers, it was beginning to show the same unmistakable signs as mine.

"You called my name. And then you said 'I love you, I love you, no matter what you did.'"

The silence that followed could have been heard in downtown Atlanta, it was so loud.

Had I said that? I tried to remember. In the throes of ecstasy, I'd cried out something, and the words Jace repeated sounded right, but surely . . .

There was no way to answer him. "If I said it, I, then I suppose I meant it."

"I thought you did." His tone was satisfied, his hands tender on my breasts. "You said it again the second time."

"I must have meant it then, mustn't I?" I turned over so that we lay face-to-face, touching from our chins down to our toes. "Do you think we should try for a third time just to make sure?"

"I think you're a pretty smart cookie," he said huskily, and that time turned out the same as the other two.

At least he said it did.

I don't know if it did or not. I don't have the foggiest idea of what I said.

At a time like that, even a sensible person loses her head.

CHAPTER TWENTY-TWO

A RINGING BOTHERED ME, the only cloud in my otherwise untroubled slumber.

One eye opened groggily to stare up at a strange ceiling.

I had the most wonderful sense of well-being, even before I woke up enough to realize where I was and who lay beside me. The bed shifted, and the warmth of Jason's body was removed as he rolled over to answer the bedside phone.

After a few sentences, Jason's part of the conversation penetrated my haze of happiness.

Someone was calling about his bull.

"It's Lochinvar," he confirmed when he hung up, dark hair tumbled so that he looked like a little boy with beard shadow. "That was Dave Waters, our farm manager. He says Lochinvar got out of his barn last night and broke down two fences to get to Steve McGilliam's cow across the road. Now he's lost in the frigging fog. Where the hell does that SOB think he's working? That cow'll drop a prize calf and we won't get a penny in stud fees."

Deducing that he was impugning Lochinvar and not Dave Waters, I made sympathetic noises. "That's too bad. Are you going to have to go see about him?"

"Reckon so. Dumb animal's as liable to run in front of a car as not."

Awake, my conscience stung.

Common sense, dormant but undaunted, was emerging from the stupor of passion.

Here I was, in love with this wonderful, terrible, gorgeous man. I'd spent the night with him, acknowledging with my body exactly how I felt about him.

And he didn't know who I was.

Nor had he asked me what I was doing in his house in the middle of the night. What was he thinking? Why didn't he ask? Did he know I'd been with Simone?

Poor Simone. I hadn't given her another thought from the moment I'd heard the door slam after her escape.

Jason, tracing a pattern on my neck with his huge hand, brought me out of my reverie.

How strange to think I had feared that hand, when all it did was give such pleasure. Little tongues of fire leapt through my body wherever he stroked me with it. I wished he would go on touching me like that forever.

As if in answer to my thoughts, he moved the hand down to my breast, going round and round the dark aureole until, as if the temptation was too great, he bent his head and tickled it with his tongue till the nipple stood straight up.

My breath came in little gasps as I reached out to grasp the hair matting his chest.

I forgot Simone. I forgot Jason's complacency. I forgot my own perfidy.

I wanted only to have this moment never end.

"Do you know you're the most wonderful woman I've ever known?" he asked after his lips had worked their way back up to mine and had kissed them thoroughly.

My anticipatory tingling of desire faded abruptly. His words filled me with unaccountable joy, but how would he feel when he discovered the truth?

"Jace. Jace." I pushed him back a little. "What's your mother going to say about us?"

"Oh, Ma knew it all along."

"She knew what all along?"

"That you and I'd end up together."

I stared. "How could she? I didn't even like you."

He pulled me against his naked warmth. "Sure you did. You were crazy about me. You just didn't know it. Now me, I knew right away. And Ma did, too. When I complained about the way you made me wipe my feet that first day, she said, 'Jace, if she can keep you in line, you better grab her, 'cause she'll be the first woman I've seen who could.' Lettie's no dummy."

"She didn't say that!"

"Yes, she did. Mind you, *I* wasn't so sure about it. But then, after you persisted in throwing yourself at me—"

"I never—"

"—and after last night." His hand reached out and the fingers spread out over my stomach, pushing gently and making my sensitive spots leap in agreeable anticipation. "First you come to the dance looking like a million dollars in that pretty red dress and make me feel like an insensitive slob. Then, after mooning about you all evening, trying to figure out how to make you like me, I find you waiting here in those sexy tight jeans."

I was the one to stop his mouth this time, hastily kissing him before he could go further and dig into things best left alone.

"You'll have to marry me," he said when we came up for breath. "You've ruined my reputation."

"I did nothing of the sort. I never intended this to happen when I came—" Belatedly, I bit my tongue and saw his tiny smile.

Not once had he asked what I had been doing in his house in the middle of the night. In the more urgent demands of our bodies, I had forgotten myself.

"Jason." There was nothing I could tell him about my reasons for being in his house last night, but I could ask him one thing, and I did. "Jason, did you kill Alan McKenzie?"

My question hovered in the air like an icy snowflake, falling gently on its way to earth to melt.

"Last night you said you loved me, no matter what I'd done," he pointed out mildly, his hand on my belly sliding away. "Why do you ask?"

I stared down the patches on the quilt covering us, saw the bruises on my arms where he had caught me at the door the past night. "I want to know, Jason. I have to know."

"All right," he said agreeably, stroking my shoulder. For such a rough hand, his touch was like silk. He moved his fingers to the bruises and outlined them gently. "I wish I'd known it was you last night." His regret was sincere. "I'd never have hurt you, Anna. No, I didn't kill Alan McKenzie. Does that satisfy you, little wildcat?"

I looked up to find him smiling again, but with an unfamiliar weariness in the golden brown eyes that I didn't understand. "Jace, who did kill him? Do you know?"

If my growing suspicions were right, he did know. I wanted desperately for him to trust me enough to confide in me.

It was his turn to look away. "Let me ask you this, Anna. Is there anything you need to tell me? I mean, if we're being honest here?" His stare came back to me, the gold in his eyes darkening, leaving them unfathomable. "Like why you're so interested in Alan McKenzie?"

The truth was on the tip of my tongue, but I couldn't tell him, not now. Later, when I'd had time to think, I would find a way to do so.

But not now. Not when our naked bodies were pressed so closely together, not while I felt my body slipping into this new state of enchantment. "No," I whispered. "I don't have anything I need to tell you, Jason."

"No?" He was unsmiling.

Heat rose up my neck, but I didn't flinch under those watchful eyes. Neither did I speak. What could I say? I'm Alan's sister and I came here to prove you murdered him?

"I answered your question," he pointed out, with a trace of his familiar smile. When I still didn't reply, he leaned over and kissed me on the mouth, very tenderly. "I don't have time to do what I'd like to do now, but when I get back, we'll do it together."

My throat was nearly too tight to speak. "I need to go home, change clothes."

"You wait right here." He got out of bed and started getting dressed. "This shouldn't take long. We can fix breakfast and then go back to bed. I'll take you home afterward and let you get your clothes."

"You're awfully honest about what you expect." I watched him buckle his belt, knowing I'd do just as he wanted.

He swaggered over and sat beside me. "I never learned to be anything but."

His eyes drank in every detail of my face, such loving wonder in them that I felt myself slipping over the edge into the depths of those shining golden pools.

"If I want a woman, I tell her. And I want you, Anna. I've been burnt a couple of times, but I always knew somebody like you would come along, somebody I could trust."

Conscience flared. I stopped him, breathless. "Jace, don't rush me."

"All right." His voice was the same as always, but with an underlying confidence that told me quite plainly he knew the outcome, even if I wouldn't yet admit it. "But you're going to have to make up your mind before Lettie gets back."

"Lettie?" I stared at him blankly.

"She won't approve of us living together unless we intend to get married." He bent down, but didn't kiss me. Instead, his fingers, wind-chafed and hard, gently followed the curve of my cheek to my chin. He sat there, his hand cupping my chin, for a long moment, almost as if he were waiting for me to say something.

"You, I, we can't jump into this, Jace," I said lamely.

His expression didn't change, but I saw a slight darkening of the gold of his eyes. What I had said was not what he wanted to hear.

His face moved closer to mine. "You love me."

"Yes," I whispered in abject surrender.

The gleam returned to his eyes. "It'll work out then." He flicked a careless finger against my cheek and got up to leave, calling over his shoulder, "I'll be back as soon as I can. If you aren't here, I'll come looking for you."

"Cocky devil," I muttered as he disappeared, but my words were without rancor.

It did not occur to me until after he'd gone that he'd never once said he loved me. Then, I couldn't go back to sleep. Though my body was relaxed and content for the first time in years, my mind whirled.

I didn't believe Jason had killed my brother. Perhaps I'd really never believed it, but now I was certain. Simone's story about him hiding the gun was untrue. We'd searched and there was no gun hidden behind the bookshelves.

Slow down, I cautioned. Everything was happening much too fast, there were too many missing pieces.

But it didn't matter. A peace unfelt in a long time flooded me in the aftermath of a passion never before known.

The memories of the past night were too overpowering. Reliving the touch of his hand on my body was too exciting. Remembering the sound of his heart under my ear was too absorbing.

There was no use trying to ignore my reaction to Jason Forrester. I was hopelessly, headily, ardently in love with him, and I wouldn't have had it any other way. Never in my life had I felt like this, but I couldn't feel this way about Jason Forrester if he was a murderer.

Could I?

No. Of course I couldn't.

After showering, I put on a flannel robe that smelled like him before going to the window and pulling back the curtains. The weather front had moved in sometime during the night, bringing light rain and fog. Everything beyond the edge of the yard was gray and dismal. Even the gorge was lost in a mist that curled up like smoke to hide its rocks and crevices.

Toweling my hair, I turned away before the miserable weather dampened my happiness. Already the room seemed less bright and the house unnaturally quiet. Without Jason to dispel it, another, deeper presence lurked. Not the demons of the gorge, but an impatient spirit that nudged me, making me as restive as it.

I looked back over my shoulder quickly, but there was no one there.

"Alan?" I whispered. Then with real pain, "Alan, why won't you tell me? I know Jason didn't shoot you."

Of course there was no answer. I was being foolish again. Clever, careful Annabelle, caught up like any other silly, lovelorn woman.

It had to be Brent.

Why hadn't I asked Jace about Brent?

Falling facedown onto the bed, I groaned.

Because I was afraid of him finding out who I was. Or because I was afraid, period. How would Jason feel when he discovered I was Alan's sister? Would he understand why I'd concealed my identity?

Perhaps he already knows.

The silence of the house made my skin crawl, while the lamps turned on by the bed didn't dispel the gloom from the gray skies outside. If only Jason would hurry back. I was ready to tell him everything and throw myself on his mercy.

Dressing, I saw the bruises on my arms where Jason had grabbed me, and tenderness welled up and flooded me. I remembered every detail of our remarkable night and wondered if he did, too.

Downstairs was as quiet and somber as upstairs. Not a sound disturbed the heavy silence. When I flipped the switch, the kitchen light spread an artificial glow no less depressing than the semidarkness caused by the clouds outside.

The churn had been put back beside the doorway, and the maple table stood innocuously in its place. It showed no signs of the use to which it had been put, no matter how hard I stared.

There was no coffee, but the fridge held a pitcher of orange juice. I poured myself a glass and drank it, going over what I would say to Simone when I saw her.

The trick was to be sympathetic but firm. We hadn't found any sign of a hiding place for a gun. Brent would have said anything, under the combination of alcohol and drugs. She'd have to make her peace with Jason in some other way.

As if on cue, the massive hush hanging over the house was broken by a car coming up the driveway. It squealed to a stop at the garage. I opened the back door to see Simone, breathless and wild-eyed, fling herself out and bound up the steps.

"Simone, what is it?"

"We were looking in the wrong place!" She pushed her hair back from her forehead. "It was the old study Brent was talking about, the one they turned into the dining room. That's where we should have been searching for the gun!"

CHAPTER TWENTY-THREE

AND SO, LIKE THE brittle, mist-laden wind that swept Simone's white-blonde tresses as she stood gasping for breath, the one nagging doubt about my lover returned to plague me.

If the gun was hidden in his house, Jason had concealed what he knew. Had he lied when he'd said he hadn't killed Alan? I hadn't thought so, but now . . .

Searching the dining room would be purely for my own satisfaction. If we found the gun, there would be a logical explanation. There would be no reason for the knowledge to go any further. No matter who was implicated.

I told myself these things, and at the time, I believed them, for all my emotions concerning Jason had fused during the past night, erasing any doubts about my love for him.

After all, if Brent was guilty as I suspected, Jace would still do exactly as he'd done. His family meant everything to him. To protect his brother, he would suffer gossip and innuendos. He would hide the gun and say nothing.

But even if the truth would make no difference in my feelings for Jason, I still had to know it. No matter how certain I was of my passion for him.

Because I owed Alan something. Besides the fact that he was my brother and I'd loved him, Alan was responsible for my present happiness. If it hadn't been for him, I'd never have met Jason, never have fallen in love.

A doubt assailed me. Was this agonizing, delirious ambience really love, or was it only lust?

It could be sex, pure and simple. I was starved for affection, especially masculine affection. I'd been alone for over a year, rebuffing any male interest or attempts at flirtation, and this was what came of it. I'd fallen like a high-school sophomore for the first persistent man who looked at me with bedroom eyes.

That wasn't true.

I loved Jason.

With every fiber, every feeling, every cell in my being.

Even though he'd never said he loved me.

Even though my head, my cautious prudent head, whispered that I was wrong, that my heart was a foolish advocate.

That was why I looked calmly at Simone after she'd blurted out her news. "Let's go look, then, shall we?"

Simone burst into tears.

"I ran away," she sobbed, the irrelevancy not striking either of us. "I let that bull loose so Jason would have to leave. I knew this was my last chance. I was so afraid he'd turned you against me."

"Don't be silly, Simone."

Despite her delicacy, she had plenty of nerve. It might be near to breaking at the moment, but she'd endured more than most.

Not because of Jace, I told myself fiercely. There was some other reason for her hysteria, such as knowing Brent was in love with Tiffany and suspecting he had a part in Alan's murder.

Simone might not be a protective wife, but if she knew what Brent had done, she'd never be satisfied to trust Jason with her husband's life.

And that constant worry in the back of Brent's eyes. If he'd killed a man, even unwittingly, he was too susceptible not to be affected. Lettie had said he took things hard, that she and Jason tried to cushion his life. All the pieces seemed to fit, perhaps because I wanted so desperately for them to.

Not true. Simone's hatred of Jason could stem from her fearing Brent's exposure. Jason, so contemptuous of her, would enjoy having a hold over her.

Or did he enjoy taunting her for another reason?

No, I refused to believe he wanted her.

Simone put her arm through mine. "I don't know what I'd do without you, Anna." She was sincere in her gratitude, pathetic in her childlike faith.

We went directly to the dining room.

The fireplace here was not as large as the one in the study, but like that other one, it was made of fieldstone and had cabinets built around it.

I began on one side while Simone started on the other.

Open shelves built on both sides reached two-thirds of the way to the ceiling. Displayed there were several pieces of Lettie's porcelain that I had helped put away at Thanksgiving. Beneath them, taking up the bottom third of the unit, were cabinets with stained-glass doors, their frames matching the chair-rail paneling in the rest of the room.

Pulling one open, I stuck my head inside and peered at the part that abutted the bricks of the chimney.

There was nothing unusual. The inside of the cabinet was made out of the same wood as the outside, smoothly fitted, innocuous to the eye.

"I can't find anything." Frustrated, Simone sat back on her heels. "I know it's here, Anna. It has to be."

"Let's swap sides."

With rising hope—Simone would be proved wrong—I checked first the shelves and then the cabinets on the left side of the chimney. Nothing.

Like its twin across the fireplace, the cabinet interior was well fitted and fastened. Only a small nail sticking out marred its smoothness. I wouldn't have noticed it except that it jabbed my hand and while nursing the ensuing drop of blood, I discerned the hiding place.

There were several inches between the side of this cabinet against the chimney and its door front. Using my hand as a ruler proved my eyes hadn't deceived me. From the door's edge to the side wall of the cabinet on the right was a hand's width and then another good inch.

Measuring in the same place on the left cabinet, the distance was barely three fingers' width.

Simone paused eagerly. "Have you found something, Anna?"

Sucking at my wound, I knelt and inspected the cabinets.

Would one or two inches be enough room to hide a gun? How thick would a .45 revolver be?

I knew nothing of guns, but I did know I wouldn't be satisfied until that side wall was wrenched out.

Carefully removing Lettie's neat stacks of porcelain bowls and saucers, I felt for a handhold and found the nail that had jabbed me earlier.

It was all I needed.

The side panel fell smoothly away from the chimney.

Simone hovered, watching. "You've found it!"

We could hardly see the opening, but it was there: a cubbyhole that looked as if it was the result of a rock coming loose and never being replaced.

When cautiously exploring the velvet blackness—the light did not extend very far into the little hole—my fingers found nothing except rough stone. Then they met soft resistance.

I drew out a leather pouch, containing something hard and heavy.

"Is it the gun?" Simone reached for it.

Still on my knees, I was already pulling at the drawstring to look inside.

One handgun looked like another to me, but I knew with unshakable conviction that this was the revolver that had killed my brother.

And I had found it hidden in my lover's home.

All my pretty speeches and all the clever theories I'd come up with meant nothing compared to my current anguish.

"I told you." Simone was quietly triumphant. "I'll be free now and Jason will be punished. Give it to me, Anna."

My knees trembled so I could barely rise with the proof Simone had insisted all along was there.

I had never believed her. Not really. Even when I'd overheard Jason taunting her, telling her he'd keep the gun out of sight as long as necessary.

Not until this moment, when I held that bag and knew that this was the gun that had been sought for all these long months since Alan's death, did I actually face the fact that Jason could be involved in my brother's murder.

Simone caught my elbow. "Anna, give me the—"

"Annabelle!"

We whirled to find him standing in the doorway.

Simone froze, shocked.

My fingers tightened on the bag.

How long had he been there? His mouth was set in hard lines beneath the dark mustache. His eyes were no longer golden.

They were black as hell.

Any hopes of an innocent explanation fled before those icy eyes. *And he had called me Annabelle!*

CHAPTER TWENTY-FOUR

"ANNABELLE, GIVE THE GUN to me." His voice was strained, the skin across his nose and cheeks pulled taut into the cold mask I hated.

"Is this the gun that killed Alan McKenzie?" I wanted him to tell me it wasn't. I wanted him to explain why it was in his house. I wanted so much that I'd never have.

"Give it to me."

"No!" Simone lunged, trying to wrench it from my hand.

He was too quick, slipping between us and holding her away from me. "You bitch! I saw you streaking across the field and figured you were up to something. I ought to kill you for putting Anna up to this."

She went at him with her nails. In one motion, he evaded her onslaught and brutally shoved her away. She fell against the hearth, dazed.

I fled to the other side of the room. He followed, cornering me. "Give it to me, Annabelle."

How could he look at me so calmly after the past night?

And after he had discovered my name.

Some semblance of order returned and with it reason.

If he knew I was Alan's sister, he could not possibly let me leave the house with that gun.

He wouldn't know I had no intentions of turning it over to the police. He wouldn't believe me if I told him I only needed the truth about Alan to free his spirit.

Reason told me quickly enough what would happen to me because he did not know and would not believe.

I wondered if he would feel remorse after my death.

There was a small wooden chair beside the fireplace. With shaking legs about to fold, I reached for its back. It was firm under my trembling hand, something solid to prop me up, help me face the man I'd thought I knew, thought I loved.

Not thought. I *did* love him. Whatever he was, whatever happened to me. The remnants of my intelligence might be fighting for survival, but he had bewitched me, truly and wholly, and I'd never again be the same.

"I love you, Jason." I was proud of my voice. It wasn't strong, but neither did it quaver.

"I know. But give me the gun now." He sounded tired, but his expression was unchanging and bleak. "You have to give it to me, Anna." There was a controlled urgency about his words.

"No, Jason, I can't." The *can't* quivered.

"Anna . . . Annabelle, I know what you're thinking, but you're wrong." There was no passion or anger in him, only a desperate sadness more frightening than either of the other two could have been. "I'll explain, but not with you holding that gun."

"I'd like for you to explain, Jason."

All the time I wondered if he would kill me and how he would do it.

Those large hands that had caressed me so tenderly could snap my neck like a twig, the way he'd threatened Simone. Or he could use one of the other guns in the study where he kept his collection. Or he could take this gun away from me. Would it still be loaded?

He took a tentative step toward me, holding out his hand.

My terror faded, and my tortured mind began to take command. "Stay away from me, Jason." I let go of the chair and started to open the bag. If it was loaded, I might bluff him into leaving.

"Don't touch it!" His voice was sharp and urgent. "Annabelle, for God's sake, put it down, if you won't give it to me. But *don't touch it.*"

His tone was so commanding that I hesitated, my hand going back to the comforting solidity of the chair.

"Annabelle, please." The bones of his face jutted, their lines stark against the gray light from behind him. "Give me the gun and let me explain."

How strange I'd never noticed before how cruel his features could be. They truly belonged to a pirate's face, for they were bloodthirsty creatures who killed without pity or regret. The resemblance was unmistakable. If only I had heeded it before.

But it was too late. I loved the face, loved the man. I wanted to do as he said and give him the gun, but reason forbade it.

"Is there anything to explain?" I asked, stalling for time.

Behind him, Simone's leg moved and she groaned. A hand went up to her head.

"You know there is." He must have seen something in my expression, for he stood unmoving, muscles tensed as if to spring. His voice softened. "Anna, won't you trust me?"

"How can I? You said you didn't kill Alan, yet you have this gun hidden in your house. It's the gun the police searched for, isn't it?"

"Yes." His eyes, unreadable, were fixed on my face. "Anna, I can't tell you why it was there, not now, but . . . Annabelle, you said you loved me. If what you said was true, you'll trust me now. Please."

I hesitated, wanting more than anything I'd ever wanted in my life to give in to him. But for Simone's, for my own self-preservation, I dared not. "Jace, I can't," I whispered, tears welling and stinging my eyes.

"It isn't a hard thing to do." His voice dropped into the husky tones I remembered so well. His eyes took on their golden sheen, hypnotizing me with their spell. "Just give me a little time, Annabelle." He put out his hand. "Let me talk to you. Let me have the gun."

"Why are you calling me Annabelle?"

"It doesn't matter. Not now. Not if you give me that gun."

I wavered, the upper part of my body of its own accord leaning toward him as if vanquished. The tears by now were streaming down my face, as every thread of my being strained toward him, wanting to have him make it right again, wanting to be safe in his arms once more.

But I was no gambler. I had never been a gambler.

I was a woman who faced the truth however devastating, and afterwards did whatever had to be done. He had bedazzled me with his body, but the common sense that was central to my core at last emerged from beneath his spell.

He took a step toward me. My nerves screamed out from the desire to run into his arms, as opposed to the heartache of knowing that I could not give in and live.

Simone, conscious enough to see what was happening, sobbed, "Don't listen to him, Anna. Run. Run away before he kills you!"

My mind, survival instinct intact, prevailed. I flung the small chair as hard as I could.

It hit him squarely in the knees, tangling with his legs and bringing him down with a thud that shook the house.

I ran, not waiting to see the results. Curses assured me he'd soon be on his feet. When he came after me, Simone could call for help.

Taking a precious second to overturn a small table and block the way behind me, I ran through the kitchen to the back door. Like a fool, I cried all the while.

The door opened easily, and this time I fled without a black figure at my heels. Anguish touched me as I remembered the previous night, but I brushed it away.

There was no time for regrets, no time for sorrow. Only for escape.

The gorge path toward my house offered the best chance. I'd use my car to go for help.

Since I'd first looked out the upstairs window, the fog had gotten worse. Where before I'd seen only occasional patches on the top rim, now the entire trail was shrouded in gray mist as thick as sheeting. I couldn't see more than two feet in front of me.

Speeding down the trail, I tripped on a root and fell. As I struggled up, I heard sounds in the distance.

A car. Simone. She'd go for help.

Then branches cracking, feet padding on the ground. Jason. He would overtake me before I could reach my cottage.

Heart nearly bursting, I came to the fork where a side path met the main trail.

Without half a thought, I abandoned the latter. I could hide until Jason had passed, then go to Matt's and get help.

Logic returned.

If Jason was protecting Brent, he would have said so. If my theory was wrong and Jason himself had murdered Alan, he would never let me leave the gorge alive.

Getting off the path, I climbed up a low bank and sheltered behind a large oak.

Footsteps neared the fork.

I pressed myself against the trunk. The rough bark cut into my cheek. The pounding of Jason's feet blended with the pounding of my heart.

The mist was all-enveloping, hiding everything but the tree I cowered against.

Good. If I couldn't see him, he couldn't see me.

Repressed anguish shook my body. I bit my lower lip to stifle sobs.

The footsteps approached and passed, continuing round the top on the main trail. He went by with a rapid, even gait, close enough to me that I could hear his sharp breathing. I continued to hug the tree until the footsteps faded, and after.

Despite the fog, I was afraid of those gold-flecked eyes and what they might see if I came out from cover too soon.

After silence completely returned, I climbed back down onto the path. Afraid to run over ground I couldn't see, I used a kind of jogging trot. I hoped it was fast enough to keep me ahead of Jason if he backtracked.

A few minutes' head start would let me reach Matt and safety. The leather bag containing the gun was still clutched in my hand, growing heavier with each step.

I was cold despite the sweat popping out on me from my desperate run, cold from the discovery that Simone had been right. Cold from the discovery that Jason had lied.

All the while he had made love to me—all the while he had stroked and inflamed and coaxed my body to heights I'd never before experienced—he had known who was responsible for Alan's death and had let me believe he was innocent.

All the while, he had lied.

Without stopping, I tied the cords of the heavy pouch through the jeans' belt loops. Its weight sagged against my hip.

The gun that had killed Alan.

Jason lied to me. Fresh tears wet my face as I struggled over the low trail.

Matt's cottage ought to be near by now. New anxieties assailed me. The path was rougher than I remembered. A fallen tree tripped me, but I scrambled up and wiped my eyes. That didn't help my vision. I could hardly make out anything more than a yard in front of me.

Taking slow and cautious steps, I started again. Everything seemed so different.

The fog swirled and soared like a dancer's skirt, tantalizing me, opening a clear patch here, another there. Even when it divided for a moment to reveal several feet ahead, I recognized nothing.

And yet it was all familiar. The jutting rocks, the gray mist smothering me, the fear . . .

Terror, sickening and debilitating, immobilized me.

I had entered my own nightmares.

When I caught myself hyperventilating, I made myself stop. "It's only a dream. It's only a dream." Gathering shreds of courage together, I plunged ahead.

I wished this wild flight were a dream. Oh, God, I wished it were a nightmare I could wake up from.

A twisted stump tripped me and nearly made me fall again. Something was wrong. The path leading to Matt's had never been this steep. And what was that rock wall blocking my path?

"Oh, no!" My cry of despair sounded eerie in the muffling gray stuff.

Back when the trail parted, the fog had obscured the way. I hadn't taken the fork to Matt's cottage, a mere ten minutes away. No, this fork led to Simone's house. The rock cliff before me marked the narrow section that I had crossed with Matt and Lew, the section that was so treacherous. One side rose up sharply, while the other plunged straight down to the rocks far below.

I was halfway down the side of the gorge on a trail that could be deadly. In the mist, the path was barely visible.

What should I do? If I turned around and went back, Jason would catch me. If I continued to Simone's house, I risked confronting Brent. Surely Simone would have called for help by now. I'd heard her car. Would she have gone home?

I chewed my lip. It didn't matter. Either Brent or Jason was a murderer, but if I had to face one of them, it had better be Brent. I'd never be able to deal with Jason.

All right. Now to cross this part of the trail like I had the other time.

The path was wide enough for one person. I'd walked sideways before, my back against the cliff. Matt had secured me to a safety line, and there'd been a sapling growing from the rock to cling to. But I'd crossed without incident, as had both he and Lew without lines.

Yes, there was the sapling pushing out, bare and dejected.

Pulling a crumpled tissue from my pocket, I resolutely blew my nose. If I was careful, I wouldn't fall. I could do it without a rope. Matt and Lew had.

Back against the cliff, I edged my right foot out onto the path.

Simone's house was close. What I did when I got there would depend on what I found. If Brent was home, he would be looking for me, because Jason would have warned him. If Simone was there, she would help me.

I slid my left foot over to the right one.

Jason. My golden-eyed, glorious lover.

Right foot out, left foot over.

In the middle of the narrow path, the tears returned. My right foot, sure until then, trod on a loose rock and I stumbled.

The sapling bent, slipped from my hand.

Down, down, down I fell.

I'm going to die.

Desperate, I clawed for a hold on the rocky face of the gorge. Bushes scratched my face. I latched onto one.

Ignoring scraped and bleeding hands, I frantically sought a foothold by digging my toes into the cliff. A notch offered a place to wedge them. Warmth trickled down my forehead. Blood from where a rock had grazed me.

Hanging there by fingers and toes, I looked down.

No, no, please God, no!

Below my feet lay nothing but fog. I didn't know which was worse: looking down and seeing the rocks at the bottom hundreds of feet below, or looking down and seeing fog but imagining what it covered.

Hysteria welled. I would not be rescued. If anyone came, I knew who it would be, and I knew what it would mean.

I could not stay here. I had to climb back up.

But I couldn't move.

Belle, my brother's voice came, *Mom always told us we could climb mountains if we tried, but I don't think she really meant you to take her up on it.*

"Damn you, Alan!" I was too frightened to cry. "You're supposed to be looking out for me."

The wind blew gently, like faint laughter.

"And I know what you'd say," I whispered. "You'd tell me to do it myself."

I could hear him finish his favorite saying: *Because ain't nobody else gonna do it for ya!*

A tear stung my grazed cheek.

Come on, Belle. You've never let me down. You'll look pretty stupid if you fall and kill yourself here. People'll say we're the dumbest family that ever came to Rahunta.

As I took a long, shuddering breath, a strange joy seeped through me. For that moment, I might really have had my brother back. "Oh, Alan. I've needed you so."

I've been here all along, silly.

"I didn't know it," I whispered.

You know it now. And you need to finish this. So let's go up, huh?

My knee found a crevice. Gathering my splintered courage, I slid one foot up and into it. It seemed a steady foothold. That gave me enough confidence to risk letting go with one hand long enough to feel the rock in front of me.

Try over here. Alan's voice, calm and amused, guided me.

I found another crack for the other foot and safely negotiated that step, too. From that point I could reach a higher bush, which I gripped while finding new footholds.

My terror was still alive, but it was under control. I could almost hear Alan laughing at me. *And you used to be my cautious sister!*

Once I pulled myself over the edge again, I lay in relative safety on the leaf-strewn path and cried.

My face, my hands, my arms, my legs . . . My whole body throbbed with pain, but Alan wouldn't let me rest.

Hurry, Belle. There isn't much time.

Carefully sitting up, I found a tissue to swipe at blood streaking my forehead.

The lump pressing into my right hip reminded me of the gun. I stood up cautiously and felt with raw fingers. The pouch was still there.

Hurry.

I plodded on with a determination that hadn't been there before.

The trail leveled out as it approached Simone's house. Not many more yards.

I should have gone back. Matt would have helped me. I would have been safe with him.

But Jason would have caught me before I got there. And Alan had sent me on. Besides, it was too late now. I'd reached the end of the trail.

The mists swirled, clearing for an instant so that I could see Simone's house in its entirety.

With an involuntary cry, I shrank back.

Tall and dark and forbidding, the black castle of my worst nightmares rose up from the fog to receive me.

I did not want to go near it.

CHAPTER TWENTY-FIVE

DON'T BE SILLY, I scolded myself. *You have to go inside. You've nowhere else to run.*

No one was in sight. The mist descended again, veiling me as I crept over to the steps leading to the deck.

The house was silent as a tomb.

At the sliding glass doors leading to the pool, I hesitated. By this time, Jason might have figured out where I'd fled. He could be here with Brent.

Trying to be inconspicuous, I peered through the glass. My emotional confrontation with Jason and the physical escape had sapped my strength. Near exhaustion, I couldn't run away again.

The pool was tranquil, the living area beyond empty. The door slid open easily.

Every cell in my body screamed to go back, to turn and take my chances in the foggy gorge. Weary as I was, instinct warned the dark house was no haven. But as in my dreams, something drove me on.

The sharp odor of chlorine assailed me. I crept over the tiles and opened the wrought-iron gate. In the conservatory, the plants offered concealment.

My caution was well-founded. Voices floated from the hall that lay at the far end, beyond the circle of chairs and sofas near the fireplace. "—know Jason won't break his promise." Brent had never sounded so agitated.

There was a pause, then the voice I had feared hearing most spoke roughly. "Don't you see we don't have a choice?"

"You promised Brent!"

Simone was here. Had she had time to call for help?

"Simone, for God's sake, let me think." I'd never heard Brent so adamant. "Jason, if she's found it and got away—"

"She could be on her way to the police right now," Jason finished for him. "Knowing Anna, she probably is. If she isn't, if she's in the gorge . . ."

Simone gave a small cry.

"Don't, Simone," Brent comforted her. "It'll be all right."

"I won't listen to this. I won't let *you* listen to this. Jason's making this up to frighten us."

"Simone, don't be absurd. I won't let Jace go to prison."

Jace. Prison. I was dying a little at a time.

"I don't care about Jason," Simone sobbed. "What does he matter to us?"

"Oh, Simone." Brent's voice revealed despair. "Darling, trust me. Please."

Almost the same thing Jason had asked of me. Only I hadn't been able to trust him.

And Simone was long past the point of trusting Brent. "Bah! You are a weakling, Brent Forrester. You never stand up to him. I wish I'd never married you. I wish he was dead."

"Simone!" Brent sounded shocked. "Simone, come back."

"Let her go. We have a bigger problem now, Brent. I've got to find Anna." Desperation roughened Jason's voice. "If she's out there in this stuff . . ."

Transfixed, I watched through banana-plant leaves as a small blur of pale pink cut across the living area.

Simone did not notice me. She carried Christopher on her hip.

I thought at first she intended to warm herself in front of the fire, but she passed the freestanding fireplace without a glance.

Setting the baby down, she surveyed the guns on the wall before unlocking the case and choosing a rifle. Its barrel reflected dully as she handled it with practiced ease. From the desk beside the door, she took a box and poured out shells.

A click and the rifle opened. Another snap and a shell was inserted. One last click and it closed, ready to fire.

The whole thing took only a moment.

As if undecided, she turned her head toward the hallway.

She meant to kill Jason.

I went cold. I could never let her hurt him, no matter what he'd done to Alan, no matter what he intended to do to me.

A little pain started in my chest, spread to my throat, but my hurt didn't matter. "Simone," I whispered.

She whirled, eyes growing big. With a quick look over her shoulder, she laid the rifle on a table and rushed to me.

"Anna, do you know Jason is here?"

"Yes." How could I ever trust anyone again? How could I ever trust my own emotions again?

She took my arm and pulled me back to the wrought-iron banister, where large palms protected us from sight of the hallway door. A nervous glance toward the deck assured me we were alone. The pool beside us lay placid, its reflection somber under the dark dome.

Outside the glass expanse, mist swirled and eddied.

"I'm going back out to look for her." Jason's grim words floated through the dome, making us shrink farther into the plants. "You think about what I said, Brent. I guess I'm tired, but I didn't know it would be so hard.'

Hard to find me? Or hard to kill me? Was he suffering from an attack of conscience? I shivered, but not from the cool air.

"Jace, do what you think best. I'm tired, too. If there's no other way—"

Footsteps walked down the hall, the men's conversation fading as Simone and I hid behind the palms. I was miserable, but she was exultant.

Her hair was loose, innocently framing her face. Had it not been for the ugly lump marring one temple—she'd have a bruise there tomorrow—she would have looked like a fair Madonna. "Don't be frightened, Anna. I won't let him hurt you," she said fiercely. "I won't let him hurt you or me ever again. Where's the gun?"

I listlessly dragged out the heavy bag. "Did you call 911?"

"No." Her wide eyes fastened on the pouch. "He came back too soon. Oh, Anna, I knew I was right to trust you."

And she was the only one I could trust.

Either Jason or Brent had killed my brother, and the other had helped conceal it. Simone had tried to warn me.

"We need to call the sheriff." Tell him that Jason . . .

She didn't answer.

"Simone? Don't we need to call now?"

Or did she intend to? If we called, she would risk losing Brent. If we didn't call, she'd have the gun to hold over Jason. The latter was what she wanted.

What did it matter? Alan was dead and nothing would bring him back.

And I was in love with a man who was either his murderer or who was sheltering his murderer. Nothing would change that.

Clever Annabelle. Always so cautious, so careful to make the right decision, so anxious to do the right thing.

The baby gurgled. Someone hadn't finished changing him, leaving him in a diaper and long-sleeved top. Seizing his chance, he toddled toward plants that comprised, I suspected, forbidden territory.

"Simone?" I asked again. "Will you call?"

Her attention never wavered from the leather pouch. "I thought he would take it away from you, but you didn't let him have it. You are so brave, Anna."

I wasn't brave at all. I was dependable and loyal and cautious and sometimes intelligent. But I'd never, ever been brave. I'd never had to be.

"If we call, Brent might be charged, too." My lips were chafed, but I couldn't wet them. My entire mouth was dry. The feeling of evil surrounded us. "I know that but I think we should call, Simone. Before Jason comes back."

"All right." I was surprised at how easily she agreed. "Give me the gun and you call."

I hated to let it go. "Simone—"

"Anna, let me have it and call 911. Tell them Jason's threatening us." She pointed impatiently toward a telephone. "I'll take care of the gun. And I promise you Jason will never bother us again."

She took the pouch out of my reluctant hand. I watched as she slipped the deadly weapon out of its covering. Her cupid's-bow mouth turned up slightly as she opened the cylinder and murmured, "Only three bullets."

Plants framed her small form. With the reflections from the glass and water shading her in silvers and grays, she seemed ethereal. Her eyes were alight with excitement and something else.

Triumph.

Numb, I couldn't share it. I didn't feel much of anything.

Except the familiar malevolence. I suspected that particular demon would never set me free. Its presence made me look back uneasily over my shoulder as I moved toward the phone. There was no demon, only a crawling Christopher, already through the gate I'd left open and rapidly nearing the pool.

Simone didn't notice him as she strode toward the living are. One hand held the gun, its cylinder still open.

Conscientious, I detoured to stop the runaway before he reached the water.

My babysitting years had left their mark, even in the present turmoil. Babies were not left unattended: that was the cardinal rule. Especially around swimming pools.

As he climbed up on the diving rock, I caught him. He was a chunk, annoyed at being thwarted. He let out an experimental yelp and squirmed in my arms.

"Shh." I bounced him on my hip with as much energy as I could spare. "Shh. Come on back with me, kiddo. You don't want to go in there."

He had the fresh complexion and clean features of young babies. When he screwed up his face to whimper, a dimple sprang out in his chin.

From the conservatory I saw Simone at the desk beneath the gun case. Scrabbling around in its drawer, she looked up and motioned feverishly. "Hurry, Anna. Call. They may be back soon."

As I started toward the phone, her head pivoted in a listening attitude.

The baby was beginning to fret in earnest. Frustrated, he kicked out his feet.

They were tiny, perfect miniature feet.

Except that the toes had webbing between them.

Like mine, I thought idiotically.

Like mine. And my uncle Joseph's and my mother's father and his grandmother before him.

Even then I didn't understand.

Jason, of course, had known what Simone had done the moment he saw my feet. He'd realized how she'd made certain Brent would collect his trust money and why Alan had died.

But I still didn't. Not even with the proof there before my eyes fastened on those little telltale feet.

Why did Christopher share my family's peculiarity? "Simone. Simone, why—"

"Simone!" Brent stood on the other side of the living area. His leather jacket hung loose from his shoulders, and his face was distorted in utmost horror. He looked at a point behind me.

I turned to see what had shocked him so.

The revolver, its freshly filled cylinder snapping shut, was held in Simone's small but skillful hands.

The barrel swung up to aim at me.

CHAPTER TWENTY-SIX

NEVER HAD I IMAGINED Simone's dainty hands could seem so formidable or so capable as they did in that moment when she pointed the revolver at me. She was entirely at ease and in command.

"Simone?" It could have been someone else speaking. My mind churned, going simultaneously in all directions.

Christopher was Alan's child and Simone held a gun on me and Brent looked shocked and where did Jason fit in?

"I'm sorry, Anna." She was quite composed. "Brent, don't interfere," she snapped as he started past the fireplace. "I'll kill her right now if you come any closer."

The angry malevolence flared with a vengeance. It surrounded me, smothering me, frightening me.

I no longer wondered at its source.

The odium emanated from Simone. All these weeks, it had emanated from Simone. She hated me, feared me, and now she intended to see me dead.

Brent stopped at her threat. "Simone, you mustn't." Fear made him hoarse. "Simone, darling, please—"

"I have to, Brent. She's Alan's sister."

"Alan's sister?" He stared at me, as taken aback by that revelation as by his wife pointing a gun at me. "My God. So that's what Jace meant when . . . Simone, you mustn't do this."

"She came to avenge his death."

"No, no, only to find out what happened!" I broke in. "I never meant to hurt anyone."

Simone didn't listen. "But she helped me. She helped me find this cursed gun when Ma—you wouldn't. Jason has made my life hell, holding it over my head—*our* heads, Brent. But no longer. We'll be free."

"You killed Alan," I whispered. My instincts had been right about Jason. He was never a danger to me. The danger was Simone, had always been Simone.

"It was an accident." Brent's haunted eyes beseeched me to understand. "When her pregnancy first started showing, she was depressed. It's hard on a woman like Simone to lose her figure, to feel unattractive. She took Jace's gun out to kill herself that night, but McKenzie saw her and tried to stop her. The gun went off. I'd seen her take the trail and followed. I came up as McKenzie fell over the edge. It was a terrible, terrible accident. It never should—" He put a hand over his face if the recollection was too much for him.

But I remembered Alan's list, the appointment he'd had at the fork. And Christopher's feet told me the truth. Alan had discovered Simone's child was his, and had set up a meeting to discuss it. Alan would have kept her secret, but Simone hadn't taken the chance that Brent might find out.

She had deliberately schemed to kill my brother.

I raised my eyes from Christopher's feet to find Simone watching me. Her realization that I knew what she'd done set her lips in a grim line.

Brent needed to know.

"Hush!" she said ferociously when I opened my mouth. "Not a word. Not a word or I'll shoot."

"Simone, you can't hurt Anna." Brent, unaware of Christopher's parentage, was concerned for me and his wife.

Simone ignored him. "When they find Anna was shot by the same gun that killed Alan, they'll blame Jason." She planned her next move aloud. "It's registered to Jason so this time they'll arrest him."

"Simone, darling, please put down the gun." Brent's plea made no dent in that implacable, beautiful face.

I wondered crossly why I had ever thought him nice. Any fool could see that this was no time for begging. He needed to do something drastic, or Simone would . . .

I deliberately closed my mind to what she'd do.

If Brent couldn't reason with her, perhaps I could.

"Simone, I never intended to hurt you." I wanted to scream, but I kept my voice calm. "I only wanted to find out about Alan. I just wanted closure. I never meant to accuse anyone of murdering him."

"Alan." Simone's lip curled. "Alan was a fool. He thought I should tell—" She caught herself and darted a glance at Brent. A crafty expression flitted across her face. Like the wraith in my nightmares, she was holding me at bay, bending me to her will while Alan's ghost was helpless against her.

As in my dreams, I was unable to move. Something terrible was about to happen, but I could do nothing to stop it. I had stepped out of reality and into another world.

"This is for us, Brent." Simone softened her voice, became seductive. "You're the only one I love, but we can't let Anna or Jason or anybody else stand in the way of our happiness."

I tried again. "Simone, I would never hurt you. If you'd just told me—"

"Shut up!" she screamed. The gun waved threateningly.

I shut up.

She shook her pale hair back and moved toward me. Her face was blank, expressionless except for a luminous quality that might be derangement. She was the first person on the verge of madness I'd ever seen.

"Put Christopher down." I'd forgotten I held him, so still had he become. As though recognizing the deadly drama going on around him, the baby had become silent and unmoving. Simone couldn't shoot me with Christopher in my arms.

And I couldn't use him as a shield.

"Please, Simone, if you hurt Anna, Jason won't protect you. Not this time. He knows I didn't kill McKenzie, that I lied to get him to help us." Brent's pleading didn't faze her.

"It won't matter. Everyone will think Jason killed Alan as well as her. We won't need protection then." She was sweetly reasonable as she moved between me and the conservatory. "Put Christopher down, Anna."

I obeyed, feeling naked as I watched him toddle away but unable to risk him being hurt.

Come to that, I had no guarantee she wouldn't shoot Christopher, too. Brent had collected his trust. And she'd never seemed very maternal.

On the other side of the room, Brent moved out of sight. Simone's glance flickered toward him, but there was no question of my going anywhere. My back was to the wall, and she was in front of the door. I was trapped.

"Simone," Brent said.

I looked over in time to see him pick up the loaded rifle from the table by the fireplace. Hope rose as he opened it, saw the shell and closed it again. "Simone, you can't hurt an innocent person. Please think about this."

Didn't he understand reason wouldn't work?

The revolver did not waver. "You won't shoot me," Simone said confidently. "You can't pull the trigger, Brent. You love me. And I love you."

Brent groaned. The rifle lowered. "God. If you hadn't taken the gun that night . . . If McKenzie hadn't been out . . ."

Simone wasn't listening. "Don't you see? The only way we can be safe is to make everyone think Jason killed Alan. We'll go away afterward, you and I. To New York or California. Maybe Europe. I'd like to go back to France, wouldn't you? Do you remember that little inn? The one where we stayed in bed all day?"

Brent was helpless against her spell.

I almost wished she would end my agony as shame eclipsed fear.

All along I had wanted to trust Jason. My heart had begged me to trust him, but my common sense had refused to listen. How would I ever make it up to him?

If I lived to make it up to him.

The long gray barrel Brent held didn't move. "I won't let Jace take the blame this time. Simone, for God's sake, don't do this."

I faced the truth. He couldn't bring himself to shoot his wife. Not to save me, not even to save his brother.

And I couldn't blame him. How could I fault him for trying to protect his wife when I had been ready to love a man who could have been my brother's murderer?

If I had listened to my heart and trusted Jason as he'd asked, I would be safe now. I would be curled in his arms, far away from the ugly revolver in Simone's small hand.

The only thing I could be thankful for was that Jason wasn't Alan's murderer. Not that the knowledge was going to do me much good. Not now.

Jace, Jace!

Would he ever forgive me for running away? I should have trusted him. But his face had been so fearsome, that of a stranger.

Simone gave a tight smile of victory and raised the revolver as her husband slumped. Her face was white except for the delicate rose shading her cheeks and the dark bruise on her temple. She was lovely as a porcelain figurine, deadly as a live cobra.

Her calculating gaze fell on Brent, its contempt telling me too late what she intended.

A strange calm descended. "Brent, she'll kill you, too. She'll kill you and me both, and blame Jason. Then Christopher will inherit everything, and she'll take it from him. You must stop her."

Brent groaned again. "God help me, I can't hurt her." He put his hands to his face.

A victorious smile and Simone tensed preparatory to pulling the trigger. I braced myself for the impact.

I wish I could tell Jace goodbye. And Christopher. I want to hold him, watch him grow up.

Images of Alan slid past like a slide show mixed with memories of Jason and Christopher and my mother and my father and Bob. My entire life in a few seconds. "Brent, please."

"I can't shoot her." Brent's words nearly drowned a quick scuffling sound.

An explosion ripped across the room.

"I sure as hell can," another, beloved voice said grimly.

I clapped hands to my chest, expecting to feel the pain of flesh being torn, the moistness of blood.

The revolver Simone held fell to the floor and skidded toward the pool. One fragile wrist bloomed scarlet and her other hand came up to cradle it as she stared at it unbelievingly.

As the reverberations died away, I remained miraculously intact. Only my ears drummed.

I couldn't hear Simone whimper, but I saw her mouth move as she backed up.

Christopher was screaming at the top of his lungs, loud enough to hear. I automatically stepped over and lifted him, hugging him to me protectively. My ears began to clear.

"You bastard!" Simone cried out as Jason started toward her. "Don't come near me!"

I could hear her, and Jason, too, as he came up beside me.

"Your fingerprints are the only ones on that gun." He was the forbidding stranger again. He advanced to within a few feet of her. "I know you shot McKenzie and that Brent didn't. He admitted he lied to protect you."

"It was an accident. She didn't mean to shoot him." Brent, dazed, held a hand in front of his face as if to block out the scene before him.

The volume of Christopher's screams did not decrease. I held on to him tightly. "It's all right, kiddo. It's all right."

"Accident, hell. She wanted your trust fund. When you couldn't get her pregnant, she tried somebody else. McKenzie was blond and blue-eyed, a perfect match. She seduced him with her farfetched tales and innocent act, became pregnant and got your money. Which she tried her best to blow."

Brent's hand fell away. "Christopher?"

"Don't believe him!" Simone screamed. She forgot her wrist, groaned when she lifted it. "He's lying to you, Brent. He's always hated me."

Jason plowed on ruthlessly, his voice rising over Christopher's cries. "We're going to tell the truth this time, Simone. You may convince a jury that McKenzie's death was accidental, but your aiming that gun at Anna was clearly attempted murder."

"You can't prove anything." The insanity was there, shining out of her eyes, plain to see. "You're the one who shot at me. You're the one who'll go to jail."

"Your fingerprints are on the revolver grips," Jason pointed out. "And on the bullets you loaded. Brent may not be able to fire a gun, but he's basically truthful. Between his and Anna's testimony, plus a

DNA test, you'll be lucky if you get out of prison before your hair turns gray."

"Brent won't let you hurt me." Simone looked toward her husband. "Brent, Brent!"

Brent, dazed from Jason's revelation, was looking at the weeping baby in my arms. He did not answer. "He's my son."

"Brent," Simone whispered.

He moved toward me and Christopher with dragging steps. "He's my son," he repeated.

I shook my head, rocking the frightened baby in my arms. "He's Alan's son. My nephew."

"Brent!" Simone sobbed. "He shot me. Your brother shot me."

Jason blocked her way still, daring her to run toward Brent.

Brent himself reached out a hand and touched Christopher's fine hair. He took a deep breath. "I understand, Simone. I'm sorry. If you'd only told me." His resolute expression, when he turned his head toward his wife, gave way to forgiveness. "You mustn't worry, Simone. It'll all have to come out, but—"

"You coward! Goddamn you all! I won't be locked up!" She turned and ran through the gate leading to the pool.

"Simone, don't run away!" Brent's plea was useless. Before our shocked eyes, she disappeared through the sliding doors.

Brent rushed after his wife. "Simone!"

I made comforting noises to Christopher. He still trembled, but his wails were lessening. The explosion had terrified him, and he clung to me like I was his mother.

"It's all right, darling," I murmured incoherently over and over. This tiny living person nestled against me was all I had left of Alan, and tenderness swelled my heart. "It's all right, darling. You're safe now."

"Are you all right, Annabelle?" Jace's touch on my arm was gentle, but his face remained hard.

"I'm fine." He had called me that in the dining room, when I'd stood holding the gun while he looked at me so angrily, and now again here. "How do you know my name?"

His mouth was unsmiling, but the upper lip curled. "Annabelle McKenzie Levee? Your lawyer told me. *Your lawyer*, Anna. Not you."

Dark eyes met mine, challenging me. "Even when I gave you every opportunity." His harsh gaze held mine for a full half minute before he made a sound of disgust and whirled.

I knew what his leaving meant. I'd had my chance and blown it. He'd never trust me again.

"Jace," I said to his back.

"Call the sheriff," he flung over his shoulder. "Don't tell them anything except that Simone tried to kill you and you don't know why." He turned at the door. "And for God's sake, *don't touch the gun!* Her fingerprints are all over it. They'll prove she . . . Tell them Brent and I are out looking for her, and that we need help to comb the gorge. You can tell them I shot her, too, to keep her from killing you, but don't say anything else."

"Jace, please." I was crying as I tried to comfort the baby and talk to Jason. Rivulets ran down my cheeks. Careful, cautious Annabelle who never cried except in her sleep. Today I'd used up my quota of tears for the rest of my life. "Jace, I love you," I said as he opened the door.

He turned with an oath. "Why the devil couldn't you . . . ? God!" He covered the yards between us in three giant strides and gripped my upper arms, looking down at me over the baby's head. "You stupid, idiotic, crazy . . . woman!" He ground his teeth. "I want to shake you. You could have died! Out there and then in here. Why the hell did you run away from me?"

"I was afraid." My throat grew so tight I could hardly speak. I patted Christopher's fine hair.

His punishing grip loosened. The sharp lines of his features softened. "Of me?"

I nodded. "You terrified me, the way you looked. So—so brutal."

"Hell, Anna. I was terrified. That gun was loaded. You had it dangling in one hand like . . . You could have shot yourself." His hands moved up and down my arms.

Christopher hiccupped, his cry down to a thin grumble. We paid him no heed.

"I'm sorry." Inadequate, but I didn't know what else to say.

"So why didn't you tell me who you were?" He was calming down.

"I was afraid, afraid you'd—"

"For somebody who's so frigging afraid of everything, you're pretty gutsy at pulling damn fool stunts like braving that gorge in this fog. What if you'd fallen?"

"I love you, Jace." Pride vanished at the chance to get him back. "Even when I thought you'd killed Alan, I loved you."

"Ah, Anna." His hands stopped their sliding on my arms. "You've done nothing but keep me turned inside out from the time you came." His eyes melted into honey. "What the hell am I going to do about you?"

I took my heart and held it out to him. "I hope you can still love me."

Gracious man that he was, he took my humble offering. "By now you must know I do, Annabelle McKenzie Levee." He bent down to kiss me over my nephew's head. His lips were warm, full of promises. His hand, smelling acrid from the gunpowder of the rifle, caressed my cheek.

Then he faded into the mist, chasing after his brother and Simone.

CHAPTER TWENTY-SEVEN

JASON WAS NO MURDERER, and he still loved me.

Left in Brent's house, I clasped the quieting baby. My thoughts were a jumbled mass, revolving around Simone's confession and Alan's child and Brent's confusion.

But always they came back to Jason, and the gleam in his eyes that was solely for me.

I was exhilarated and frightened at the same time. I was terrified for him out in the gorge, but I was ecstatic because he loved me.

He loves me, my heart sang over and over. *He still loves me.*

He knew who I was and what I'd done. And he still loved me.

And he was out there in the foggy, dangerous gorge chasing a murderess.

The poor quivering baby clung like a leech to my neck, hampering my efforts to speak distinctly into the phone as I called for help.

At last I made the person on the other end understand, and a sheriff's patrol car soon appeared.

I'd forgotten how I must look, dirty and disheveled from my fall, until I saw the deputy's reaction to my appearance as he questioned me.

"I don't know." I remembered Jason's instructions. "I fell on the trail. I came here and Simone . . . She's crazy."

"What happened?"

"If Jason hadn't come, she would have shot Brent and me." I told him about Jason confronting her. "Then she ran away, and Jason and Brent went after her. You've got to find them." My urgency was real.

Soon the mist-laden woods were aswarm with people.

A woman deputy came, trying to coax more information from me. I admitted nothing beyond what I'd already said. Until I found out what else Jason wanted me to say, my story wouldn't change.

This officer was brusque but efficient. It was she who found Jenny's number and had me call her to come to help with Christopher. And it was she, shortly after Jenny's arrival, who told us that Simone had fallen and rescue teams, hampered by the mist, were at work trying to get to her.

That lovely, treacherous gorge.

It showed no mercy and claimed what belonged to it with ruthless tenacity.

And Simone, beautiful and delicate, had turned out to be just as treacherous.

"Where did she fall, Treva?" Jenny, acquainted with the deputy, had no compunction about asking. "That point where it's so narrow?"

The deputy, a plump woman with a cynical face, answered readily enough. "No. It was up where this trail joins the main path, before it goes on up to Lettie Forrester's house."

The same place where Alan had met his death.

Somehow I was not surprised. Was it purely accidental that Simone had fallen there, too? Or was it like all the other strange coincidences?

A memory returned of the moment when my foot had slipped on the path, and I fell, despairing of survival before I caught the bush. Had Simone felt that same despair?

I shivered.

Sometime later, two men came to the deck and conferred with Treva. Afterward, she came into the den where Jenny and I watched Christopher play. "Jenny, can you reach Lettie? She needs to be here."

Jenny and I stared at her, my heart turning cold. They wouldn't be calling Lettie for Simone.

"Why? What's happened?" Jenny asked.

I blurted out, "It isn't Jason, is it?" Both women looked at me, but I didn't care.

"It's Brent." The deputy's face softened as she patted my hand. "When Simone fell, she got caught on a rocky point. Jason and Brent found her before the others caught up to them. Jason went back to his house for rappelling gear, but Brent wouldn't wait."

"Oh, sweet Jesus." The horror on Jenny's face was the first real expression I'd seen there.

"He went over the edge. The crew at the bottom just found him."

"Dead?" Jenny asked her.

The deputy nodded.

I closed my eyes. Brent, so caring, so decent, so *nice*! His only crime was in loving his wife.

It wasn't fair.

And Jason, so protective of Lettie and Brent—How would he cope? Oh, God, I wanted him with me. I wanted him safe.

"Sue's coming back with Lettie," Jenny said after calling Palm Beach. "Lettie's tough. She'll bear up."

I could only think of my own mother's pain when she'd lost her son.

As the afternoon turned into evening, the baby went down for his nap and I paced.

Later, Jenny fixed a light supper.

In the middle of our trying to eat, another deputy arrived, shivering with cold. "Jason Forrester and that new doctor managed to climb down to where Simone was hung." He accepted coffee gratefully. "They lifted her out, but a helicopter's coming to take her to the hospital at Chattanooga. She's pretty bad."

Soon afterward, Treva picked up her things and went away, saying I'd be notified when to come in to make my statement. Jenny and I were left to stare at each other.

I dreaded hearing what story Simone would tell. The coming months, with all the publicity and fresh rumors about Jason, would be a nightmare. Lettie would be heartsick.

"It's her own fault," Jenny told me, misinterpreting my silence as grief for Simone. The day's events had left her talkative. She'd had to leave a family gathering, but seemed more resigned than annoyed. "I always figured something like this would happen. She was real unstable. Up one day, down the next. Jace warned me when I first took the job."

"Jason hired you?"

"Uh-huh. I was a nurse in Nashville till my mother got sick and I came home to take care of her. When she died, Jace asked if I'd stay on awhile and look after Christopher and *her.*" The disdain was patent.

"He thought Simone needed help?" I was still trying to find reasons for the tragedy. Alan, no matter how I'd loved him, had sowed the seeds. His weakness where women were concerned had caused his own death as well as that of Brent and perhaps Simone.

No, that wasn't true. Alan was weak but not evil. Simone was to blame. Her greed had wreaked this havoc on people I loved.

"Jace thought she needed watching," Jenny said in her matter-of-fact way. "She liked men too much and Brent was kind of innocent. Jace would have died before he disillusioned Brent about her doings, but he had me keep my eyes open. Whenever she got too public, he'd put a stop to it."

That explained why Jenny always seemed to be around. "I noticed her with Matt."

Jenny shook her head regretfully. "He's like Brent, too gullible for his own good."

"She didn't care about Christopher." I remembered the casual way Simone spoke of her son.

"No, but he's what got her the money. After he was born . . . Well, one time she nearly let him drown, and after that, Brent had me stay until he came in every night. He thought she didn't know how to take care of a baby, but she didn't give two hoots about anything or anybody except herself."

Jenny showed no pity.

"It's hard to understand someone like that." Despite what she'd done, I felt no anger toward Simone. A great numbness blunted everything except my emotions concerning Jason. Of him I was certain, but everything else . . .

Jenny sighed. "There's lots of people like her. Some are better at hiding it and some are worse. Most of them don't go to these lengths to get their own way, though."

Sensible words from a sensible woman. They should have been reassuring, but they meant nothing.

I'd lived through my nightmare and was beginning to realize it was over. If I could only see Jason safe, everything would be all right. Calls to his cell went directly to voicemail. My messages went unanswered.

Finally, about eight-thirty, he came in. Hearing his truck pull up, I rushed to the kitchen and flew into his arms and buried my face in his filthy yellow jacket. For the first time since the nightmares had begun, I felt safe.

"I'm sorry," I said. "I'm so very sorry about Brent."

He held my face between his hands and looked at me. "I know. I'm glad you're here." He kissed me gently before cradling me against him, his face nuzzling my hair.

"Go on in the den. I'll fix some fresh coffee," Jenny said, diplomatically, after following me to the kitchen.

"How's Christopher?" Jason asked.

"He's fine. He's asleep." My voice broke. "How're you?"

"I'm okay."

I looked at him and saw it was true. His grief for Brent was there, but he had himself tightly contained. He would have to come to terms with what had happened later, but for the moment, he was dealing in his own way.

I hurt to realize that he and his brother were Simone's victims as much as Alan.

I drew him over to the sofa. "What about Simone?"

"She's dead. She died on the way to the hospital."

I couldn't mourn. Nor could I imagine the flitting fairy princess cold and silent in death.

Jason shrugged out of his jacket. "Funny thing, she came to as we loaded her onto the helicopter. She was hysterical, claimed she was pushed."

"Pushed!" Still trying to frame Jason. Would we ever be free of her?

Jason picked up my hand. His words were deliberate. "She said she was pushed by Alan McKenzie."

"Alan?"

We sat in silence for a while, the warmth of our touch reassuring, making me bold enough to admit, "He came to me, Jace. I fell up there, on that narrow place between here and Lettie's, where Matt made me use a safety rope before. Alan spoke to me, shamed me into climbing back up."

"You fell!" Jason's eyes widened, his mouth gaped. "The part where the trail narrows over the cliff?" His voice rose. "You fell *there?*"

I nodded. "I guess I would have hung there till I fell into the gorge if Alan hadn't come."

"Anna, you must be mistaken. There's no way you could have climbed up from that spot. I couldn't have climbed up there. Nobody could have." Horrified, Jason stared. "There's sheer rock underneath that ledge. There's nothing to hold onto under it. If you fell there, you'd be dead."

"Alan was there. He helped me get up."

Jenny's arrival with sandwiches and coffee stopped further dissent. As Jason ate, he told her about Simone, and she agreed to stay the night with Christopher. "Figured I might need to. I brought some clothes."

When he'd finished eating and we were alone, Jason chewed on his lip. Finally, he said, "When I left here, I didn't know where I was going. I just knew I had to find you. Before I got up to the main road, something made me turn around and come back." He hesitated. "I could have sworn somebody said 'Go back. Belle needs you.' It was as plain as if someone was speaking right beside me. That's why I turned around and came back down."

"It was Alan. It must have been, Jason. He sent you to help me."

My love gave a long, audible sigh. "I don't believe in ghosts, Anna. But maybe I should. Anyway, it's for sure he didn't come to help Simone."

"Maybe it's for the best," I murmured, wondering what Simone must have felt at the end, believing Alan was there beside her, pushing her over the edge.

"I think it is." Jason had on the same clothes he'd put on that morning when he left to get Lochinvar, the flannel shirt and jeans stained with dirt from the gorge. Lines of fatigue were pronounced around his eyes and mouth, but he spoke with his usual decisiveness.

"I talked to the sheriff, told him you're Alan McKenzie's sister. He thinks Simone killed your brother and tried to kill you. I didn't tell him different." He looked at me. "You can give him the details if you like."

He seemed to make it a habit, giving me a choice. Though I suspected he knew I'd do as he suggested.

This time.

I kissed him on the mouth.

"There'll be some questions for you, but not tonight," he said, coming up for breath. "I'll run you home if you're ready."

"The baby . . . Christopher. Can't I stay? He's my nephew, Jace."

"He'll be more comfortable with Jenny tonight. He's used to her. You've got plenty of time to get to know him."

In the car we went over my story. I'd walked to Brent's house and was shocked to find Simone aiming a gun at me. Jason showed up in time to keep her from shooting me. I didn't have the faintest idea why she was trying to kill me.

"Just stick to that," Jason advised. "They suspect the gun is the one that killed your brother, and tests will prove it. They think Simone found out who you were, convinced herself you were out to nail her as Alan's killer, and decided to do away with you."

"All right." There were so many things I wanted to ask him. "Jason, what happened the night Alan died?"

He rubbed his face with his hand, drained as I'd never seen him. "It was . . . We all kind of lost our heads that night. Brent wanted to protect Simone so when I got there, he spun a story about her trying to kill herself. He said he got the gun away from her just as your brother came up to help and it went off, hitting Alan. He begged me to help cover it up."

"Simone told him that's what happened, but she went there deliberately to kill Alan." I shuddered at her coldhearted murder. "I found a schedule Alan had made up for that day. He was supposed to meet her there. She planned it, Jason."

"I don't doubt it. I should have guessed earlier about the baby. If I had . . . Well, it's too late now. Anyway, that night Brent was so upset, I agreed to help conceal what happened. It wouldn't have mattered if you hadn't come along."

My hand reached out to caress his cheek.

He kept his eyes on the road but caught my fingers in his. "Your brother didn't suffer, Anna. As soon as Brent came for me, we took my truck to the bottom. It couldn't have been more than twenty minutes before we reached him, but he was already dead. He must have died when he first went over."

I bit my lip. "Thank you. I'd wondered. I couldn't bear the thought that . . ." I didn't finish, knowing that with Brent's death, Jason would go through his own regrets, his own conjectures.

"Added to everything else," Jason went on, pretending he didn't see me furtively wipe my eye, "I'd found out that same day that Tiffany was in love with McKenzie."

"It must have been awful for you."

"Oh, I liked Tiffany well enough, though her folks and mine were the ones who really wanted the engagement." He shrugged. "But I knew what people would say if I let Brent take the blame. They'd say Brent was covering up my killing McKenzie. I thought if we took McK—your brother's wallet and jewelry, it'd look like a mugging that went wrong and maybe . . . Anyway, Brent hid that stuff while I took the gun. After a day or so, I came to my senses. I put two and two together, figured Brent was covering up for Simone. But he wouldn't admit it. Later, I found out she'd sold some of—some of your brother's things to buy that damned ring she flaunted."

The woman at the pawn shop must have been Simone. I could easily see her slipping away from Brent when he took her shopping in Chattanooga, putting on a red wig and entering the shop. Her eyes would have been sparkling and her smile brilliant as her small fist clutched Alan's rare coin.

I remembered how angry Jason had been when she showed off the ring. He had been angry because he'd known how she'd bought it.

Disgusted, he shook his head. "I told her how stupid she was, that it would lead right back to us. But she didn't care. Money was all that mattered to her. Money and men. She tried to seduce me the week after I met her. Charming, eh? Poor Brent. He never had a chance."

The bitterness was dulled, as if he was too tired to hate her anymore. "I took the rest of your brother's things and threw them away so she couldn't pawn them, too. Then you had to go and find them."

I mutely pressed his arm.

His hand covered mine. "I thought you and I could work it out. When I saw your feet, I did some checking. I kept hoping you'd tell me yourself. I waited for a while, wanting you to talk about it. Then, when I saw how Simone had persuaded you I was some kind of monster, I told Brent I couldn't keep lying."

I cringed at how I'd behaved toward him this morning. "Jason, I apologize. I wanted to believe you about Alan. I wanted to tell you I was his sister. But I was so scared. The way you looked . . . It all came about so suddenly, I didn't know what to think, who to believe."

And I'd nearly lost Jason.

Love was more important than revenge, perhaps more important than truth. I might have unraveled the mystery of Alan's death, but it had nearly cost me Jason. If I could have relived that terrible moment when he begged me to trust him, I would have chosen differently. If I'd been truly wise, I would have listened to my heart when he asked, would have given him the gun.

Then none of this would have happened. Brent would be alive and so would Simone.

I hung my head. "Even when I ran away, I loved you."

"That's what counts, isn't it?"

That was all. His hands on the wheel were as competent as they had been on my body. The square fingers rested there carelessly, steering as though driving was second nature to him.

He reached over with one large hand to pick up mine and put it to his lips. A warm glow swept through me. I was forgiven.

"That day I fell into the pool, did someone shoot at me? Was it Simone?"

"I think so. She must have used a silencer and shot from the trail, hoping I'd get the blame. I've seen her shoot skeet and she's good. She learned how to shoot from an uncle in Canada."

"She wanted to kill me because she knew I was Alan's sister." She'd seen my toes that day we'd shopped in Helen.

"Probably. When that didn't work, she decided to use you another way. I kept her in line by threatening to give the gun to the police. It was the gun that killed your brother and her prints were all over it. She intended to get it and set me up for killing you."

"Getting rid of both of us." And Brent. I shivered and gripped his hand tightly with both of mine. I wouldn't tell Jason what I suspected she'd intended for Brent. Not yet. "I shouldn't have listened to her."

"She was very convincing."

Only the sound of the truck engine broke the silence on the twisting road to the top of the gorge.

At my cabin, he came inside. I didn't want him to leave, but didn't know what he would say if I asked him to stay so I put off finding out by using the old tried and true.

"Would you like some coffee?"

"I've had two cups in the past hour. I'll be up all night now." He pulled me into his arms and I did not resist. "All I really want is you."

We clung together.

"Except I'm so damned tired," he said, his whiskers rough against my cheek. "Why don't you get some clothes and come home with me, Anna, darling? I'll be rested in the morning. And afterwards, I'll cook you breakfast. My bacon and eggs are pretty tasty."

I liked the way he called me darling. I liked the way he thought he was enticing me.

"I don't want to leave you," he added when I didn't immediately agree. "I need you too much right now."

"Then stay."

"I can't stay here." He sounded affronted that I'd asked.

"You can if you want to." I looked up at him, holding onto him for all I was worth, using his own argument against him.

He hesitated a full five seconds. "What the hell. I hope your bed's big enough for two.

It was.

Other Fiction

by

Cheryl B. Dale

Romantic Suspense

Intimate Portraits
The Man in the Boat
Set Up

Paranormal Romance

The Warwicks of Slumber Mountain

Light Mystery

Taxed to the Max
Overtaxed and Underappreciated

Vintage Mystery

Losing David

If you enjoyed this book, please consider leaving a review to help others discover it. Among sites that offer places for reader reviews are:

http://www.amazon.com

and

http://www.goodreads.com

If you do have the time and take the effort to leave a review, please accept my sincere appreciation and thanks.

www.cherylbdale.com
cherylbdale.blogspot.com
cherylbdale@hotmail.com

www.ingramcontent.com/pod-product-compliance
Lightning Source LLC
Chambersburg PA
CBHW032004170626
46807CB00006B/2634